T0064228

INFATUATION

INFATUATION

Character Is Destiny!

(A collection of short stories)

Ravindran Pottekkat

PARTRIDGE

A Penguin Random House Company

Print information available on the last page.

To order additional copies of this book, contact
Partridge India
000 800 10062 62
orders.india@partridgepublishing.com

www.partridgepublishing.com/india

CONTENTS

FOREWORD/ ACKNOWLEDGEMENTS

I started writing short stories, in Malayalam, from the age of 22. Many of them have been published, in various journals. I had a collection of such short stories with me and many of them were in the form of novelettes. Many years back, I had decided to publish this collection of short stories in the form of a book. Dr. Chandrika Thalayar, noted poet and critic and former Professor of Malayalam, in Government College, under Kerala University, wrote a preface also. But, due to various reasons, I could not publish the same. Now, when I look back, I feel disappointment, in the failure and express regret to Dr. Chandrika Thalayar, for the lapse.

For many years, while in service, I could not find time for literary works. After retirement, I have temporarily settled in Bangalore. Now, there is ample time at my disposal, to read and write. Hence, with the persuasion of my daughters, Junitha and Thanuja and son in laws Sinish Gopi and Sathyajith, I ventured for this attempt.

First and foremost, I thank my daughters for their inspiration and relentless persuasion, to restart literary activities. After completion of the manuscript, the editing and typing the same in Google were done by them. Mr. Sathyajith was instrumental in finding out the publisher. He contacted Penguin Publishers first and then Partridge Publishers, India and done all follow up works. I thank my daughters and son in laws, for their sincere inspiration and help, in publication of this book.

My thanks are due to my friend Sri. Vijayan, Kondrappassery, my brother P. G. Chandran and uncle P. S. Kuttan, for their valuable advice and guidance in this endeavour. Finally, I thank my wife, Smt. Prasanna and our relatives Sri. E. K. Sahadevan and Smt. K. K. Bhanumathi Amma for reading the manuscript and suggesting necessary changes and modifications.

This book is dedicated to the memory of my parents, Late Smt. Bhargavi and Sri. P. S. Gopalan, Manalur, Thrissur District, Kerala.

Bangalore,
16-10-2015.   Ravindran Pottekkat.

DIAMOND NECKLACE

It was an autumn evening, in the year 1996. A chilly wind was blowing from the north, with clouds of dust and smoke. Maya got down from the taxi and walked towards Kalyan station. When she was checking the coach position, she heard the announcement "The superfast express going to Kanyakumari via Ernakulam will arrive on platform No. 2 shortly'.

The station was overcrowded with passengers. Maya struggled through the crowd and reached platform no. 2 and then the train was standing on the platform. She boarded the train and found out her berth. By the time she occupied the seat, the train left and picked up speed.

Maya's mind was cloudy and agitated but she concealed it from the co passengers. Her face was bright and cheerful like a white dahlia in the crimson light of the setting sun. She looked hardly 40 and some strands of hair had turned grey near the temple.

Maya watched the co passengers with curiosity. There were two couples and a ten year old boy. They were talking in Malayalam about the anti South Indian attitude of the Shiva Sana. Although Maya could understand Malayalam, she was unable to speak even a word in that language.

The train was running at high speed, and slowed down when it reached the ghat section. It was drizzling when it passed Lonavala. When the train reached Pune station, Maya took out a packet from her handbag and opened it. It contained four pieces of bread with butter and she finished it within no time, and watched the other passengers, who were sitting opposite to her. The boy smiled at her and she returned the smile.

'Aunty, are you going to Kerala?' The boy enquired Maya.

'Yes, I'm going to Thrissur in Kerala'. Maya replied.

'We're going to Ernakulam'.

'What's your name?'

'Aunty, I'm Sanjay and this is my mummy, Smitha and papa Viswanath. The others are Annie aunty and Joseph uncle' Sanjay said touching one by one.

"Where're you living in Bombay?" Maya enquired.

'All of us're working in private company at Ambernath and are living in adjacent quarters there.' said Smitha.

'Are you Marati?" asked Viswanath.

'No, I'm Sindhi'.

In a short time, they became friends and the conversation continued for hours and went to sleep at 8.30 pm.

Next day dawned. Maya woke up at 8 am. The train was running through paddy fields. She thought it must be Andhra Pradesh. She noticed that a major portion of the landscape is dry and arid and remained uncultivated. Various types of grocery items are growing in abundance where irrigation facilities are available

Sugarcane fields stretched out in all directions, as far as the eye could see and the workers were toiling in the fields with only a piece of cloth around their waist.

The train was running through paddy fields again and the heat was unbearable.

'Why're you going to Thrissur?'. Smitha enquired.

'My husband is a malayali and he hails from Thrissur.'

Smitha and Annie were very talkative and Maya participated in their conversation for a long time while Joseph and Viswanath slept in the top berth.

'Have you visited Trichur earlier?' Smitha enquired.

'This's first time I am going there'. Maya said.

'Do you like Kerala?' Annie asked Maya.

'Of course, I have heard that it is God's own country. It is very beautiful and enchanting like Kashmir, but I had no luck to see that place, so far', said Maya.

'Why don't your husband take you there', asked Annie.

'My husband's parents did not want a city born daughter in law. For long 18 years, I was not taken to his house and none of them talked to me over phone either. I hoped that they will reconcile after some time, and invite me to their house;but nothing happened. So, I am going there uninvited." Maya's eyes became wet and tears rolled down her cheek and she wiped it with her sari.

'How many children have you got?', asked Smitha.

'None. I'm still undergoing treatment, visited many temples, in Maharashtra, and north India and spent a lot of money". Maya's face became gloomy.

'Did your husband undergo any treatment? In my opinion something is inscrutable in not taking you to his house even after 18 years of married life". Smitha expressed her opinion.

'My husband has met many doctors in Bombay and Dubai, but he has not undergone any treatment. He used to say, that he is OK and everything is in the hands of God.' Said Maya.

'I have valid doubts, about his sincerity. He may be having a family in Kerala; otherwise, there is no reason to hesitate, to take his wife to his house, in Kerala'. Smitha said.

The conversation went on for hours, and finally Smitha consoled Maya by her soothing words "Don't worry everything will be alright soon. Annie has no issues and she is also under treatment.'

The train was running through Tamil Nadu.

'The train will reach Thrissur by 6 am, tomorrow. Please, go to sleep early and get up at 5.30am' Annie told Maya.

'OK, we can meet in Bombay after coming back, good night' said Maya.

Maya shook hands with Smitha and Annie and went to sleep by 8 pm.

The train reached Thrissur by 6.10 am and Maya alighted from the train, with her luggage. Before getting down, she wanted to say goodbye to her friends, but they were in deep sleep.

When the train left the station, Maya noticed that it was very dark outside and she walked straight to the ladies waiting room.

At 7 am, Maya went out and hired a taxi and showed the address to the driver.

Suresh M. K, Meloth House, Padiyam Road, Anthikad.

It took about one hour, to reach the destination. The driver had to enquire, at two places, to find out the house. Maya got down from the taxi and stood at the gate with amazement. It was a sprawling three storeyed building, standing in an extensive compound, with full of coconut trees. There was a small garden in front of the house.

Maya hesitated for a moment and then went inside. She pressed the doorbell and waited anxiously. Suddenlyl, the door was opened and a graceful old lady looked at her and asked.

'Who are you?'

Maya smiled and fumbled for a reply 'can I see Suresh?'

'Come inside.'

'Thank you.'

Maya sat on the sofa available in the living room and looked around. It was a neatly arranged sitting room with picturesque scenery on the walls. A Malayalam and English newspapers were lying, on the teapoy.

'May I know who you are?' The old lady repeated.

'I'm Maya from Bombay. Where's Suresh?. Please call him' Maya said in one breath.

Then, a lovely girl in her teens dressed in churidar appeared and enquired 'Are you papa's friend?'

Maya's face became reddish and heart began to beat loudly. She groped for words and said loudly.

'Yes, I'm papa's very, very close friend'.

The girl giggled and ran inside.

'Papa, papa, somebody came to see you'. She called aloud.

Then, she heard sudden footsteps, somebody descending the staircase and approaching the living room.

Suresh and Maya saw each other. On seeing Maya, Suresh was startled and a lightning passed through his head. For sometime, he remained mute and speechless, staring at Maya. Maya broke into tears.

And Suresh stood there transfixed as a statue. Maya cried uncontrollably and and her sari was drenched in tears.

After some time, Suresh got back his senses, and he struggled to console Maya.

'I'm really sorry Maya. I'd to depart for Kerala without informing you, since father was not well'.

Suresh was terribly shocked and somehow he managed to say some words to console Maya.

'OK, you are very smart. What I feared was true. You are a cheat. Why did you spoil my life? I have nobody in this world. I can not share my husband' Maya lamented uncontrollably.

Suresh came and sat by the side of Maya and caressed her and wiped her tears with his dhothi.

There was a sudden commotion and all the people in the house rushed to the living room. People looked at one another and murmured. 'Bombay wife has arrived.'

Maya wept incessantly and finally slept in the sofa. In the meantime, a car came to the house and a middle aged lady went out with a girl and a boy.

Maya slept for about one hour and woke up. Suresh's father talked to her in English and broken Hindi. "Beti, I know what happened. I'm really sorry, and you can also live in this house. We'll accept you as our daughter in law'.

But, these words did not soothe her mind. Maya looked like an insane person and she did not listen to what Krishnakutty master said.

Maya kept on lamenting and despising her fate. Suresh compelled her to fresh up and after some time she got up and went inside and returned with a renewed vigour, to face Suresh and she sat opposite to her husband. Somebody brought a cup of tea and she gulped it down in one breath.

'Maya, you're most dear to me than anybody else. Please, forgive me if I have wronged you' Suresh apologised over and over again.

'Tell me, have you another wife?' Maya blurted out.

'Yes, I am sorry for hiding it from you so far. You are my most beloved and without you I am zero. The other lady is my cousin sister imposed by my mother. She is an innocent woman and cannot find fault with her'.

'Have you any children?'.

'Yes, two elder girl and younger boy. Daughter is studying in college for MA and son in 9th standard'.

'Why did you cheat me? Why did you spoil my life?' Maya sobbed again.

'I was infatuated with you and feared I will lose you, if I told you the truth'. Suresh was choking with emotion.

That night, they slept together in the same bed, but Maya did not utter a word. Maya's thoughts wandered to the good old days.

Suresh was a graduate Engineer, working in a Tata Firm. Since it was difficult to get a job in Kerala, he went to Bombay in the year 1976. He was living with a friend at Ambernath. One day, while going to catch train, a very pretty girl with a bag slung over her shoulder, came opposite to him. When she took her kerchief from the side pocket of the bag, something fell down. Suresh bent over it and it was a hundred rupee note. Immediately, he called her by clapping and handed it over to her.

She smiled and the same was returned by him.

'What's your name?' Suresh asked.

'Maya'

'I'm Suresh, electrical engineer in a private co.'

She left and Suresh went to his company. That night, Suresh could not sleep. Maya's face appeared in his mind over and over again. He tossed in bed to left and right, till daybreak. He took leave the next day and waited for Maya but could not meet her. After a week he happened to meet her again. They became friends and met frequently. Friendship slipped into love.

Maya was in the last year of her BA degree. She told Suresh everything about her. She was the only daughter of a Sindhi business man. At the time of partition, her grandfather and family came to India from Sind, in Pakisthan. He had a lot of properties and big business establishments there. He rushed to Delhi, leaving everything behind. They were in refugee camp for one year and after that with the help of government started a small scale industry in Meerut. Business flourished and thus life became secured. Maya's father took his degree from Agra. After the demise of grandfather, they moved to Ambernath, Bombay. Maya's father started a shop of electrical appliances, in Kalyan and it was a big success. He Purchased a flat in Ambernath and invested in stocks and shares. They had many close relatives in the Sindhi colony of Ambernath.

Suresh told her that he took his degree in electrical engineering from Trivandrum Engineering College. His parents were high school teachers and had one sister. Father had worked in many government schools at various parts of Kerala as headmaster and acquired some properties and he inherited the ancestral house, through partition. His mother was working in a private school, in their village.

His father, Krishnakutty master is a strict disciplinarian, but mother is a simple gracious woman. She was very pious and used to go to Guruvayoor temple, every week.

One day, Suresh asked Maya to accompany him to the subregistry office at Thane and she readily agreed without any hesitation and skipped class that day. Some of his friends were waiting there when they reached there. After marriage, she was taken to a flat at Dombivilli and her parents were informed by a special messenger.

Next day Maya's parents came to the apartment. Suresh was available at that time. Maya broke into tears on seeing them. Suresh touched their feet and begged forgiveness.

'Don't worry beti, we have approved your marriage.' Maya's father said smiling.

They blessed both of them and invited them to their house. Maya's mother could not control her sorrow and hugged Maya and caressed her cheeks and said. "We are alone there and you can come and stay with us".

'We'll consider this request after some time' Suresh said.

When parents left, Maya began to sob uncontrollably, since she felt guilty conscience, for her mistake. Maya's parents loved her deeply and did everything for her but, she ignored them and eloped with a stranger.

'Maya cool down, they have wholeheartedly approved our marriage and no need of guilty conscience' Suresh patted her and consoled.

Suresh took one week leave and Maya skipped class during this period "They went to Goa and spent one week in a luxury hotel. During evening, they will go to the beach and spend time in sightseeing. Once, they went to the outer sea in a boat and it was a terrifying experience for Maya.

Next week, they went to Maya's house. Maya's parents were very happy. During their stay there, they had some visitors from Delhi and they were distant relatives of Maya. All of them were very much impressed, by the personality of Suresh and they spoke to Maya's mother "Suresh is a perfect match for our Maya'.

'Why don't you invite your parents to Bombay?' Maya's mother asked Suresh.

'Mummy, my father is a strict disciplinarian and won't approve of this marriage. He wants a Malayali daughter in law and that too a village born and convent educated girl.

'Did you inform them about the marriage?'.

'Yes. I sent a letter immediately after the marriage'

'What's their response?'.

'They're really angry'.

On hearing this, Maya's mother dropped that subject and never asked anything about his parents in Kerala. She enquired about Maya's studies and shifting residence to their house etc.

'Maya can continue her studies and a degree is highly essential for a job' said Suresh.

Days, months, and years rolled by and Maya passed BA degree in I class and joined MA in the same college. Suresh made two trips to Thrissur, leaving Maya with her parents. Maya was in a happy mood and pursued her studies well. She also started learning Malayalam, with the help of Suresh.

During vacation, Suresh and Maya went on a tour to North India. They visited Delhi, Agra and Meerat and visited some relatives of Maya at these places. Also, they visited Jaipur, Pushkar, Ajmeer and Jaisalmer. For Maya, the palaces of Jaipur and Udayapur evoked wonder and amazement. The Amber fort was another wonder. During this journey they purchased a lot of items for themselves and Maya's parents.

In the meanwhile, there was a lot of problems for Suresh in the company. There was a strike in the factory and Shiv sena's demand for expulsion of South Indians from the factory. Following this, many South Indian workers and executives resigned their jobs and left. Many of them got jobs in gulf countries and the remaining left for Kerala.

One day, Suresh was in a depressed mood after returning from office and told Maya that he was going to resign the job, since there was hostility from the local workers and the attitude of the management was disappointing.

Maya became aghast and began to cry. Suresh consoled her by saying "If I go to gulf I will take you with me and no need of panic.'

'I'm afraid, please tell me what is the real problem?" Maya asked Suresh in a terrified state.

'There's no threat for life, but the locals are creating problem everyday and it is difficult to continue there longer'. Suresh explained.

In the meanwhile Suresh appeared for some interviews in Bombay and got selected as engineer in a powerhouse in Dubai and after getting their offer he resigned the job and left to Dubai leaving Maya in the care of parents.

After joining duty in Dubai, Suresh sent letters to Maya frequently. He was staying with some tamil friends there. After receiving first salary, Suresh sent a letter to Maya stating that he was wonderstruck on receiving the first salary. It was ten times, the salary he received, in Bombay. He also enclosed a D/D for Rs 10000/-.

Within six months, Suresh moved to a luxury apartment near the creek at Marina and took Maya to Dubai. Maya thanked God, for the love and care she received, from her husband. Maya's parents exulted in the good fortune of her daughter and made some offerings to the deity, in Ambernath temple.

Suresh had only very few Malayali friends, and they were either from Travancore or north malabar side. Most of his friends were North Indians or Tamilians. He used to take her to all important events, in Dubai, evading the eyes of his relatives and friends from Thrissur.

Maya had a lot of relatives there and she used to visit their houses occasionally with Suresh and they in return used to come to their house. Maya's relatives were mostly businessmen and she was happy and contented even though she had no children.

Suresh purchased a costly car and he took driving licence. He taught Maya to drive and she also got licence.

Thus, Maya began to drive through the streets of Dubai and other emirate countries. Maya used to call her parents every alternate days. They rejoiced in the prosperity of Maya and Suresh and kept reminding them about consulting a doctor. As requested by Maya Suresh took her to a famous gynaecologist there. After thorough examination she remarked that Maya had no problem. However, she prescribed some medicines and asked Suresh to undergo some tests.

After some months, Maya asked Suresh. 'Doctor had asked you to undergo some tests, did you complete it.?'

Suresh laughed loudly and said. 'I am OK and will pray to God Almighty, to show some kindness'.

Maya was worried. Months and years have passed, after coming to Dubai and she did not conceive. Suresh planned a Europe trip during the month of May, when temperature had soared to 50 degree celsius. They visited London, Paris, Amsterdam, Switzerland and Spain. The journey was memorable and worthy to be cherished in memory for ever. They spent the three weeks, virtually in heaven. Maya thought that she will become pregnant after the trip, but in vain.

On one week leave, they visited Bombay and during this trip mother took her to a gynaecologist in Jaslok Hospital. She also made thorough investigation and said "No problem is detected ask your husband to meet a good physician.'

Suresh told Maya. 'OK, we can meet a good physician in Singapore. I'll arrange a trip to Singapore, shortly.'

Suresh got very few letters, from his parents. Maya used to ask him, 'Why don't you send letters to your parents regularly?'

'OK, they're fine'

Next year, they planned a trip to Singapore, Malaysia and Hongkong. It was also a memorable trip. In Singapore they met a Chinese doctor. After discussing with both, he said "Jogging daily, protein rich food and meditation. He advised them to take raw groundnut regularly'.

Suresh started jogging daily, after that trip. Maya also used to accompany Suresh, for jogging but she stopped it after a fall, during jogging.

One day, Suresh came from the office and said. 'I am going to Kerala, on a three day trip. Are you afraid to remain alone in the flat?'

'I'm not afraid. Why are you going there urgently?'

'Mother's not well. She had a fall in the bathroom and sustained some head injury' Suresh said.

'Suresh bhayya take me also with you to Kerala. I want to see your parents and that enchanting landscape.' Maya entreated.

'Time's not ripe to go there. I'm telling this, only in your interest. If they misbehave with you, it will affect our life, adversely.'

'I've a longing to see my in laws. Even if they do not want to see me, I love them dearly'.

'OK, I'm not coming. Please ring up, let me talk to my mother in law. I love her as my own mummy'

'Please wait for some more time and everything will be alright'. Suresh tried to console her.

'You're unkind and cruel to me. Even after 10 years of marriage, you're reluctant to take me to your house. This is nothing but cruelty to the spouse, and is unpardonable.

God's wrath 'll fall on your head, if you continue like this.' Maya began to sob, but Suresh did not budge or buckle due to remorses or curse.

Maya spent three days in her flat alone. She spoke to her cousins, that she was alone and would contact them, in case of any emergency.

Long 10 years have passed, after coming to Dubai. With the passage of time, some changes have come to the looks of Maya and Suresh. Maya has become more charming than before. She is not in the habit of visiting beauty parlour or applying facial cream and still her face has become more beautiful. Only one or two strands of hair had turned grey near the temple and she did not pluck it off or dye it. But, there were a lot of grey strands in the hair of Suresh and his face has become darkish with age, but he maintained his youthful vitality by daily jogging exercise and meditation. Maya's body became plump and obese due to lack of exercise and overeating. She has turned to spirituality, in recent times and has a collection of books of Hindu mythology, Vedas and upanishads and books written by Swami Vivekananda. She is deriving mental peace and tranquility, by reading these books.

Suresh has made enough money, with 10 years of service. He has purchased many plots of land, in his native village and deposited huge sums, in fixed deposit, in several banks, in his home town. Once, Maya advised him to invest in stock and shares and acquire some landed properties in Bombay but he did not show any interest.

One day, Maya put forward a suggestion to Suresh.'Suresh bhayya, we can adopt a child, a baby girl, from any of the orphanages of India. How long can I live like this?'

'Don't worry, we can think over it later. Let me try, whether I'll get a child from my own family circle. If there's any orphaned child in your family circle you can try for it. I'm least interested to take a child from orphanage'. Suresh consoled her, by his soothing words, but he did not do any follow up work.

One day, Suresh and Maya went to a music night organised by the Malayali association. Maya relished the programme very much. While coming out of the venue, Suresh happened to see a relative in the crowd. Suresh became aghast and pulled Maya's hand and slipped out of the hall hurriedly'. Somehow, they got into the car and escaped from being caught red handed.

'What's the matter?, whom did you see in the crowd to get upset?Seeing the embarrassment on the face of Suresh Maya asked.

Suresh kept mum. Maya saw a kind of terrified look, on his face and asked again 'Why do you avoid Malayali friends? I have seen your aversion to Malayali friends, on many a time. Why are you afraid of your own people?'

'I don't want unnecessary friendship. Many of them are gossip mongers'. Suresh said in shaky voice.

As a bolt from the blue, Maya got a phone call from mother. "Papa is not well and he was taken to a famous doctor in Jaslok hospital and on his advice he was admitted, immediately'. Mummy was in a disturbed mood and was weeping, while talking to Maya.

Maya flew to Bombay the next day itself. Papa had occasional gidiness and palpitation. He had also breathing complaints and fainted once. Immediately, he was shifted to ICU and thorough investigation was made. Suresh was informed and he rushed to Bombay to help Maya. Suresh spoke to the doctor treating Papa and he replied gently 'Sidwani is having kidney problem. He had all types of ailments, like BP, sugar and asthma. Continuous intake of medicines, has adversely affected the functioning of kidneys. We are going to start dialysis immediately. Kidney transplant is the only alternative. Please, try to find out a donor at the earliest'.

Suresh was shocked. He apprised Maya about the present condition of Papa but kept it secret from mummy. 'I'm willing to donate my kidney to Papa', Maya said wiping tears. "Maya, I'll find out a donor immediately. I've already contacted some agents here and they have assured me that, a donor will be arranged from Tamilnadu, at the earliest. I'll meet the entire expenditure, don't worry", Suresh consoled Maya.

Dialysis was started the next day onwards. Suresh and Maya were in the hospital throughout. He has paid an advance of one lakh rupees to the agent, for bringing the donor. On the second day of dialysis, the condition of Sidwani suddenly became worse and he breathed his last. Maya could not control herself. Suresh also wept seeing the lifeless body of Papa.

Sidwani's body was cremated in an electrical crematorium the next day. So many friends and relatives had gathered in and around the house. Entire people of Ullas Nagar colony had assembled there, to pay homage to the departed soul. Maya's mother Anjali lay motionless, for days together, since the loss of her beloved life partner was unbearable to her.

'Did you inform your father, bhayya?', asked Maya.

'Yes, I had phoned him from the hospital. He has expressed deep condolences', replied Suresh.

Maya's grief was boundless. She stood for hours looking at Papa's photo and wept for many days.

Sidwani's ashes were immersed in the Ganga. Later, Suresh took Maya and Mummy to Varanasi, Dwaraka, Allahabad, Haridwar and Rishikesh on a Pilgrimage and prayed for the salvation of Papa's soul.

After coming back, Suresh purchased a new car for Maya. Papa's shop remained closed for weeks, following his demise. It was reopened after completion of the rites and rituals. Maya gave necessary instructions to the staff and legal proceeding for transferring the ownership to her name was initiated.

"I'm not coming to Dubai along with you, since mummy's condition is very pathetic. Let her come round to normalcy, then I'll fly back", Maya told Suresh.

Suresh had no complaints and he returned to Dubai alone. After that, Maya could never go to Dubai. She had to take care of mummy and run the business. Suresh used to visit Bombay occasionally, stay for few days and fly back. More and more hairs of Suresh turned grey and a dark colour appeared around his eyes. Maya became fairer and she had reconciled to her fate. Her business was running with good profit. She had no financial problems, still Suresh used to send DDs, every month.

Long eighteen years had elapsed, after their marriage and for this marriage anniversary, Suresh arrived in Bombay. He and Maya visited the Ambarnath temple and returned home. He then took out a box from his suitcase and gave it to Maya and said. 'This is my gift to you, on the eighteenth anniversary of our marriage'. It was a costly diamond necklace. Maya did not rejoice on seeing it and in a depressed tone she said, 'Suresh bhayya, I thank you for the gift, but I will not wear it. I'll keep it as an eternal relic of your love.'

Maya did not wear it even once. She used to open the box and gaze at the beauty of the glittering stones for a while, and keep it back in the locker. Those were emerald stones. Its beauty kept on increasing day by day.

One day, Maya made a call to Suresh in his office phone. One Lokesh from Delhi, who was Suresh's assistant, attended the call.

'Boss has gone to Kerala two days back' Lokesh said.

Maya was startled. This is the first time he is leaving for Kerala without informing her. That night she could not sleep. She tossed in the bed to left and right and still sleep did not embrace her. Unnecessary thoughts, kept on tormenting her mind and finally, she decided to visit Thrissur, uninvited'.

'Let it be a surprise' Maya thought to herself.

She decided to go by train, in the ordinary compartment and she reserved a berth, in coach S-6 of Bombay Kanyakumari Express. She did not know that, this journey will turn her life topsy turvy and the relation will be snapped, once and for ever.

At Suresh's house, Maya spent a sleepless night and thoughts wandering through the past events of her life. Suresh was sleeping peacefully, by her side, and no nightmares or apparition tormented him. Maya rose at 6am, had her bath, changed clothes and went direct to kitchen. Suresh's mother was in the kitchen and the maid was making breakfast.

'Amma, I'll help you' Maya said.

'No, beti thank you' Suresh's mother said in broken English.

'Amma, I can understand malayalam. Where is Rajani and children?'.

'She has gone to her house with children. Only seven days left for Rohini's marriage.'

'Who is Rohini?'

'The daughter of Suresh. The groom is a doctor'.

'Amma, I'll go back to Bombay shortly'

'Beti, don't spoil the marriage' Suresh's mother pleaded Maya with folded hands.

'No amma, never, I will go back before that. I came here to see the house of my husband with whom I have lived for long eighteen years'.

That day, she had an accident. she slipped and fell from the staircase and sustained bruises on hands and legs. She was immediately taken to the hospital, by Suresh and they gave first aid and sent her back, since the injury was not serious.

Next day, she called a taxi and went outside.

'Take me to collectorate'. she asked the driver.

The taxi was parked inside the collectorate compound and she opened the door and left asking the driver to wait. Maya went, direct to collector's chamber. The confidential assistant tried to block her entry, but she ignored him and burst into the chamber, like a hurricane and wept like a child.

The collector was a North Indian, named Biswas mehra and he was taken aback, on seeing the lament of Maya. He asked her to sit down and explain her story in detail. After sometime, Maya regained her composure and narrated her tragic story. On hearing it, collector's mind was touched deeply and tears appeared in his eyes.

After hearing everything, he said 'Do you want to punish him, for the treachery, meted out to you?"

May's face looked terrified and she stared at him, with horror.

'Please think over it peacefully and answer. He can be arrested and sent to prison, if you give a written complaint to the police. But, you have to fight, a long legal battle. He will lose his job, in the gulf and will get jail, for many years.'

Maya kept mum, and remained pensive, for some time. She did not want to see, Suresh languishing in jail, after being convicted, in a criminal case'.

'What is to be done, tell me clearly?' Collector asked again.

'No Sir, I don't want to send him to prison even though he has spoiled my life. He has a big family to look after and his daughter's marriage is due to take place after one week. I want to separate from him and that is all' Maya said in a pathetic tone.

'Then OK, I will send my ADM to your house tomorrow morning, to find a solution. I will speak to the panchayat president also in this regard.

Maya thanked the collector, for his sympathy and help and left the chamber, with a crestfallen face. She returned home in the same taxi and nobody asked her, where she went or what was the motive behind it.

Amma gave her, rice and vegetable curry, for supper and she slept in the same bed, as before, upstairs.

Next day, ADM arrived by 10.30 am, in his staff car. The Panchayat president and ward member had reached the house, by that time.

The negotiation continued for two hours and finally arrived at an agreement.

1. Since the marriage is registered, divorce also has to be registered.
2. A compensation of Rupees three lakhs to be given to Maya, by D/D.
3. A flight ticket to Bombay to be arranged.
4. An amount of Rupees five thousand to be given in cash for incidental expenses.

Suresh agreed to this decision, without any objection, and Maya wept profusely, when the mediators left the house.

Next day, the divorce was registered in the office of the District Registrar, Thrissur in the presence of panchayat president and ward member.

After completing formalities, in the registration office, they took Maya to the Cochin Airport. Maya sat in front seat and others including Suresh in the back seat of the car. During the journey, the Panchayat President and ward member talked about the various schemes, to be implemented, during the current year. Suresh and Maya kept silent, till the car reached airport.

'Let us part ways.' Maya will go to Bombay and we back to Anthikad'. Panchayath president spoke in a humorous style.

Maya got down from the car, wiped tears from her eyes with kerchief and walked towards the departure lounge.

Before going inside, she waved her hand several times and others waved back. Suresh, who wore a brave face so far, turned back and walked towards the car, with a haggard face. His eyes were brimming with tears. He opened the door of the car and screamed like an insane person.

There is only five days left, for the marriage. After parting with Maya, Suresh spent two days in despair and mental agony in his room upstairs. He was in a mentally crumpled state. Mother went upstairs and compelled him to come down and eat something but he did not budge. He spent two days with only one packet of biscuit and one bottle of water.

Amma again went upstairs and asked him to eat something but Suresh shouted at her and said, 'Please give some peace of mind. I have no appetite for anything'

'There is only five days left for the marriage, please, bring Rajani and children'. Asked mother.

'No amma, after a couple of days'.

She did not compel him and went down with a worried face.

Next morning, after a cup of tea, Suresh went out, for jogging. After Maya's arrival, he has not gone for jogging.

Suresh returned home, after one hour. He looked very tired and panted excessively, while climbing the steps, of the staircase.

At 9 am, amma again went upstairs, to call him, for breakfast. Suresh, was lying in the bed, with face pressing the pillow.

'Suresh come down and have breakfast'. Mother said patting his shoulder.

No answer.

'Suresh wake up' she said again.

No answer.

She was very much worried and shook him violently.

No answer.

Fear gripped her and she began to lament, loudly.

'Oh! Suresh, Suresh, my son'. She lamented, hysterically.

On hearing the cry, father ran up and shook him and turned him over, with face upwards.

Immediately, the doctor was called in and he, after examining Suresh said.

'I am sorry, masterji, he is no more'.

Father, could not stand the news and he sat on the floor and sobbed.

The news spread like wildfire and the entire people in the locality rushed to Meloth house.

The funeral ceremony was conducted next day. The house and compound became a sea of humanity. A large number of people of that village had assembled there, to pay homage to the departed soul. Rajani fell unconscious, when the body was taken for cremation. The Panchayat President and local MLA participated in the funeral. The body was cremated, at the southern side of the house, after funeral rites. The pyre was lit by his son, Sunil.

The news was communicated to Maya, through a telegram. After one week, the postman brought a cover, to Krishnakutty master. It was from Maya.

Bombay,
05-05-1996.

Beloved papaji,

Even though we were separated, he was the light of my life. God was cruel enough to put out that light. Hereafter, there will be only darkness, in my life. Sorry papaji, Amma, Rajani and children, my deep condolences.

Yours lovingly, Maya.

The marriage of Rohini was postponed to a date, after six months. Invitation was sent to Maya also. On the eve of the marriage, a lot of relatives and friends had gathered at that house. A big Pandal (shamiana) had been erected on the eastern side of the house and the entire compound has been decorated, with festoons and flicker lamps.

A taxi came and stopped in front of the house and a charming lady with a 3 year old boy got down, from the car. She walked to the house. It was Maya. She came straight to the living room and put her vanity bag on the sofa. All people in the house rushed to the living room and encircled Maya.

'Where is my daughter, the bride?", asked Maya. Rohini came forward and touched her feet and Rajani came and hugged her. Maya blessed Rohini warmly. Tears streaked down Maya's cheek and Rajani came forward and wiped it. Maya opened her vanity bag and took out a jewellery box with inscription, Zavery Brothers, Bombay, and she extended it to Rohini.

'This is my marriage gift for you", Maya said and hugged Rohini. Rohini smiled at Maya and opened the box. It was a diamond necklace of extraordinary lustre, made of Ruby stones. Rohini's mind thrilled with ecstasy and kissed Maya over and over again.

'Papaji, I've to catch the return flight to Bombay. I'm leaving now itself". said Maya.

"Whose child is this?'. Asked Amma.

"He is a distant relative of mine. His parents died in a car accident and was in the care of a neighbour's family. I've adopted him after completing the legal formalities.'

The boy called her 'Mama' and she called him 'Beta'.

They got into the car and closed the door. Maya and the boy waved their hands and the crowd gathered at the gate waved their hands in return. The car moved slowly, picked up speed and disappeared from sight.

********* END *********

A PALMIST IN SINGAPORE

Mr. Rajaram was dozing in his cabin, after lunch, in the 20 storeyed Samson tower, of Singapore. His office is situated in the 7th floor of this building. This office was opened two years back, after resigning his job, as manager of an Insurance Company.

Then, the telephone rang and he answered the call. It was from his niece Dr. Lakshmy from Chicago in US.

'Uncle, I'm Lakshmy from US. How're you?, how's your family? I'm coming to Singapore to attend a medical conference, on 21st instant. Dr. Richard, is also coming with me. Please, arrange hotel accommodation for three days. After the conference, we have a plan to tour the entire island.

Rajaram was surprised on receiving such a call. After coming to Singapore, about twenty one years back, he has not heard anything from her. It is a mystery, how she got the phone number. In a flash of memory, he recollected the past events, in his ancestral house, on the bank of Nila - the Bharathapuzha. When the river is in full spate, it is a beautiful sight, from the balcony of the Kovilakam (house of royal family). After the annual examinations, his nephews, nieces and cousins will flock together, in the Tharavadu (ancestral house) and they will go back only after the vacation. There will be a festival like situation, in the big three storeyed Kovilakam. During summer, the Nila will shrink to a narrow stream, and the remaining portion will be sandy plane, stretching for kilometers. Their main playground will be the sandy plane, on the riverbed, from which the river receded to a small stream. They will play football and cricket on the riverbed and then take a bath in the stream and walk to the Kovilakam. The girls also will take part in all the games and dip in the serene and placid waters of the Nila and run fully drenched to the privacy of the bathroom, in the house for changing dress. There were five nieces and all of them were very pretty and good at studies. Altogether, there will be not less than fifteen guests, in the house, during summer vacation.

When he met Lakshmy, last time, she was in the fourth year, of her MBBS, in Calicut Medical College. Rajaram was reluctant to mingle with his cousins, nephews and nieces, because he had failed in the SSLC examination and was roaming with friends for various social activities. He was very smart and energetic and still he had a fear, whether they would sneer at him for his backwardness in studies. He had the image of a hero, among his friends and hence many complaints had been received in his house about him. He was a pampered and spoiled boy, in the eyes of his relatives and neighbours.

After MBBS, Dr. Lakshmy went to London for FRCS and then moved to US, married an American and was working in a famous hospital, in Chicago. After her departure to US and subsequent marriage, he did not have any chance, to meet her. She had come to Kerala, with her husband and held a grand reception, in a star hotel, at Ernakulam. But, he had left to Singapore, by that time.

Rajaram was looking after the landed properties and agriculture of the Kovilakam, till he left to Singapore. He will take necessary money, from the coconut account and live lavishly with his friends. His elder brothers were in Singapore and father Ramavarma was working as manager of a star hotel, in Panaji, Goa. There was no dearth of money, in the Kovilakam and they lived in luxury and splendour. For many years, Rajaram did not think of a job, for himself and lived lavishly with the income of the Kovilakam. On the compulsion of his brothers, he appeared for a supplementary examination after many years and completed his SSLC.

One day, Rajaram met a palmist in the temple compound at Thrissur.

'Can you read my palm?' Rajaram asked the palmist.

'Yes, show me your palm.' The palmist asked.

Rajaram sat in front of him and produced his palm.

'You hail from a royal family. You have come out successful, in an examination, recently. You have many notorious friends. Give up their company and go to your brothers. You will occupy high positions and become very rich. You will have three children and then break away from your wife and children and return to your Kovilakam and ultimately, become a sage.'

Rajaram was an atheist and he did not believe in astrology and palmistry. He was surprised, on hearing the prediction, of the palmist.

'How do you know that, I hail from a royal family?'

'It's written on your face,'

'Where are my brothers?'

He pointed his fingers towards east and said 'Beyond the seas.'

'What shall I do to become rich?'

'Go to the place, where your brothers live'.

He paid ten rupees to the palmist and returned home.

After a few days, he had to go to Thrissur and he met the palmist again and said. 'I want to learn palmistry. I'll give you anything, if you teach me this science'.

The palmist agreed and told Rajaram. 'You can't learn this science, without a guru'.

'OK, I'm agreeable for anything. I want to master this science'

'Guruji, what's your good name?' where's your house?'

'Son, I'm Velayudhan and belong to kanakkans gramam, near Pullazhi'

Rajaram paid his guru, a dakshina of fifty rupees and touched his feet.

'Lord Muruga, show kindness to me and bless my disciple, Rajaram'. He closed his eyes and prayed for some time and placed his hand, on the head of Rajaram and blessed.

It lasted for six months and at the end of the lessons he gave him a book titled Hastharekhasasthram.(Science of palmistry).

Rajaram paid him an amount of Rupees five hundred as fees and guru became pleased and said 'If you've any doubt, you can come to me, any time and I'll be here.'

One day, he read the palm of his mother and said 'You are going to become widow'.

Mother was completely upset, on hearing the prediction, of her son. She went to Guruvayoor and many other temples and paid offerings and arranged poojas for the long life, of her husband. Rajaram tried to console his mother and said 'I don't know, whether palmistry is true or not. Nothing will happen to our father. Don't worry.'

After a couple of weeks, Ramavarma came to Kovilakam in a taxi, without any prior intimation.

He was seriously ill and immediately taken to Mission Hospital, Thrissur. He lay in the hospital, for about six months and ultimately, breathed his last. A lot of money was spent for the treatment of father and still they could not save his life. Misfortunes, began to haunt the Kovilakam, one after another. After father's demise, his sisters demanded partition of the ancestral properties. They attributed that the income from the property was being misused by Rajaram, for wine and women. This accusation was unbearable to Rajaram and his mother. Rajaram in a fit of anger stopped irrigation, of the coconut palms, during dry season and neglected the paddy cultivation. Coconut fronds became dried up completely, after stoppage of irrigation and woodpeckers made holes in the trunks of the dried coconut trees and parrots and kingfishers began to live in these holes. Headless trunks of hundreds of coconut trees, stood looking at the naked sky and this was a poignant sight and caused bitterness and sorrow to everybody.

Rajaram made a trip to Goa, to bring home the belongings of papa and was ashamed to hear that his father had another family there, with one school going daughter. He met papa's friend Pereira, who was working in the reception dept. of the hotel and he took him to that lady. She and her daughter were living in a rented house. She was a Goan catholic named Sophia and was running a beauty parlour. The daughter, Shimna was studying for BCom, in a private college. Rajaram returned home in anguish and mental agony. He kept it a secret and did not tell anybody He did not stay at the Kovilakam for long and left for Singapore one day after informing mother.

Rajaram's arrival, was a surprise to his brothers Radhakrishnan and Chandradas, who were in better positions there. Elder brother Radhakrishnan was senior accountant in a ship maintenance company and he had four daughters and three sons. The younger brother Chandradas was working as an Officer in the Sports control board and he had two daughters and one son. He was a close friend of the union leader Devan Nair, who later became President of Singapore They had their own apartments and their children were studying in prestigious institutions.

Rajaram stayed with Radhakrishnan and he learned accountancy from him and appeared for the government examination in accountancy and got through. He was immediately selected by an insurance company, as assistant. He was very able to canvass people, to take life policies by means of his amiable nature and palmistry. His predictions became true for some chinese clients and they made big publicity of his ability, to tell future, by reading palm. In one case, he predicted an accident to her husband and in the second case he predicted that her daughter will secure first rank, in her higher secondary examinations. Both these predictions became true and thus there was a gold rush to meet Rajaram by Chinese ladies and all of them took new policies from him. On the basis of the business, he ranked first in the company and thus he got out of turn promotion and became Asst Manager and then Manager in a short period. He married a bengali lady, named Nanditha, working in the same branch and purchased a new apartment and car.

Rajaram woke up from his reverie and started his work as Medical Consultant. He had a number of highly qualified doctors at different parts of the world. Patients can consult these doctors through video conference and without going to hospital, their problems were solved. 50% of the fees charged will be credited to the accounts of the doctors. There was a well equipped lab in his complex and thus consultation and investigations were done simultaneously. He had also employed a lady physician, named Dr. Neeraja in his office. In case, anybody wanted direct consultation, they can meet Dr. Neeraja. In addition to this, he used to read palm at the request of customers for pushing life insurance policies. In a short time, Rajaram became a rich man. One day, he accidentally met Devan Nair, in a function who was then President of Singapore. Rajaram shook hands with him and examined his palm.

'Devanji, your palm says that you'll resign and leave Singapore.'

'Why should I resign? I'm very cordial with our PM'

'You are going through a very difficult period'.

'I don't believe in palmistry' He laughed.

After a few months, he resigned and left for US.

On 21st, Rajaram went to the Airport, in his Benz car and received Dr. Lakshmy and husband.

When they boarded the car, Lakshmy asked 'Uncle how far away is the hotel?'

'It's nearby, we can reach there by 30 minutes.'

She would have thought that, Rajaram will be working in some company, as chauffeur and he has come with the company car to receive them.

After running for about 30 minutes, the car reached an independent house, on the top of a hillock. Rajaram stopped the car and asked them to get down. Dr. Lakshmy and husband followed Rajaram to the house and they were received by a smiling Nanditha. It was a surprise for Lakshmi and Richard when they heard that the four bedroom bungalow belonged to them Dr. Lakshmy could not believe, on seeing their three sons, Rajiv, Rajesh and Ranjith. speaking English, in American accent.

They stayed with Rajaram and family, for three days happily and left for US after seeing some important sightseeing places. When they left Rajaram jumped in joy and told his wife' 'Lakshmy thought that, I'm only a company chauffeur and that, I'm still that old good for nothing uncle. She has realised that we're living in more luxury and comfort than she.'

Rajaram got an urgent message from brother Radhakrishnan, His youngest son Pramod was admitted to hospital with high fever. The doctors did everything possible to save the life, but he breathed his last. They could not diagnose the illness. Radhakrishnan and Prameela were in great shock and anguish. Rajaram and his wife went there and tried to mitigate their grief, but in vain. Days, weeks and months, passed and still they could not reconcile, with the loss and hence they decided to go back to India. Chandradas, Rajaram and all of their friends and relatives tried to dissuade them, from the hard decision, but they did not relent. One day, they set sail to Chennai. After reaching the Kovilakam, Radhakrishnan wrote a letter to Rajaram and it was really a touching account of his love towards his son who left them at such a tender age.

Shornur,
25-8-1990.

Dear Rajaram and Nanditha,

We arrived here safely. We feel that, our beloved son Pramod is still with us. After landing at Chennai, we stayed in a hotel for two days, to arrange reservation for onward journey to Thrissur. At Chennai, the children made a lot of problems, saying that, they want to go back to Singapore. The reason was the dirt and filth and the unhygienic conditions of our roads and streets. It took much time and energy to convince them, that India is a very big country and is on the path to development. Here, we cannot expect the neatness and high hygienic conditions of Singapore. Hence, we took them to Mylapore area which is more beautiful and healthy.

Finally, they agreed to remain here and we heaved a sigh of relief. From Chennai, we got reservation in AC coach and the journey was very comfortable. During train journey, Prameela got up from sleep and cried, saying that, she saw Pramod lying by her side and when she woke up, he disappeared.

Rajaram, I have saved enough money for the future life, including children's education. It was my wish, to take them home before the national service commences. After completion of the national service, we can not do anything against their wish.

Amma is having all kinds of ailments and still she is pulling on, with the help of some servant maids. The Kovilakam is in a dilapidated condition. A commission had come to measure the property and nothing heard after that. It is better to be partitioned, at the earliest. But, I don't think it possible, since the heirs are at different parts of the world and some have left this world already.

Hope you are fine. Convey our enquiries to all others.

Yours lovingly,
'Radhakrishnan.

Rajaram has got a close friend named Chandramohan. He hails from Kodungallur and is a leading advocate, there. He has married a Chinese lady and have two children out of this wedlock. He is very rich and living in the lifestyle of a Chinese millionaire. His wife is a doctor and both the sons are studying for medicine. He used to come to his consultancy office and spend hours discussing various problems related to Singapore.

'We Indians have no problems here. There's no unemployment and no discrimination against Indians and other minority sections such as Malaysians, Jaffna Tamils etc. All are living in perfect love and harmony. We don't know what'll happen after Lee. He's such a visionary and great leader and it's his efforts which made Singapore a prosperous nation, without any ills of our society. There's no natural resource here and the only resource of Singapore is manpower and with this resource Lee has created a wonderful world here. He's really like our mythological king Mahabali who made a rich kingdom, in Kerala, without any vices of modern world'. Chandramohan said once.

Rajaram took the palm of Chandramohan and read it. He was startled and was hesitant to say the truth.

'What's the matter? You look embarrassed. Tell me the matter'. He requested him with folded hands.

'There's some problem for you, be careful.'

'What's the problem?'

'You'll separate with your wife, within six months'

'Is it true?'

'Yes, your palm says so.'

'I don't believe.' He laughed and ignored it.

The prediction became true. For a minor issue, he fought with his wife. The two sons supported mother and pushed him out of the house. He took a rented house and started living there alone. Even after six months none of his family members rung him up or came for reconciliation and hence, he applied for divorce and it was granted. Then he went to Kerala, married a beautiful girl and brought her to Singapore.

Rajaram had a lady secretary named Nalayani, a JaffnaTamil. She was very hardworking and will sit very late in the office to clear pending works. With the irony of fate, he became very close with her and began to live like man and wife secretly. One day, that secret became public and his wife quarrelled with him and that ended in divorce. But, they could not live long. Nalayani's brother arrived one day from Malaysia and took her forcefully to his house, in Kuala Lumpur

Rajaram had two rented houses. One is occupied by him and the other was rented out to a widow, named Rajashree Iyer, from Kadalur, Tamil nadu. She had two daughters and they are employed in Canada. They invited her to Canada but she did not go and was staying alone. She used to come to the consultancy office, occasionally and spend time, discussing various topics.

One day, Rajaram said 'Rajashree We are going on a tour to Canada and US, Do you join us?'

'Yes, I'll come anywhere. Tell me, when you are planning to go?.'

'It's part of a tour package. About fifteen people have already registered their names'

'How many ladies are there?.'

'Most of them are couples. I'm alone and have no company'.

'Then I'll give company to you, don't worry'

It was a three weeks' tour programme and the journey started on a Saturday after one week.

It was really a thrilling experience for Rajaram and Rajashree. Both of them were leading lonely lives for years. They both lived in one room and went to meet Rajashree's daughters together.

'Uncle she's leading a boring life, for years, after demise of our father. Please, give company to her and dispel her boredom.' Both the daughters told Rajaram, in one voice.

After that Canada- US trip, Rajaram took her to various parts of the world and dispelled her boredom and loneliness.

'I'm going to Kerala. Do you come with me?'

'Certainly. I haven't seen the God's own country so far'

Rajaram took her to his Kovilakam and met mother who was bedridden due to various ailments.

Amma kissed his hands and enquired 'How is your wife and children?'

'They are well off. Wife has to go to office and children are studying'.

'Who's this lady?'

'Her name's Rajashri and she's my friend. She has heard about Kerala and came with me to see it.'

Amma smiled and blessed her son and his friend.

They visited all their relatives, including his brother Radhakrishnan who is living in a beautiful house, constructed recently in Thrissur town. His children are studying in various colleges and he is running an Accountancy coaching institute, in the town.

Brother scolded him for his wayward life and asked him to look after the children properly.

'How dare you bring such a lady to our house. This is not Singapore. There, you are at liberty to do whatever, you like'.

'Sorry, If you don't like me walking with her, I'll not bring her again. Excuse me this time. Nanditha and children have no financial problems and still I'm helping them. I've given my house to them'. Rajaram said.

Rajaram took Rajashri first to Goa and stayed there for one week. During his stay there, Rajaram took Rajashri to a beauty parlour and enquired about Madam Sophi. The new owner of this parlour was one Mumbai lady, Remla and she said.'I purchased this shop from one Neetu Menon, some two years back and I have no idea of Madam Sophi'. He spoke to some shop owners in the vicinity and they had no information about this lady or her daughter. So, they boarded a train to Cochin. After spending two days in Cochin, they proceeded to Thekkady and then to Moonnar, Alappey, Trivandrum and Kannyakumari and then went back to Singapore.

After a few months, Rajashree flew to Canada, since the marriage of her elder daughter had been settled. Thus Rajaram became lonely again and without company. After reaching Canada, she had telephoned and invited him for the marriage. He could not go and sent a greeting. After marriage Rajashree became ill and could not return to Singapore.

One day, brother Chandradas came to meet Rajaram. His visit was to invite him for the marriage of his eldest daughter Gita, who is a doctor. The groom also is a doctor by name Nagaraj. His parents migrated to Singapore from Andhra Pradesh only a few years back.

'What about Sudarsan? Where is he working now?'

'He has married a Chinese lady, some time back and is living separate. He's an engineer in Siemens and his wife also is working in the same company.

From the talk, Rajaram realised that his brother is not happy in the selection of the life partners by his daughter and son. He consoled him with some soothing words 'Brother, this is Singapore nobody can question them. They can select anybody as their life partner. We have no moral right over them and the only alternative is to approve their selection.'

Rajaram had gone to attend the marriage. It was conducted first in a church and then in a Hindu temple and the reception was arranged in a small auditorium. Then only, he came to know, that the boy is a christian, though his name is that of a Hindu boy. The attendance in the marriage was not more than hundred. It was obvious, that, he had not invited more people. Chandradas had a large friends' circle there and still he did not spend much for this marriage. Rajaram thought that his brother's mind has to be purified since he is still behaving like an Indian even after having lived in Singapore for over forty years. Indian boys and girls born and brought up in Singapore have broad outlook and considers all communities and nationalities as one. Those born and brought up in India, has to be reformed, to reach the social standards of Singapore.

Rajaram is very fond of Thai girls and used to go to Bangkok occasionally and stay there for weeks. His life was very miserable for want of company. He once thought of marrying again, since leading a lonely life in a flat of a skyscraper in Singapore is very horrible, but his friends and wellwishers were against such a gamble. They advised him to reconcile with his old wife since she is still a young lady. But, he was not interested and said 'Age is advancing rapidly, and nobody can stop old age. If I reconcile with her, she may drive me out again or when I'm laid up she'll settle score with me.'

One day, a terrible news reached him when he was talking with a client in office. 'Adv. Chandramohan had a massive heart attack, while arguing a case, and he died instantly in the court premises, before being shifted to hospital. This message was conveyed to him by brother Chandradas. Rajaram was shocked out of his wits, and rolled down in a speechless condition.

Dr. Neeraja was available at that time and she immediately gave an injection to reduce his tension.

Rajaram was advised to take rest for about one hour, for release of tension and when he came round to normalcy, wanted to go to the residence of Adv. Chandramohan immediately and Dr. Neeraja arranged a driver to take him to the house of the deceased.

Rajaram could not control his grief, because he was so much attached to him, for years. There was a huge crowd in that lane, where he was living. He managed to go inside, and had a look, and came out. He accompanied the body to the crematorium, and returned to his house. Rajaram was completely shattered on the demise of his close friend. He did not go to his office, for two days and was in uncontrollable grief. He was really heartbroken, and took to drinking, for peace of mind.

Memories came flooding to his mind, and he was restless, and in great mental agony and could not sleep alone in his flat. So, he came out and started his car and went to his old house. When he pressed the calling bell, a chinese boy opened the door.

'Where's Nanditha?' He asked.

'No Nanditha here. This's the house of Dr. Chiang Semin'.

'They were staying here.'

'Yes, that Indian lady, I can remember now. She has sold it to us, some three years ago and went somewhere.'

'Do you know where she went from here?'.

'No, I don't know. You please speak to my Papa'

Rajaram did not wait further to meet the doctor. He walked back to his car, started, and went to the house of brother Chandradas. He is visiting that house, after so many years.

'Rajaram, how did you find out the house?' Chandradas asked.

'Sorry brother, sorry, for not coming here, for so many years'.

'What sorry, you don't know the value of blood relation. Here, there are only two families and still we do not meet each other and share our difficulties. You're living for enjoying life and it'll be a waste of time and energy to discuss with you, about family relations and problems. You can't do anything in this respect, I know'. Chandradas was furious.

'Brother, I'm sorry. I came here for some peace of mind, and you are trying to drive me out. OK, I'll go now itself.'

Rajaram turned back to go, and then Chandradas came, and hugged him, and dragged him to his house.

Both of them began to cry, and then Gita came forward, and pacified both of them.

'Gita, where'is Nandhitha and children.? I want to see my children. Even though, I'd divorced my wife I've still great love towards Nanditha and my children. I went to see them in my old house, but it's now occupied by one Chinese doctor and family.

'They have left Singapore. They have gone to Australia, about six months back. Rajiv and Rajesh have passed engineering, and they have been trying for a visa to Australia, and now they got it, and all of them left together, for a better life.'

Rajaram was completely shattered, on hearing this news. 'They could have at least made a call to me, before leaving this place. They didn't do it. OK, they have won and I've failed' Rajaram could not control himself and he began to cry like a child.

Rajaram returned to his flat, after some time, and did not stay that night with Chandradas and family. He could not sleep that night, and opened one bottle of whisky and started drinking.

Next day, he flew to Calcutta, and from there to Buddha Gaya by road. He got his head tonsured, and became a buddhist monk. Stayed in Gaya for two weeks and returned to Singapore. Rajaram telephoned his brother Chandradas, and said, 'Brother, I have converted to buddhism and became a monk. I'm entrusting the consultancy to you. Dr. Neeraja will run it well, and you simply look after everything, including my two flats and car. After a couple of days, I'll go to Kerala. From there, I'll go on a long pilgrimage to Himalayas.

Rajaram reached his Kovilakam and touched the feet of Amma. She was very much pained, on seeing him in the new saffron attire. Neighbours and old friends came to see him. That evening, he went to Thrissur temple compound and searched for the palmist, his guru Velayudhan, but he could not find him anywhere. He asked some palmists sitting there, and one of them said 'He is dead and gone. His son is here and I'll bring him'.

After fifteen minutes, he brought a lungi clad man from the other side of the temple compound.

'This's the eldest son of Velayudhan. He is also a palmist'

'What's your name?'

'Andavan'.

'Where's your father, my guru?'

'He's no more. He died five years ago"

Rajaram took out a handful of currency notes from his pocket and thrust it into his hands and said. 'Your father is not an ordinary human being, but he had the powers of God Velayudhan. He is my guru and he had predicted that, I would become a sage. His prediction has come true, but before that, he has gone'. Rajaram laughed and then, he walked briskly towards the Vadakkumnathan temple.

********* END *********

ELEPHANT ROCK ESTATE

Usually, coffee plants bloom during the month of March or April. In the event of pre monsoon rains, the entire valley will be in bloom, within a few days and the air will be filled with a pungent fragrance. It will attract millions of butterflies, from far and wide, for pollination of these flowers. These multicoloured butterflies will fly together, and it will look like multi coloured clouds, floating in the sky.

A day in April 1998, the ghat road lay under the blanket of fog. In the yellow fog light, Senthil could hardly distinguish between the road and the protection wall. After climbing 9 hair pin curves, he reached the valley of fragrance. At 7.30 am, nothing was visible and the whole valley lay prostrate in front of him. He got down from his car and looked around and everything looked like phantoms.

Senthil Kumar was awe struck and he stood there, till the sun poked its head above the faraway mountains and then the fog melted away within no time. He then started his car and went forward and stopped near a market and asked a villager. 'Where is the elephant rock estate?'

'It is there' He said pointing to a mountain chain lying in the east. He looked at the mountains and stood there in wonder and amazement for some time. He was impressed by the beauty of the landscape and serenity of the atmosphere.

'How can I go there? Where is the road going to the mountains?' He asked again.

The villager showed him the road and said 'It will take more than one hour, to reach there'.

Senthil kumar turned the car to the tarred road going eastwards. On the way, he saw thick coffee plantations on both sides of the road. They were in full bloom and a penetrating odour wafted to his nostrils.

After going about 1 KM, he stopped at a steel gate with a security cabin and an indistinct sign board.

'Is it elephant rock estate?'

'What do you want?' The security guard asked.

'I've to meet Sunder Lalji'.

'Please write down your name and address and purpose of visit' The watchman placed an old worn out register before him.

He wrote down as below.

> Address
> Senthil kumar. B,
> Senthil Enterprises, Hyderabad.
> Purpose- Business discussion.

Senthil started the car and went forward slowly, since the road was full of potholes. He stopped in front of the bungalow. On the way, he saw a school, dispensary, leaf collecting centre, market and Estate office. Also he saw workers' quarters called paddy and a number of small type bungalows.

'What do you want?'Asked the gate watchman.

'I want to meet Sunder Lalji'

'What's the purpose?'

'To discuss some business matters'.

'Write your name and purpose'. The watchman gave a piece of paper and Senthil wrote the name and purpose.

The watchman went inside and returned within five minutes.

'You can go inside and meet him now'.

Senthil went inside and he was warmly welcomed by Sunder Lalji. Senthil was very much impressed by the hospitality of Lalji. Discussion continued for about one hour and then he came out of the bungalow, thanked the watchman and left'.

Two months elapsed, after the visit of the stranger from Hyderabad. One day the Manager and Laison Officer were called to the bungalow of proprietor Sunder Lalji. At that time, Mr Senthil and his friend one Mr. Venugopal, chartered accountant from Calicut were also there.

'This is Mr. Joseph Mathew, Manager and Deepak Liaison Officer', Lalji introduced them to the guests.

Senthil and Venugopal shook hands with them.

'Mr. Joseph Mathew, the estate has been sold to Mr Senthil from Hyderabad. Negotiation has been going on for the last two months and agreed to the price quoted by him.' Lalji said.

'How much is the price?'Manager enquired.

'Seven crores 'Lalji said.

'It' s very low. The extent of the estate is about 1200 acres and it is in perfect condition'. Said manager.

'This's a labour oriented industry and it is hard to make much profit. Further, tea price is falling day by day. Now Russia is not participating in the auction and new bidders are reluctant to come to Cochin. Many companies have started local marketing and some are selling the tea from their factory itself.'Venugopal said. He was thorough with the market trends of tea industry. Talk continued for some more time and they were served with tea and biscuits. When Mr Joseph Mathew and Deepak left, Lalji called his wife Hema and introduced her to Mr Senthil and Venugopal.

'My wife is not well and we want to go back to Pune at the earliest. We are alone here. Daughter was given in marriage to a businessman in Bombay and son went to London for higher studies in medicine. He is a doctor and has no interest in plantation. His plan is to practise in Bombay after his MRCP. I was studying in Bombay, when my father purchased this estate from an englishman in the year 1950. Forty eight years have passed after that. My father was very much interested in plantation business and liked this place very much. There are so many big, big estates, here, but most of them are in the hands of companies like Poddar, Harrison Malayalam, Elston, Assam brook etc. but very few proprietary concerns like ours All these forests were cleared and converted into tea estates by Europeans and they left one by one after independence'.

Sunderlalji waxed eloquent about the history of plantations in Wynad.

'Who were the owners of these forests?' Senthil asked'

'These forests were owned by some families and Europeans had taken them on lease and after hundreds of years nobody will come to claim them. They have taken too much pain in clearing the bamboo forests and planting tea saplings with silver oak for shade and constructed beautiful bungalows at the top of hills. They have braved the wrath of wild animals like elephants, tigers, bears, boars etc. They brought cheap labour from Tamilnadu and made paddys (quarters)

for them to stay. Whatever we see today, is the sweat and tears of the British people mainly.

They have also taken labour from here to their plantations in Malaysia, Surinam, Figi, Morasia etc.

'We were completely ignorant of the role of Europeans in our plantations.' Venugopal said.

'How old are you Mr. Senthil?' Lalji asked.

'I'm forty. I was born and brought up at Vanchiyoor, Trivandrum. Father was in the service of Maharaja of Travancore. I was in gulf for a period of 15 years and invested my money in real estate at Hyderabad and Chennai. After returning from Gulf I opened my present office in Hyderabad. My main business is real estate and granite quarry at Sathyamangalam. Senthil introduced himself and Venugopal remained silent.

'Venugopal where is your office at Calicut?' Lalji asked.

'It's near Christian College'.

'How did you become friends?'

'I was working as chief accountant in the company where Mr. Senthil was Sales Manager. After returning from Gulf, I started practising and Mr Senthil went to

Hyderabad. Even though, we were far apart he used to take advice from me in each and every case'. Said Venugopal.

'Are you married Mr. Senthil?' Lalji enquired.

'No.'

'Why, so late?'

'I did not find time to think about marriage or rather I was afraid of marriage'.

'Mr Senthil, I came to Wynad at the age of 30, immediately after marriage. Till then, I was living in the house of my uncle in Bombay. My father fell ill, and mother asked me to come over here to take the reins of the estate. After short illness father passed away and mother followed suit. The estate came to my hands, since my brother had his own business in Nairobi and Sister was living in Pune. After coming here, I rarely went to Bombay or Pune. My children were born here and had their education in Bangalore. My wife is an extra ordinary housewife, with no demands. I am very much worried since she is not well.' Lalji's eyes became wet.

They talked for a long time and left on the assurance that the registration will be done within two weeks. After registration, Lalji and family went to Pune. A big joint send off was given to Lalji and family by the various associations of the employees. They were given a send off by the Wynad planters association also.

Senthil took over the charge of the estate and started living in the Estate Bungalow. It is really a palatial bungalow, with six wide bedrooms, living room, dining, kitchen and a conference hall upstairs, three balconies, servant's quarters, garage, and a restroom for watchman. There were innumerable exotic flower plants in pots, in front of the house and in the terrace upstairs. If we look from the balcony on the northern side the valley lying to the west and north can be seen including Kalpetta town. It is really marvellous, to see the valley under green blanket for kilometres as far as the eye could see. After night fall, the atmosphere will become very cold and chilly and without sweater, room heater, or fire it is rather difficult to live there.

The stillness and tranquility of the night is broken by the whistling sound of the beetle and cricket. Occasionally, the hooting sound of owl and sweet music of lark can be heard. The night is always cold at the bungalow. Senthil will use a sweater and a thick blanket in night for easy embrace of sleep.

For few days, food was brought from a resort at Kalpetta since all servant maids had gone along with Lalji and family to Pune. In the meanwhile, Deepak, Liaison Officer, brought a lady from a far away paddy for cooking food for Senthil. Nalini the new cook was surprised when Senthil spoke to her in Tamil 'Sir you speak very good Tamil, are you from Tamil nadu?'. Nalini asked with love and respect.'

'I'm from Trivandrum, but my mother tongue is Tamil' Senthil said.

After a few days, a new lady by name Prema joined Nalini in the kitchen.

In a short time, Senthil studied every thing about the estate. He prepared a dossier about all types of staff from tea plucker to Manager. Also he made an inventory of the assets of the estate. Also, he collected data of the total chapp(leaf) plucked daily, total production of tea and average monthly revenue from auction and monthly expenditure for salary, electricity, diesel, pesticide, fertilizer, taxes and miscellaneous items. He was really shocked to find that the profit during the last one year was negligible.

One day, Senthil was brooding over the ways and means for reducing expenditure and increasing production. then Mr, Joseph Mathew came to the bungalow to discuss some urgent issues.

'Please be seated, what is the news?' Senthil asked with a smile.

'The worker's unions have submitted a joint charter of demands for consideration of the new management'.

'What are the demands?' Mr Joseph Mathew please read out the demands one by one' Senthil asked with curiosity.

Mr. Joseph Mathew read out the demands.

1. Bonus to be enhanced to 15 % from the present 8,33 %.
2. Daily wage of the workers to be enhanced by 20% to all section of workers. Leaf pluckers should be given allowance irrespective of their output. The plucking charge to be enhanced by 50%.
3. Special allowance to the pesticide spraying staff.
4. Special allowance for workers in night shift in the factory.
5. Posting of a doctor in the dispensary
6. Conveyance to be arranged for students living in far away paddies.
7. Issue of blankets to all sections of workers.
8. Immediate maintenance of all paddys.

Senthil became aghast on hearing the demands and said 'Within one month of my take over they have come with unreasonable demands. I am not going to accept any of these.' Senthil said.

'We can not reject this outright. We can tell them that demands with high financial implications can not be considered now, since the financial position of the company is pitiable'.

'OK, you deal with them and settle the problems. At presen, the estate is running on loss. You have to convince them with facts and figures and avoid unnecessary strike.'. Senthil said.

'OK Sir, I will try'. Joseph Mathew said.

Joseph Mathew called the union leaders for a discussion after two days. He put the proposals before them but they did not accept. Unions submitted a notice for indefinite strike. Then, Senthil called the leaders to his bungalow for discussion and requested them to put off the strike.

'Now our financial condition is precarious. I will consider your demands when financial position improves'.

'Tell us, when the financial condition will improve?' Asked one leader in an agitated mood.

'You are aware, that I am new in this field. I have already taken a huge loan for purchase of the estate and another loan is not possible at present. The estate is running on loss, for the last two years. Without increasing production, I can not consider any of your demands'. Senthil was very firm and hence the talk failed. They gave notice of indefinite strike.

Indefinite strike started. There was no plucking of chapp(Leaf)., factory, school, dispensary and office remained closed. The workers gathered in front of the office and demonstrated.

Manager Mr. Joseph Mathew and Liaison Officer Deepak used to meet Senthil in his bungalow and review the strike situation.

'Is there any news from the union leaders?' Senthil asked.

'They are very adamant, but the worker's condition is very pathetic. If they do not get the pay their condition will be pitiable. They can not pull on beyond one month. There will be penury and privation in paddys if it is a prolonged strike.'

'Shall I call them for another round of talks?. Now, two weeks have passed'. Senthil said.

'No sir, let us wait and see whether they will have second thoughts. The ordinary workers are ready to come for work. But hardcore workers are threatening them with dire consequences'.

The strike has entered the sixth week. There was abject poverty in paddys. Children are crying for food. Many fell il, but they have no money to take them to hospital at Vythiri or Kalpetta.

One day, Mr Joseph Mathew and Deepak were coming out of the bungalow of Senthil after review of the strike position then a group of people attacked them with sticks and rods and ran away. Senthil heard a shout and then a scream and ran to the gate, but by that time the assailants had escaped and two persons were found lying on the road. He and the watchman ran up to the spot and found Joseph Mathew and Deepak lying in a pool of blood. Immediately he took them in his car to a missionary hospital at Vythiri and then to Calicut Medical College Hospital. From Calicut, he telephoned the police and registered a complaint. Joseph

Mathew sustained serious head injuries and Deepak's hand was fractured. The police arrested four workers of the estate and they were remanded to police custody for two weeks. Later, police came and enquired with Deepak and Joseph Mathew in the hospital. Deepak gave a full account of the incident, but Joseph Mathew could not speak anything, due to the injury.

Joseph Mathew was admitted to the orthopaedic ward first and later shifted to the neurology section since he had severe head injury. His family at Kottayam was informed and they came to the hospital, immediately. Senthil stayed at Calicut for two days and then went to his estate bungalow after giving some money to the wife of Joseph Mathew and father of Deepak for hospital expenses.

The strike has entered the eighth week, and no solution was in sight. The workers began to go outside in search of work in coffee plantations. There was starvation in all paddys, and still they did not compel their leaders to settle the strike. There was a hostile atmosphere in the estate and Senthil had many apprehensions about his safety. But he did not seek police protection.

Nalini and Priya wanted to go home, but Senthil did not object and they did not return. The watchman also was found missing. Senthil started to live on bread, banana and black coffee.

One night, Senthil looked through the window of his bedroom, upstairs and saw shadows moving near the gate. A sudden fear crept into his mind. He thought that they were planning to kill him. He could not sleep that night and stood at the window for hours, looking outside. At 5 am, he slipped out of his bungalow in disguise, after locking it and went outside through the short cut road. He was in dhothi and used a cap on head and a shawl and nobody recognised him.

The workers found the house closed and next day all newspapers reported that the proprietor had escaped cheating the workers. Next day, a flag was hoisted in front of his house and workers started relay hunger strike at the gate of the bungalow. Thus strike entered the 10th week and no sign of settlement was visible.

Deepak was discharged from hospital, but Joseph Mathew remained in the hospital since prolonged treatment was required for him. Deepak lodged a police complaint regarding the disappearance of Senthil, because he was afraid of his life. Police made thorough investigation but no information was received. Deepak contacted the Hyderabad office but they had no information and then he contacted his friend Venugopal at Calicut, and he also was not aware of the whereabouts of Senthil. Deepak, then went to his house at Trivandrum, but there was only a lady there, and she did not know anything about Senthil. On enquiry, she told Deepak that she is the second wife of his father. He collected the address of Senthil's sister and went to Thirunalveli.

There, he met his mother and sister and on their direction, Deepak went to an ashram near Neyyar dam and Senthil was found to be safe and sound there. Senthil was surprised on seeing Deepak.

They returned to Calicut and stayed in a hotel. By that time, the workers union had expressed their willingness to negotiate and a meeting was arranged in the presence of labour commissioner and the strike was withdrawn on condition that one month salary should be paid to them in advance and other demands can be settled through negotiations. Senthil agreed to their demand of advance pay and from next day itself all of them came to work.

Senthil did not rejoice. He arranged payment of the advance pay within two days with the amount available in the bank. Thus, that nightmare is over and normalcy was restored in the estate within two days. After reopening the estate, Senthil and Deepak visited the medical college and met Joseph Mathew. 'His condition has improved and can be discharged shortly.' said duty doctor.

'Prolonged treatment is required for him. He is unable to walk even now and prolonged physio therapy has been advised by doctor.' His wife said in a sad and pathetic voice.

'How are you, Joseph Mathew?' Senthil asked by patting him on his shoulder.

'I'm OK, needs some rest. There is some difficulty in walking and it can be corrected by physio therapy.' Joseph Mathew said smiling at Senthil.

'OK, I'll give you 3 months leave with full salary'.

'Thank you sir, thank you, for your big heart'.

Senthil paid a cover containing an amount of Rs 20000/- to Joseph Mathew and he accepted it with thanks.

Senthil returned to the estate with Deepak. On the way, Senthil asked Deepak to look after the duties of Manager, till he rejoins duty and Deepak agreed. After reaching bungalow, Senthil issued necessary orders in this regard.

Next day, he got a message from Murugan requesting him to reach Hyderabad immediately. Senthil started to Hyderabad that evening and reached there in the morning. He went to the office at 10.30 am and Murugan was waiting for him.

'Sir, Bank Manager Kameswar Rao called me several times.'.

'What is the matter?' Senthil asked.

'Non payment of interest'.

At 11 am, they went to the bank and met the manager.

'Interest was not paid'. Manager said.

'Sorry sir, I'll arrange it shortly'.

'Were you out of station? I had rung up several times.'

'I had gone to my estate in Wynad. How much I have to pay?'

'It works out to Rupees 24 lakhs for the first quarter. If you don't pay it immediately penal interest also will be levied.

'OK sir, I'll arrange it immediately.'

Senthil assured the manager and left his cabin.

After reaching office, Senthil told Murugan 'Murugan we have to arrange 1 crore urgently. Fifty lakhs for paying the interest for two quarters and balance for repayment of bonus to the workers. in the estate'.

'How to make one crore?' He asked himself and started brooding over this question.

Finally, he decided to borrow one crore from a Marvari money lender. For this, he will have to mortgage his estate.

Senthil spoke to the money lender and he agreed. But, he is to be taken to the estate and show the documents. Thus Senthil returned to the estate with the money lender named Prahlad.

Prahlad spent two days in the estate and returned to Hyderabad with Senthil. Loan was received next day itself. Senthil paid 48/- lakhs towards interest for two quarters and 50 lakhs was transferred to his account at SBI. branch, Kalpetta.

On returning to Wynad, Senthil arranged for the disbursement of bonus amount to the employees.

But, from that day onwards Senthil was gripped by a kind of tension, fear and anxiety. How to settle the loan amount of Marvari, began to torment his mind always.

'God will show me a way out '' He prayed.

Senthil was an atheist from school days. He has suffered a lot during his childhood. He has seen his mother crying like a child due to the harassment of his wicked father. He had to fight with his father and on the advice of mother he went to his uncle's house at Nagarkovil and he completed his BCom with the help of uncle Chokkalingam pillai who was a merchant. It is his uncle who financed him for his gulf trip. When sister was married to a school teacher at Thirunelveli, mother's plight became pitiable. One day, he brought a lady from Parasala and mother fled to the house of her daughter. Later, they heard that father died in an attack and the new wife became the owner of the property there. Senthil did not go to that house later and went to sisters house whenever he came from Gulf. He had an uncle in Chennai and it is he who advised him to invest in real estate. in big cities, like Chennai and Hyderabad.

After coming back from Hyderabad, he visited Medical College, Calicut to meet Joseph Mathew but he had been discharged and taken to his house at Kottayam.

One day Senthil asked Deepak.'How much tea is available with us.?'

'I'll give a reply within a few minutes, let me contact the Asst Manager in charge of store. Deepak called back within ten minutes and said 'about two loads'.

'When is the auction?'

'Next month'.

'How much we will get out of that? How many loads we can send at that time?"

'We may get about 30 to 40 lakhs if production is at it's peak.'

Senthil did not say anything. He thought to himself 'Ive done a big mistake by purchasing such a white elephant. I've lost peace of mind My properties in Hyderabad, Sathyamangalam and Chennai had to be given as security to get a bank loan of 7 crores. Had I sold those properties it would have been better. Now I can not do any thing with these properties.' Senthil cursed himself for his mistake.

Next day, he gave an ad in all leading newspapers.- A well maintained tea estate for sale, area 1200 acres with new factory. Contact Venugopal, Chartered Accountant, Near Christian College, Calicut.

Many people contacted Mr Venugopal and he took them to the estate, but nobody quoted more than 6 crores. Senthil was dejected. He thought ways and means to dispose it, to free himself from the loan of Marvari. How to get one crore immediately was the question.

In the meantime, Senthil interviewed and posted a lady doctor in the dispensary. She was from a christian family of Thariode. She had taken her MBBS from Trivandrum Medical, College.

Senthil liked Geetharani for her robustness and outspoken nature. She will come to the dispensary on her scooter and go home on the same scooter.

'Can you come on Sunday?' You can take off on some other day"

'No sir, I have to go to the Church.'

'OK, I asked you, because there will be more patients on Sunday. OK no problem the compounder will manage. They'll attend all house calls in case of emergency'.

In the meanwhile, there was a fire in the factory during night. Even though fire brigade came the factory and store room were completely gutted. The workers on duty fled on seeing the fire and and nobody tried to douse the fire. Hence, nobody sustained any injuries due to burns. They could have saved the factory, if they wanted to, but they didn't do it. In the initial stages, the fire spread very slowly. The fire was due to short circuit. Before the fire brigade came every thing had been reduced to ashes Even though, the fire died out automatically, Senthil had to pay a handsome amount to the fire fighters.

Senthil was aghast on hearing the news of fire. Everything was gutted in the fire namely factory, machine, plucked chapp, processed tea and old stock of tea etc. The loss due to the fire incidence was was big and it has shattered Senthil very much and he was laid up with fever and high BP after the fire hazard. Dr. Geeta Rani came and examined Senthil, BP 180/130., Temp 103 degree celsius, and gave one dose of medicine to him, to bring BP under control and reduce temperature. She spent about one hour with him, in his room. Nalini brought tea for both of them.

'Please relax, don't worry. Your high BP is purely due to tension, every thing will be alright.'. Gitarani consoled him.

'Problems are coming one after the other. I am a fool, really a fool, for purchasing this estate without a thorough study and enquiry. I thought, I can mint money. Peace of mind is gone for ever'. Senthil was in a depressed state and he began to sob.

Geetha patted him and tried to console him, but in vain.

'Please relax, we can find out a solution for the problems troubling your mind. I am going now,'

Geetharani went out of the bungalow, started her scooter and left.

Next day, the insurance people came and took a number of photos, verified the documents and left. After that, Electrical Inspector and team came. They made thorough examination of the site took samples of ash, verified the guy wire taken to the factory and collected details from the eye witnesses etc. He is the most important person in the case of a fire accident. His certificate is of great importance for getting insurance claim, compensation etc.

Deepak asked Senthil to pay an amount of Rs 10,000/- to the Electrical Inspector and he paid it most confidentially and without being seen even by the company employees or anybody else.

Following this, KSEB people came and they also had to be pleased. Then came, police to verify the sabotage angle and they were treated well and met their demands. After this, the Plantation Inspector came and made a general enquiry and left. He does not have more jurisdiction in this case. Finally, the revenue people, the Tahsildar came along with Village Officer and ADM. They were taken to the bungalow and given lunch. They behaved well and did not accept anything. When all people left one by one, Senthil heaved a sigh of relief. His BP shot up and found refuge in bed.

Continuously one week, Geetharani came to the bungalow to take BP, Temperature etc.

'Unless you relax and take rest, I will have to give tranquilizer'

'Doctor, even with tranquilizer my BP will not come down.' Senthil said.

'Then tell me, what is your actual problem?' Geetharani asked'. If you tell me the truth, perhaps I may be able to help you.

Senthil lay motionless for sometime and said 'How can I share my problems with you?'

'Then I am going now itself'.

Senthil tried to smile, but could not. Doctor I am in a trap and only suicide can solve my problems'

'What is the trap?'

'In the trap of a bank, money lender and the workers of my own company'.

'How much is your debt?'

'Eight crores'

'It's a huge amount and we people can not do anything'

'Loan is 8 crores, but I have assets worth Rs 20/- crores., but all are under mortgage. They can not be released easily'.

'What is your immediate requirement?'

'1.5 crore' Senthil said a rough amount for freeing from Marvari and paying interest for 6 months.

'I can give you that much amount'

Senthil could not believe.

'How can you arrange so much money?'

'It's not my money. My friend is in search of a property at Vanchiyoor, Trivandrum. If you are willing to sell your ancestral property there, you can make that much' Geetharani smiled

'But, I've no property at Vanchiyoor, who told you that I've a property there.?'

'You've a house and 80 cents of land with an old house there. It'll fetch that much'.

'How did you know about it?' Senthil asked

'Don't ask me anything now. Your step mother is living in that house. Why don't you give something and ask her to vacate. She has no right to possess it. Give me the address with a sketch of the plot and road leading to it.'

Senthil was surprised and he said 'How can I ask her to vacate?. She is my step mother.'

'Don't be sentimental Your mother had to run away because of her. As long as your mother is alive, she has no right. Don't drive her out, give her some four or five lakhs and she will vacate willingly and no question of guilty conscience.'Geetharani said.

Senthil thought she is not a doctor, but an advocate. She is having plenty of practical wisdom.

'I want 3 day's leave. I'll go myself and settle everything.' She said.

Senthil gave her the address with sketch showing the route to the above place.

Geetha went to Trivandrum, stayed in her friend Radhika Thankachy's house and visited the house of Mr Senthil in her friend's car. The house had a special charm even though it was old They were received by a middle aged lady. 'Who are you?What is your motive?' The lady questioned them with dread and fear.

'Do you sell this house?. We want an old model house and liked this house.' They said.

'What is your source of income?'

'I'm getting destitute pension. There is nobody to look after me'.

'In whose name is this house?'.

'It' s in my husband's name and he died some years back'.

'People say your husband has other legal heirs - wife, one son and a daughter.'

'Yes that is true. I was brought here on condition that I will be paid 5 lakhs to nurse him till his death. But without paying that money he left. He did not keep his promise.'

'So this house belongs to his legal wife and children and you have no right on this property.'

'Yes, I admit. I have nursed him and looked after him for three years. Let them take the house and I should get what he promised.'

'What was his illness?'

'He had severe BP, diabetics, heart complaints and what not?'His one leg was amputated and lay in bed for 2 years'. I was a home nurse and hence I could look after him well. Non of his relatives came for the funeral.' She sobbed.

'How much do you expect'.

'The promised amount of 5 lakhs. Then, I will go to my brother's house at Parasala.'

Geetha felt sorry for that lady and said 'We'll ask them to give more than 5 lakhs'

After talking for about one hour, they returned to Thankachi's house and next day Geetha returned to Wynad.

She went to the hospital next day and after duty went to see Senthil in his bungalow. She told everything in detail about his step mother and then asked him 'You give 10 lakhs to that lady and she will vacate the house immediately without any murmur.'

After a couple of days, Senthil went to Thrunelveli and told his mother and sister that they would get back their ancestral property on payment of Rupees ten lakhs. His mother Jagadambal and sister Rethi Devi rejoiced at that news. Senthil told them that there are certain liabilities to the estate and the money received from the sale will be utilised for that purpose and they will be made partners of the company and they agreed. From Thirunelveli, he went to Vanchiyoor and met his stepmother. She was happy to meet him but suspected that he had some ulterior motives, in his visit.

'Ilayamma (step mother), I have a Tea estate at Wynad. You can come and stay with me there. I'll look after you well, till your death. I am thankful for the selfless service rendered by you in looking after my father till his death.'

'Senthil, I'm not coming with you. My brother is living at Parasala and he'll look after me. So, if I get the promised amount, I will vacate the house with my bag and baggage'.

Senthil paid her Rupees 5 lakhs and assured that he 'll send her a monthly pension of Rs 3000/-. She agreed and Senthil locked the house with a new Godrej lock and accompanied her to her brother's house at Parasala. Senthil returned to Wynad from there.

He called Geetha and said 'The house has been vacated and now your friend can quote her price'.

'They will take it at the present market price and no need of bargaining. I'll speak to Thankachy now itself'. Geetha said. Thus the property was disposed off at the rate of Rupees two lakhs per cent and Senthil got I crore and sixty lakhs. Mother and sister had come to the sub registry office for registration.

Senthil told mother and sister that the amount will be divided into three equal parts and one part each will be given to sister and mother and their share will be given after a period of one year. They agreed and the entire money was taken by Senthil. Senthil also enquired whether they wanted share in the company and their reply was negative. After the registration and handing over of the property Senthil took them in his car to Wynad along with his brother in law Subramania Pillai.

They spent one week in the bungalow. Even though Senthil invited them for a Wynad tour they declined and spent the entire time in the bungalow. One day, Geetharani was called to the bungalow and she spent a lot of time in their company and all of them liked the lady doctor very much.

'Amma I'm going to marry this doctor. What is your opinion?' Senthil said in the presence of Geetha and all of them broke into peals of laughter.

All of them liked Geetha and they expressed a genuine doubt whether her parents have agreed for this marriage. Senthil said in a joke 'We'll elope to Tirunelveli, if they did not agree'. Geetha looked at Senthil and laughed again.

Senthil's guests left for Tirunelveli after one week They liked the estate and the bungalow very much. He took them to Calicut Railway station and they boarded a Chennai bound train to Coimbatore. They said at the time of parting 'We'll catch a bus from there to Tirunelveli and that is better than catching train from there. The Kollam Shengottai road is in a very bad shape and this route is far better than that'.

Senthil was relieved of a big burden. He paid off the debt of the Marvari and heaved a sigh of relief. One day Senthil gave a cover to Geetha when she came to the bungalow. She asked 'What is this?'

'This is a small gift for your sincere help. I would like to give you a gift of 5 lakhs. You should accept this.'

She refused to accept it and said 'I have a satisfaction that I could do something for my boss. If that gift is accepted that happiness will desert me'. Then she stood up and left in anger. For many days, Geetha did not come to the bungalow, but Senthil talked to her over phone and apologised for the mistake.

Since the factory was gutted the chapp (leaf) had to be taken to another factory for processing. Every day, two loads will be transported to Rippon estate and the same will be processed and given back at a special rate. Since the rate was found to be high, Senthil made a deal with another factory at Pozhuthana

The compensation claim submitted to the Insurance company was rejected on the ground that sabotage is suspected since the workers had a grudge against the management that their strike was crushed and they had decided to teach the management a lesson and the fire is a handiwork of some disgruntled workers and hence compensation can not be considered. Senthil filed a case in the civil court and fought the battle for over one year and then a judgement came in favour of the company and allowed a compensation of Rupees eighty lakhs. It was another victory of Senthil. He then placed an order on a Mumbai based company for construction of a modern factory in his estate.

His loan has come down to 6.5 crores and then he requested the bank to release his granite quarry from mortgage and the bank agreed. This land was lying unused because of the fear of Veerappan the forest brigand and now a party approached him for a big sum wih the idea of starting 'mining there and since the rate quoted was reasonable he accepted their offer of Rupees two crore and seventy lakhs. He remitted an amount of 2.2 crores towards the loan and thus reduced the loan to 4,3 crores. After this, the bank agreed to release one Chennai property and that was sold for a very high price. In this deal he got 3.3 crore and the entire amount was paid to the bank. and the loan came down to 1 crore only. Subsequently, two more properties were released by bank and now Senthil has enough free property to support him. The bank is prepared to give any amount without security, since he has proved that he is a real businessman. By this time, he received a huge sum by way of auction of chapp and on receipt of this amount he paid some incentives to the workers and other support staff.

Now, there is a glitter in his eyes since he has managed to tide over many crisis and innumerable problems. He has now sufficient bank balance and a special fund for crisis management. The factory work was commenced and there are no labour problems and the company is running smoothly. He paid 50 lakhs to his sister and deposited 10 lakhs in the name of mother Smt. Jagadambal.

Mr. Joseph Mathew resigned the job since he is still unable to walk properly in spite of physio therapy for a long time. He was given a compensation of Rupees 10 lakhs. Mr. Deepak was promoted as Manager and a new Liaison Officer named Pradeep kumar was appointed in his place.

One day, Geetharani came to the bungalow with a cover and gave it to Mr. Senthil and said' 'Sir, I am going to resign and join for MD in St John Medical College, Bangalore and this is my resignation letter'.

Senthil was shocked and his mind sank within him.

'Sorry Geetha, due to lot of problems I was unable to speak with you in recent times. Don't take it as an offence. One day, I'll tell you every thing in detail. I've managed to tide over almost all the problems and now my bank loan has come down to the minimum of 1 crore and they have released most of my properties given as security. Your help has paved the way for quick solution of the problems. Thank you Geetha, you are really a practical girl and I am happy to accept you as my wife, if you're willing.'

Senthil said this much in one breath and looked at Geetha.

'Sir, I came to thank you for your love and affection. I love you very much, but my mother will not approve a marriage out of our community. It's she who brought me up after my father expired and I brooded over it over and over again but I could not take a decision, against the wishes of my mother.'

'Then Geetha, I'm very much indebted to you. Will you be kind enough to accept a small gift from me?'.

'No Sir, thank you. After joining MD course, I'll call you.' Saying this Geetha shook hands with Senthil and went out. It was really a bolt from the blue. He peeped through the window and heard the sound of a scooter moving away. It's sound became thinner and thinner and finally died out. Senthil sank into the sofa and sobbed.

********* END *********

FINAL RETURN
TO CHENNAI

After graduating from a famous college in Chennai, Sujatha joined JNU for MA Economics. She was born and brought up in an orthodox brahmin family, of Madurai. Her father, Sundareswan was a Major in Indian army and her mother Bhagyalakshmy a mathematics professor, in government college, Chennai. Sujatha's mother was very rigid in her attitudes, but, father was a bit flexible', Sujatha was liberal in all respects. She observed brahmin customs at home, but outside she was an entirely different person. She loved students, from all communities and was benevolent towards the poor students in her class, from childhood. Without being seen by others, she used to extend small monetary help, to the needy, irrespective of caste, creed or religion. She had the magnanimity of seeing all castes and religions alike. Mother used to remind her frequently 'Sujatha don't forget that you're a Tamil brahmin girl. Don't bring friends belonging to other communities, to our house'.

Sujatha's ambition was to become an IAS Officer. For BA, she secured fourth rank in the final degree examination. Her previous records were also brilliant. Hence it was the wish of her father to send her to Delhi for post graduation. Sujatha thanked papa, for sending her to Delhi. She thought that, she could improve her English and Hindi, which was highly necessary for UPSC selection.

Sujatha's room mate in the hostel was one Niranjana, from Orissa. Her ambition was also to get through in the Civil service examination. They both liked the extreme climate of Delhi, it's wide roads and cosmopolitan culture.

'Sujatha have you been to Bhuvaneswar?' Niranjana asked her once.

'No, not Orissa, I have visited almost all other cities and important places of India.'

'The temples in Puri, and Conark are world famous. Orissa though poor is a cradle of ancient civilization. Have you heard of Kalinga? that is Orissa. It is the Kalinga war that transformed emperor Asoka as a Buddhist monk.'

Sujatha smiled and said 'Oh!, are you teaching me history? what's the use of history?. Here there's no difference between man and animal? Animal is better, because they've only one motive ie. to hunt for food and procreate. They live in the same environment, drink water from the same pond and live without any protection from sun and rain. Man lives in compartments called castes and higher hierarchy people look down upon others and some are treated as untouchables and we make lofty talk about our civilization and culture. In the book 'Freedom at Midnight' Dominique Lappierre and

Larry Collins have remarked that in India every occupation had it's caste, splitting society into a myriad of closed guilds into which a man was condemned by his birth to work, to live, marry and die. The five divisions of society had multiplied into almost 5000 subcastes out of which 1886 in Brahmins alone. This is India, the great land of Rishis and Upanishads. I hate sage Manu for creating varnasramam in Indian soiety.' said Sujatha.

Niranjana was wonderstruck on hearing the lecture of Sujatha.

'Are you a communist?'

'I'm a communist, socialist, humanist and above all a true Indian. My mind weeps on seeing the stark reality of poverty, inequality, injustice and discrimination in all walks of life. The corrupt politicians are responsible for this pathetic state of affairs in India.'

'I admire your views, but what can we do to reform the society?.'

Niranjana thought that Sujatha may be a member of one of the lowest, downtrodden, sections of society, aspiring for upliftment. Sujatha was dark in complexion, and never uttered a word about her community. Further, she rarely talked about her father or mother but was eloquent about her friends in Chennai and Madurai.

Every month, Sujatha will get a money order from Chennai and occasional letters from papa and mama. Promptly, she will send replies to them.

Niranjana's brother was a Chartered Accountant working in a private company in Noida and used to come to the hostel every week. One day, Niranjana introduced her brother to Sujatha.

'This's my brother Anupam Babu.'

Sujatha greeted him 'Namesthe'

'You're from which place?'.

'Chennai."

'Why came all the way from Chennai?'

'I want to better my English and Hindi'. There at Chennai we use only Tamil in campus as well as in house.'

Sujatha liked Anupam and used to exchange pleasantries whenever they met.

During Christmas holidays, Niranjana planned a trip to Jaipur in Anupam's car and invited Sujatha to join them.

'I can't accompany you without mama's permission.' Sujatha said.

'I'll get permission for you, give me the phone number of your mother.' Niranjana asked.

Niranjana called Sujatha's mother from a booth and spoke to her. 'Aunty I am Niranjana, Sujatha's room mate. We are planning a trip to Jaipur for christmas vacation. All local students have gone to their houses and only a few girls like us are left behind. Shall we take Sujatha with us to Jaipur?. My brother will accompany our party and there is nothing to worry.'

After a lot of questioning, she gave her consent on condition that she should call her from Jaipur.

One Rhea, from next room also came with them. It was a pleasant trip. They started in the early morning. After entering Rajasthan they were ashamed to see hundreds of marble quary workers sitting on their haunches behind the pine tress lining the road. The initial picture of pink city was very ugly and pathetic. Sujatha became very much depressed and gloomy on seeing this sight and she did not look outside till they reached Jaipur city. They spent two days at Jaipur and visited all palaces of Jaipur and also Amber fort. Sujatha relished the trip very much and moved very closely with Anupam. That trip sowed the seed of love between Anupam and Sujatha.

Anupam once told Sujatha that he wanted to marry her, but Sujatha kept mum. When the request was repeated she wrote to her papa and mama stating that Anupam is a handsome gentleman and earns a very good salary and belongs to a rich brahmin family of Bhoovaneswar. In his reply, papa told her to study well and complete her MA and try for civil service examination and think about marriage only after that. Mama wrote a lengthy letter in which she has repeatedly mentioned that she is a Tamil brahmin girl and told her plainly that she would not approve any groom outside her community. She also reminded her that Oriya brahmins like Bengali brahmins are fish eaters and hence they could not be considered for her only daughter. She further mentioned that, if she selected a boy from Tamil brahmins migrated to other states, it wouldl be considered.

Sujatha was in great dilemma. She thought a marriage without parents consent is out of question and hence she tried to withdraw from the love affair. She avoided Anupam for about one month, but he then resorted to letters. She got frequent letters from Anupam and her mental peace was completely shattered. She avoided sending replies to Anupam and her mind became more strained. She had no friend to seek advice and hence she was in great mental agony. She thought of discontinuing studies and going back to Chennai, but she did not want to go back to her mother. Hence she again wrote to her father for advice. He in his reply again emphasised his ambition to see his daughter becoming an IAS Officer and told her not to think of marriage till that objective is attained.

One day, Anupam came to the college and met Sujatha and asked her to get into the car. She hesitated but he compelled her to accompany him to a restaurant, in the city. Finally, she had to obey. He took her to a Punjabi restaurant nearby and and ordered tea, sweets and icecream.

They sat there for about one hour and discussed the case of marriage.

'My parents will not approve our marriage and hence I can not do anything. Let us wait some more time till completion of the course.'

'My parents're compelling me to get married and if you do not agree I'll marry an Oriya girl.

Anupam took Sujatha to her hostel after some time and went back to his lodge.

Sujatha lost her interest in her studies and was in a pensive mood always. Having seen her condition Niranjana once asked. 'Sujatha, what is your problem? You are always gloomy and thoughtful. Tell me everything and I will find out a solution. You are always brooding over something and you have secured very few marks in the last examination.'Niranjana said.

When compelled over and over again Sujatha opened her mind and told her everything.

'OK, I will ask my brother to retreat. Don't waste your life by going behind love and marriage.

Love is not advisable during college days, because it will spoil our studies, career, future and everything in life. We will not achieve our goal, if we got involved in a love affair.

So, stop it now itself and no further meeting and letters. Obey what I say, or you are doomed. Further, my parents will not approve a bride out of brahmin fold'. Niranjana advised Sujatha.

'I'm very much depressed due to the opposition from my parents. If they don't agree, I will discontinue my studies and go home. If I reach Chennai, my mind will become peaceful.'

'Sujatha let me ask you one thing. Are you brahmin?'

Sujatha did not say anything and kept mum. She booked a ticket by train to Chennai and left after a few days. Anupam had come to the station to see her off.

'Don't worry Sujatha. After sometime your parents will approve our marriage and till that date I will wait for you. Don't discontinue your studies.'Anupam said.

After reaching Chennai, Sujatha called Anupam and Niranjana. She spent one week in Chennai. During this period mother took leave and spent time with daughter. She made a number of sweets for her daughter and took her to many temples, in the city. Sundaresan telephoned from Amritsar and talked to Sujatha for about half an hour. He told her to forget everything and study well to achieve the goal of an IAS cadre. Sujatha heard everything and said yes to all his demands.

'Please obey mama. She's a very very practical woman' Papa put down the receiver after saying this.

Mama, one day called her to the pooja room and asked her to pray to Gods that she would not disobey parents and would be loyal to them till the end of her life. Sujatha simply said something silently, closing her eyes.

Mama was very happy and thought that she would never dare to disobey her parents

One day, Bhagyalakshmy made her sit by her side in the sofa and advised 'Sujatha think over it and withdraw from the love affair. We have saved too much for you. If you disobey that will be given to some charitable organisations or temples. Sujatha tried to convince mama that she is unable to forget Anupam.'Mama he is such a nice guy, educated, handsome, rich and brahmin.'

Then, she became very angry and said 'Stop this nonsense. If you do not obey, you will cease to be our daughter and you will have no right whatsoever on our wealth.'

Sujatha's father was not so rigid as his wife Bhagyalakshmy, but fully supported her views on life. He directed his elder brother Ramaswamy whom Sujatha called periyappa with great respect and love, to go to Chennai and advise Sujatha. Periappa was a kind hearted man and was unable to wound anybody, especially Sujatha. He, immediately boarded a bus from Madurai to Chennai.

After reaching there, he called Sujatha to his side and said 'Sujatha study well and appear for the civil service examination and come out in flying colours. After becoming a District Collector, we can think about marriage and children. If you marry now, your education will be spoiled and you will become big zero. So, forget that boy and obey what mama and papa say. I say this in your wider interest. If you don't obey, it will lead to a permanent break up of relations.'

'Sujatha was adamant and said 'I'll not marry anybody other than Anupam'.

Periappa left for Madurai after lunch and Sujatha returned to Delhi the next day. Anupam received her at the station and took her to hostel. While going back they took a decision to marry after one month.

Thus, on a wednesday they married at the Birla mandir in the presence of a small crowd of friends and relatives. Sujatha was later taken to his new residence at Noida. Sujatha wrote detailed letters to her papa, mama, and Periappa regarding the marriage. No greetings or letters were received from any of them. Thus Sujatha decided to face the challenge.

From next month onwards, the money orders and letters stopped Sujatha did not waver or weep. She decided to discontinue her studies, Anupam asked her to continue her studies and offered to meet all the expenses but she did not relent. Thus Sujatha became a housewife and homemaker.

She began to prepare food for Anupam. In the initial stages Anupam did not like the taste because it was in the south indian style. She learned necessary guidance from Anupam and began to make food in the Oriya style. She prepared fish curry and mutton curry for Anupam and he found them tasty. Sujatha continued to be a vegetarian, even though she prepared non vegetarian dishes. Gradually she learned to prepare very tasty food and stole the heart of her husband.

In the meantime, Anupam got a job in a famous Tea estate, in Dibrugarh, Assam as chief accountant and he accepted the offer since it was a highly paid job. He resigned from the present company and moved to Assam.

Dibrugarh is an enchanting hill station, with full of tea estates. Anupam joined duty immediately and he was provided with a beautiful bungalow with one maid and gardener. In the next week he went to Delhi and shifted his residence to the new station. He was given a company car with achauffeur. Sujatha liked the place very much. But, there was one problem. The local people showed some kind of hostility to outsiders especially Bengalis. In the recent times many cases of riot against Bengalis had been reported. So, people were afraid to go out after nightfall since criminal gangs were very active in that area. Many times the company executives had been kidnapped and huge sum demanded for their release. Hence for the security of the assets and staff the company has formed a protection force recently.

Anupam came to know about the security threat, only after joining duty, He was really afraid, but there. was no other alternative. So, he continued there and was vigilant always. Whenever he has to go out, he will requisition the services of armed security guards. One day, he was returning to office after taking cash from the bank and the jeep was ambushed and cash stolen. Anupam and the driver had a miraculous escape. Both of them jumped from the jeep and hid behind the undergrowth, but the two security guards sustained serious bullet injuries and money looted.

. Hence, all company officials were given instructions to be careful while going out of the company premises. Sujatha shuddered like anything, on hearing the attack and looting of cash. After this incident, company posted more security guards primarily goorkhas or ex servicemen to counter extremist attacks.

One year rolled by, after reaching Dibrugarh. When they reached this place, she had sent a letter to papa and mama, but they did not reply. Then, she sent a letter to Periappa and after one month she got a reply in which he had mentioned that her father was promoted as Lieutenant Colonel and transferred to Udampur, Jammu. He had also mentioned that, mama is very adamant and advised her to send occasional letters to mama and papa, whether they sent replies or not. He had also enclosed the new address of Papa. Immediately, Sujatha sent two letters, one to papa and the other to mama. Every day she will expect a reply either from papa or mama., but no reply received. After two months, she wrote another letter to periappa with great anguish and desperation. In the next letter periappa asked her to make a trip to Chennai and beg forgiveness from mama.

Thus, they reserved two tickets to Chennai in Gawhatti Chennai express. Anupam took one month leave and proceeded to Chennai. After reaching Chennai, they took a room in a hotel, and made a fresh up and then went to K K Nagar, in taxi. After reaching the apartment, Anupam Pressed the doorbell and waited. The door was suddenly opened and mother's face appeared. She stared at Sujatha and Anupam with a kind of disgust. Sujatha smiled at mama and thought that she will be affectionately hugged by mama and taken inside.

'Who're you?, why did you come here?. I've no daughter, I'd one but she's no more 'Saying this she closed the door.

Sujatha and Anupam waited there for ten minutes but the door remained closed. Then they decided to return to the hotel. When they boarded the car Sujatha was crying like a child.

'She's not a mother, she is a devil. No mother can behave like this to her daughter and husband. She is so unkind and cruel to meet out such treatment to me' Sujatha lamented.

After lunch, they slept upto evening and then checked out and went straight to the bus stand and caught a bus to Madurai. They reached there next day morning. and went straight to periappa's (elder brother of father} house in the agraharam on the bank of river Viga. They were received with great warmth and affection. They were given two tumblerful of water by periappa's daughter Rukmini and then came Valiamma Seethambal and embraced Sujatha. and said 'You are my daughter and I shower you with blessings.'

She placed her hand on the head of Sujatha and prayed. Then Sujatha touched her feet and Anupam who was standing near her also bent and touched her feet. She blessed Anupam also.

'Where's periappa?' Sujatha asked.

'He's just now gone out and will be back in a short time'.

Then, Sujatha placed the suitcase inside and took Anupam to the back side and showed him the bathroom.

After bath, they were served with idli and sambar. Anupam liked it very much and ate too much.

When they were taking breakfast, periappa came and talked to them for a long time, about mama's behaviour. In the evening they were taken to Madurai Meenakshy temple by periappa. and Anupam remarked 'It is marvelous. It is really a riddle.' That night they stayed in that house and wanted to go back to Assam. But periappa suggested that they take out a South Indian tour. They liked the idea and went to Kanyakumari. They spent two days there and then moved to Trivandrum. On the way, they stopped at Thakkala to see Padmanapuram palace. Anupam liked the palace, very much. At Trivandrum, they saw museum, Padmanbha Swamy temple, Kovalam beach etc and then went to Alappey and Cochin. From Cochin, they caught Gawhatti Express and reached Dibrugarh within 15 dayas and hence cancelled the balance leave and joined duty.

Two days after return there was a shocking news that Chennai Gawhatti Express derailed near Calcutta and many people died and hundreds sustained injuries.

Two years have passed after marriage and Sujatha became pregnant and gave birth to a baby girl. She was like Anupam, very fair and with chiselled nose etc. After delivery Sujatha again wrote three letters to mama, papa and periappa regarding the arrival of new member in the family with name Suchithra. Periappa replied immediately and congratulated both Anupam and Sujatha with blessings to the newborn. Papa sent a letter of jubilation after one month, with blessings to the granddaughter. Sujatha was overjoyed on receiving the letter from papa. But mama did not send any letter or greetings and she began to hate her mother. Many people came from Anupam's house including Niranjana. She had got a job in the central secretariat and gave up civil service ambition. She secretly told Sujatha that she is in love with a section officer in the same department. who hails from Bihar. 'Is he brahmin?' asked Sujatha.

'No, he's from Yadava community'.

Don't delay, get married at the earliest.'

A couple of days after the arrival of guests, Sujatha received a telegram from periappa saying that her papa Col. Sunderesan died in an encounter with infiltrators. Sujatha was shocked and she fell unconscious on hearing the news of papa's tragic end and she was immediately taken to a private hospital in the town and she remained there for two days. The guests left the bungalow after Sujatha was discharged from the hospital.

Sujatha and Anupam jointly wrote a letter to Bhagyalakshmy, consoling her in the great loss. Mother did not relent and no reply was received.

Suchithra has become two years old and is now a very naughty girl. Anupam brought a maid to look after Suchithra and her name is Aparna. She is Bengali and aged about 50 years, unmarried and was living in the care of his brother in a remote quarter of the estate. She was very happy in the assignment and looked after Suchithra as her own daughter. She also taught Sujatha Bengali and Assamese. Sujatha began to call Aparna as mama and she was very much delighted on hearing it and she thanked Sujatha for calling her as mama.

Two years passed after the demise of papa. On his birthday and on the anniversary of martyrdom Sujatha went to a Kali temple there with Anupam and performed poojas. In the meanwhile, they got an invitation from periappa to the marriage of their daughter Rukmini to a boy called Ganesh working as Asst Manager in a Nationalised Bank in Madurai. Immediately, they reserved tickets to Madurai and attended the function. Anupam and Sujatha paid ten thousand rupees to Rukmini, as gift. Immediately after marriage, they returned to Dibrugarh. Bhagyalakshmy, did not attend the marriage on the pretext of illness. If she had attended the marriage it would have caused much embarrassment for Sujatha and Anupam. Sujatha was very much relieved in the absence of her own mama and prayed to God to bring about some changes in her character.

Suchithra started going to play school in the kindergarten school of the estate. Every day Sujatha and Aparna will go to bring her home after the class. One day, when they were about to go to the school Anupam came to the house in a jeep and informed Sujatha a shocking news 'There was a phone call from a Malayali residing in the same apartment that Mrs Bhagyalakshmy had a massive stroke, admitted to the Vijaya hospital and she is still in a critical condition.'

Sujatha was shocked and fell down unconscious. Immediately, she was taken to the hospital in the company jeep. After one hour, she regained consciousness and began to cry aloud. Anupam was in a dilemma and could not take a decision as to what is to be done. Finally, he decided to go to Chennai at once. He arranged a vehicle up to Calcutta and caught flight to Chennai. She had expired before they reached the hospital and the body had been shifted to morgue. Mr Ramachandran, who was living in the adjacent flat, traced out the address of Anupam and Sujatha from the diary of Bhagyalakshmy, tried many numbers of the company with the help of the local Exchange and finally got the GM of the estate and he passed on the information to Anupam. Mr. Ramachandran who was the occupant of the adjacent flat handed over the key to Sujatha and said 'She was leading a reclusive life for quite a long time and it is my wife who nursed her and took her to hospital when she fell ill and she kept on talking about you in the hospital bed and asked me to hand over the key of the house to you only'.

The body was taken to the KK Nagar residence and all friends and relatives informed. Next day, her body was cremated in an electric crematorium, Chennai and ash kept in urns. Periappa and family were informed about the sudden demise of mama by Sujatha after they reached the hospital and periappa started immediately and reached the KK Nagar residence before starting funeral rites.

After the funeral rites and cremation Sujatha and Anupam returned to their house with Periappa and family. She loved and respected her mother but did not have a deep sense of remorse because of her stubborn and uncompromising attitude. Sujatha sent a lot of letters to her, but she did not reply. When Anupam was taken to her house he was ill treated and shut the door before him. She did not give any value to her only daughter and tried to impose her will over others. Sujatha did not do a heinous crime, but married an educated handsome brahmin boy drawing high salary and still she did not show any kind of consideration of the hopes and aspirations of her only daughter. She did not even greet Sujatha when she became a mother. Thus Sujatha had started to hate her mother. Periappa and family stayed there with them and helped Sujatha in conducting poojas for the salvation of the departed soul. After all rites and poojas were over periappa asked Sujatha and Anupam to open all the almirahs and lockers to find out the actual savings of Bhagyalakshmy and Sundaresan.

They were surprised to see many long term fixed deposit receipts, of several nationalised and private banks, shares, debentures, bonds and documents of several properties, Insurance policy etc. In all cases, the nominee was Suchithra of Sujatha's daughter.

The key of bank locker was traced out, but locker can be opened only after the legal heir transfer formalities are completed.

'Where's father's savings?' Sujatha asked.

'It's to be probed. We'll get a clear picture, if we open the bank locker, but it will take time since legal heir transfer has to be effected.'

'Periappa do you know where the landed properties are located?' Sujatha asked.

'I don't know. We've to trace it out. There are two houses in Chennai and these are occupied by some people. I don't know the details of any other properties.'

'Who're the tenants?' Asked Sujatha.

'I've seen the flats, but I don't know the tenants.'

A lot of legal proceeding are required, to transfer these properties to my name. Further, the nominee is our Suchithra. It can be claimed after she becomes major.' Sujatha said.

'Death certificate is to be obtained in respect of both the cases. Then only. we can proceed with legal heir transfer.' periappa said.

Insurance company is likely to challenge the claim on the ground Bhagyalakshmy had all the ailments like sugar, BP, heart complaints etc.. We have to meet an able advocate to deal with the cases.

That night, Anupam and Sujatha spent a lot of time discussing how to recover the properties, owned by mama and papa.

'We've to be here for conducting the cases and pursuing the claims etc. Prefer the claim of the Insurance policy first. I request you, to resign the present job and shift to

Chennai urgently. We can start a consulting agency here in Chennai and that will be better than the job in the estate.' said Sujatha.

After one week, they returned to Dibrugarh After reaching there, Anupam submitted his resignation letter to the GM. He was told that the same will be accepted after a period of one month. So Anupam worked for one month, got discharge, settled all liabilities and packed all furniture and all other items, in a truck and they went to Chennai in their car.

Opened the flat at chennai, cleaned and the couple photo of Smt Bhagyalakshmy and Sundaresan was hung it in the living room. and Sujatha placed a big garland over the photo. and then she stood in front of the photo with folded hands and prayed. She later, lit a lamp in the pooja room and prayed for the peace of the departed souls. Then, Sujatha walked to the balcony and looked outside. A mellow breeze came and caressed her cheeks and went away. Sujatha, then jumped up and said 'Anupam my parent's souls are wandering here. They've hugged me, spoke something in my ear and left'. Anupam came running and saw Sujatha sitting in the pooja room meditating, with both eyes closed.

********* END *********

DREAM CITY

It was a friday, the weekly holiday in the dream city, Dubai. People were flowing to the metro station, from the day break to enjoy the holiday at any of the tourist locations of the emirate. Sreeja looked from the window of their apartment near the metro station and watched the surging mass of people.

'Devetan, people are enjoying the holiday and we are sitting idle, here. I have been living here for the last thirty years and still I don't know the tourist spots of Dubai. I've seen only the Bhurj Khaleefa and nothing else' Sreeja said in a complaining tone.

'The tourist locations of Dubai are miracle garden, global village, Dubai mall, aquarium, Burj Khaleefa, Desert safari, a night in the desert village for tasting Arab cuisine, a ride on camel back, and enjoying belly dance and a boat journey to the outer sea through the creek etc. I'll take you to all the sightseeing places, before we pay adieu to this land,' Devan said. Then, the doorbell rang and on opening the door Devan was surprised to see his friend and next door neighbour Rajdeep, from Delhi, standing with a packet of sweets.

He came inside and sat on the sofa for a short time.

'It's heard you are going back to Kerala after retirement. Is it true?'. He asked.

'I'm about to complete 41 long years in Dubai. My children are studying in India, and there should be somebody to guide them. I'll complete 60 years shortly, and then I'll retire and leave for Kerala'.

'OK, that's good. It's always better to live in our native place in the evening of our life.

'My daughter, Sumithra has completed 18 years of age. She is studying in UK and hence her birthday was not formally celebrated here'. Rajdeep said and he left after talking for about ten minutes.

Devan became nostalgic for sometime and recalled for a fleeting moment his childhood days in his village and the daring journey to Dubai. He risked his life and hence he got a bright future in Dubai. Had he remained there. he would have become a petty official in any of the departments of the state, or centre, and will be struggling to make both ends meet. He has been living in this apartment, for the last twenty years All the buildings in this street are owned by the Dubai government, and the rent is only nominal. The ground floor is occupied by shops and business establishments and the three floors above are flats for rent. It is a miniature India and most of the flats belonged to Indians, hailing from different states. The only drawback is that there is no lift, and the ceiling height is more and the occupants have to scale a flight of stairs, to reach their homes. The shops belonged to the people from India, Pakistan, Bangladesh, Sri Lanka and Philippines. There are two dispensaries owned by Indians, one hotel by Palestinians and one beauty parlour for women by Sri Lankans.

Indians and Pakistanis live as neighbours in love and friendship, in adjacent apartments. Devan is already 59 and wants to retire and go home, at the age of 60, from this beloved Dream City. He came to this land about forty one years back, when he was only 18. After matriculation, he learned type writing and shorthand from an institute at Chavakkad which is a haven of nonresident Indians working in Gulf countries. There are thousands of them in the gulf countries and the village has become opulent with hundreds of palatial residential buildings and thriving business. Many of them went to gulf, braving their lives in launches or country boats. Many have perished in the sea, by drowning. Those who risked their lives had a bright future. Later, they took their friends and relatives to the gulf by flights, after arranging necessary documents.

Devan had many dreams, when he was a student. Bu, the financial condition at home did not permit him for going to college. He did not regret and was in search of a job for a better life.

He was living in his uncle's house, since his father was in the army and mother eloped with a nomadic muslim trader, when he was only two and his sister three years old. Nothing has been heard about his mother after that. Father used to send money every month to his uncle and he and his wife looked after them very well as their own children.

When Devan was studying in 9th standard, his father returned home after retirement and started a grocery shop near his house and married a widow without encumbrances. Father and his new wife came and invited Devan and his sister to their house, but they did not go and lived happily in the house of their uncle. He had a friend named Kunhammed in the typewriting class and and he decided to go to gulf in a launch and invited Devan to accompany him.

One day, Devan went to his father and put forward one demand. He had a fear whether his father will become angry with him, but he was very happy on hearing his demand.

'Papa, I want to go to gulf. There is a launch at Chettuva, taking people to gulf and my friend Kunhammed is going next week. If I get five hundred rupee, I can also go with him.'

OK, I am happy to hear that you want to go to gulf. It is a good idea and I'll give you six hundred rupees for this purpose.' Father smiled at him and said.

After one week, the launch set sail to gulf. The launch sailed for two weeks The life in the launch was very horrible Water was scarce in the launch and they were given only two glasses, for the whole day and due to thirst they could not eat anything. One day, they were awakened in the dead of the night and asked to jump and swim to the shore. Devan and Kunhammed, jumped and swam and reached the shore easily but some unfortunate fortune hunters, sank in the water and drowned.

They hid in a thatched hut near the beach for two days. During day time, they will remain in the hut and after sunset they will venture out to the market area, without being seen by others. They were shocked to see people speaking hindi and they looked like Indians. One enquir, it was rerevealed that the place was a coastal village of Gujarat.

They were very much disappointed in the failure of their first mission. Devan had Rs 100/- with him hidden inside the waterproof jacket. They went to Bombay, where Devan had a cousin named Rajan. They met him and returned to Kerala with his help. After reaching hom, they went and met the owner of the launch Krishnan and his mind melted on hearing their woes and ordeal and assured them that they would be taken in the next journey. Krishnan, admitted that the compass of the launch was faulty and all the people were unloaded near Gujarat coast, by mistake. 'I'll make necessary arrangements, for taking you to the gulf in the next trip.'Krishnan consoled them

After one month, they again set sail to Dubai. This time they reached Dubai shore. The launch reached the creek of Dubai in the early hours and all the passengers were asked to jump and swim to the shore. Devan and Kunhammed found out an Indian after reaching the shore, and he took them safely to a temporary camp. They spent many days under the love and care of Indians there, without paying anything. At that time there were only very few business establishments in Dubai, and the remaining areas were lying barren. The work of an Airport was going on and they got work as coolies there. They worked hard and earned something. There will be checking by the police occasionally, and if there is news of any check they will hide some where.

At this time, there was an accident near Dubai port and many Indians died in that boat wreck. A boat from Bombay with many Indians sank near the Dubai port and many people died. This incident, touched the mind of the magnanimous Sheik and he ordered immediate issue of documents to all people living there illegally.

Devan and Kunhammed got visa and they travelled to Bombay by flight, after one year of their adventurous journey to gulf. They came to India for one month leave, with many items purchased from gulf. But, most of these items were taken by Custom Officers at Bombay Airport. They came empty handed and similar items were purchased from Thrissur town and given to their dear and near ones.

After one month stay in Kerala, they returned to gulf together from Bombay. They went to Bombay by train and stayed there for two days and caught a flight to Dubai ;After reaching Dubai Devan joined an exporting firm run by a native of Labanone, as clerk, and Kunhammed started a small business at Al Rashidia. Devan improved his English and learned Arabic by joining an institute.

For two years, Devan did not go to Kerala and saved money, for the marriage of his sister, Pushpalatha. Uncle had written once that a proposal has come from a boy working in Air Force.

That proposal was settled, after thorough enquiry and marriage fixed, after three months.

Devan went to Kerala to attend the marriage. He met the entire expenditure of the jewellery and marriage arrangements and food. His father and uncle gave two bangles each, as present to the bride. Devan was in great joy and ecstasy in the marriage of his sister to an employed youth, belonging to a good family. The ignominy due to his mother's elopement, did not affect the marriage.

After returning to gulf, Devan began to save money for purchasing some assets in his village.

After ten years of service in that firm, Devan became Asst Manager, with better salary and perks. At this time, he got a letter from uncle, in which he made a request to conduct his marriage with his daughter, Sreeja. She is now studying for BEd, after completing degree.

She, is a nice girl with good manners and affable character. Devan liked that alliance and wrote to uncle that he was willing to marry Sreeja After six months, Devan went to Kerala on one month leave and married Sreeja, his cousin sister.

After expiry of leave, Devan returned to Dubai. Sreeja passed BEd examination and then applied for passport. Devan arranged family visa for Sreeja, after receipt of passport.'

Devan took a flat in an apartment near the port area and then went to Kerala on one week leave and brought his wife to Dubai. They lived in that flat for one year and then moved to Sharjah, since the rent in port area was very high. He also purchased a second hand foreign car for going to office and back. Their life was very happy and harmonious. He had many friends and they met occasionally, in the apartment of any of them. His friend Kunhammed, had grown to a big businessman. He is now running two big grocery shops and has purchased many properties in his village and built a beautiful house, near his old house.

Sreeja became pregnant and she gave birth to a baby girl in a hospital, in Dubai. After birth, he required the help of a lady for postnatal treatment and preparing food etc. He met an agent, there engaged in the supply of domestic maids, and got a lady aged 50 years. Her name was Sadiya and belonged to Pattambi. Devan liked the lady and offered to pay her a handsome salary.

Devan and Sreeja liked the maid very much. She is very efficient in all works, namely housekeeping, child care, postnatal care and preparation of food. Devan took a lot of new clothes for her and a separate room was also given to her.

'Where is your house? Who is your husband? How many children have you got?' Devan asked Sadiya.

'Sir, I have nobody. My husband died two years back and I have no children, to look after me.

After the death of my husband, I was staying with his sister, in Pattambi'. Sadiya said.

'What was the occupation of your husband?'

'He was a trader of antique items. He'll visit houses and purchase these items and sell them to a dealer, in Palakkad'.

Devan and Sreeja felt pity on her and treated her well as their sister. After her arrival in the house, Devan had no tension, regarding the newborn child or his wife. She did not allow Sreeja to rise from bed, except for daily hot water bath. She will rise in the early morning and prepare food for breakfast and lunch and then apply medicated oil all over the body of Sreeja and bathe her in hot water. Hot water will be splashed on her stomach portion and then massage with her hands. The bath will last for one hour. When the child wakes up, it will be smeared with oil and then face, nose and head shaped with her hands and bathed in lukewarm water. Then, medicines will be given to Sreeja, at the stipulated time, at least three times daily.

Sadiya, one day requested Devan 'Sir, keep my monthly salary with you and give it to me when I go to my native place'. Devan agreed to the request.

'When're you going home?' Devan enquired.

'I 've nobody there and will remain here till my death' Her eyes became wet and began to sob.

'Don't cry. You're like a mother to us. We'll do as you desire'.

'Let me call you son'.

'You can call me son and Sreeja daughter. We're happy to hear it'.

Devan had written to uncle and father about the birth of a new member in the family and also mentioned about the maid, who is like a mother to them. He invited them to Dubai, for a short period to see his daughter and for a tour of the emirate. His uncle and wife accepted the invitation and arranged to take passports. Devan arranged visa for them, for a period of three months. On their arrival Devan went to the Airport to receive them.

Sreeja's parents were in great ecstasy, on arrival in Dubai. When they reached home, Sreeja and the maid went to the door, to receive them. On seeing them, Sadiya retreated to the kitchen and put on her burkha(veil) and went to talk to them.

Devan did not like this behaviour on the part of Sadiya and said 'Sadiya thatha(sister) what is the use of burkha, inside the house.?'.

'It's our custom that we should wear burkha while talking to strangers'.

'They're not strangers. They're our family members

'But, Sadiya was adamant'

She began to wear burkha always and Devan did not object.

Deven took his guests to different parts of emirate for sightseeing, leaving Sreeja and daughter in the care of Sadiya. When they returned, Sadiya was sleeping without burkha and Ramakrishnan the father in law of Devan was startled on seeing the face of Sadiya, the maid.

'This is my sister, Bharathy who ran away with the muslim trader'. He told his wife secretly.

This was overheard by Sreeja and she told Devan.

Devan realized that the maid Sadiya is non other than his mother. He became angry and asked Sadiya to get out. 'I don't want to see you since you are so cruel and unkind to run away with a stranger, leaving behind two little kids, at home.

Ramakrishnan tried to pacify Devan, but he could not control his grief.

'She's not a mother, but a devil, an amorous and lusty devil, who had no compunction to discard her loving husband and two little infants, for her own pleasure.' Devan lamented.

Ramakrishnan and his wife were in the ecstasy of meeting Bharathy, after many years and they talked with her about her life, after she left the house.

We can't call it an elopement, but it was an abduction. The trader Sulaiman was an expert in witchcraft and black magic. One day, he came to the house when children were sleeping and enquired whether there were any old and antique items. He said that he would give high price for those items. She had some bronze items, which belonged to time immemorial. She wanted to sell them to the trader and went inside to take them. He came behind her, caught her, overpowered her, subdued her and raped her.

There was nobody in the surrounding and her cry was not heard outside. After that, he began to come to the house frequently and she became pregnant. There was only one way to escape from the ignominy and it was suicide. Sulaiman gave something to her and she became calm and quiet and went with him to his house at Pattambi. She later, gave birth to a boy, but the child died a few months after the birth.

Bharathy was taken to Ponnani and converted to Islam and name changed as Sadiya and she did not object. She did not get peace of mind for many years and always had a guilty feeling that she had discarded his loving husband and two kids of the age 2 and 3 years, for the sake of a stranger and debaucher. She went to many jarams(tombs), of soofi saints and prayed. She paid offerings to many temples and prayed standing outside the gate, for peace of mind. Sulaiman stopped his business abruptly and remained at home. He was suffering from a lung ailment and it was later diagnosed as lung cancer and he died within a period of two months. Sadiya became lonely and hence she went to the house of her sister in law, some distance away. One day, an agent came and told her that there is chance for ayas in gulf countries and asked her to take passport. The agent took her and some other ladies to Bombay and after immigration formalities, sent them to Dubai by flight.

Devan heard everything peacefully, and was very much disturbed. Whom to blame for his mother's present plight?, he did not know. Finally, he came to the conclusion that it is not mother's fault, but due to the circumstances beyond her control and not due to her lust.

He consoled himself that it was due to fate or destiny and it is not correct to blame mother and God is to be blamed, for the same. We are suffering for the sins of our earlier births, according to Hindu mythology and he asked himself whether it is fair to punish an innocent man or woman for the sins of their earlier births, about whom they knew nothing.

Devan began to call Sadiya 'amma' and she loved him immensely and helped him in all possible ways, and also his wife and kid. Sreeja gave birth to a baby boy after many years and all the birth related treatment and care were given by her. She lived with them peacefully for over fifteen years, and died there. Since she was still a muslim, her burial was conducted in a cemetry of a mosque there.

The rent of the flat was enhanced astronomically by the landlord, in Sharjah, and hence Devan and family moved to an apartment near the main Airport, Dubai. This was owned by the government. It's location is very ideal and convenient and rent very reasonable. They stayed there, for long twenty years. Deven continued in the same company and he became in due course Manager, AGM, and then DGM. He was happy, for attaining such a high position with only matriculation certificate as qualification. He has saved enough by landed properties, fixed deposits and share in some companies.

Devan's daughter, Sandhya passed higher secondary from an Indian School in Sharjah and then went to Bangalore for medicine. After three years, son Vijesh passed higher secondary and he was sent to Chennai for Engineering. He is occasionally sending money to his father and sponsored the education of his son Dileep, from his present wife, He has given monetary help to many people, for education and medical treatment.

One day, Devan happened to meet his old friend kunhammed and was surprised to learn that he is now in the business of hyper market at many parts of emirate, Muscat and Qatar. Devan was in great joy on learning that his friend has become a billionaire and one of the high dignitary NREs of India.

'Devan, why do you return to kerala. You can work here, even after 60 years, on payment of a small tax.?' Kunhammed asked.

'Thank you for your suggestion, I've thought about it over and over again and came to the conclusion that the' remaining life should be spent in our country. I've to look after the children and guide them properly for their future. My daughter will finish MBBS, next year and if any better proposal comes, to be given in marriage. Regarding my son, I've no worries and I'm sure that he is able to look after himself." Devan said.

'It's better, not to go to Kerala. It's in political turmoil and compared to Kerala this land is heaven on earth. There is full security here for our families, since the rules are very stringent and rulers very impartial and perfect. They have no fear or favour and the administration is found to be corruption free. In India, ladies are afraid to go out after night fall and and it has become a land of scams and swindlers. Many of the people, are lazy and unprincipled and their motive is to make money, by by hook or by crook.

An iron hand is required to set things right.' Kunhammed spoke eloquently.

'What you said is cent percent true. It is difficult to live in Kerala or any other state with unnecessary hartals and strikes. As NRE, what can we do, to reform the society?' Then, by the by, what about your children?'

'They are in US, both sons are studying for medicine, there'.

They shook hands and parted.

Devan submitted necessary papers for retirement. He will get huge amount at the time of retirement and made necessary planning for investment, in a judicious way. He planned to utilise that amount to purchase small plots, in Thrissur town. The price of land is shooting up and if we invest in land it will never fail.

After retirement, he visited all his friends and colleagues and paid adieu. He went to meet Kuhammed, but he was in US. He was sorry for leaving the Dream city, a city which made him what he is. Even if, he went to his native place and enjoyed the sweetness of home, this city will loom large in his mind, as a beacon, till his death. The work culture, discipline and fear of authority is unheard of in India. Without discipline and respect of authority nothing can be achieved. In Kerala Devan may feel frustrated and he may come back to Dubai or some other place in the emirate. But, nothing can be predicted now, Devan and Sreeja waved their hands to all their friends and well wishers and boarded a Gulf Air flight to Nedumbassery.

********* END *********

MADAM BRIJITHA

Dr. Lakshmanan, was the medical officer of the Gemstone Tea estate, Ooty. His lovely bungalow is standing on the top of a hill. It was designed and constructed by his father, Mr. Grifith. He was an Englishman, Engineer by profession and was the manager of this estate for a long time. His wife was a Malayali lady, named Mythili Sreedharan, from Tellichery, Kerala.

. For a few years, he had worked as manager of Volcarts Brothers, Tellichery and during this period he happened to see the daughter of his accountant, Mr. Sreedharan. She was fair, tall, slim and beautiful and had an angelic look. He felt love at the first sight and wanted to make her his wife and hence discussed this matter with Mr. Sreedharan and on his permission married her. In north malabar, such marriages were common during those pre independence days. There were many European companies, like Aspinwal, Volcarts Bros and Piers Lessly and the british staff of these companies used to marry Hindu girls and their progeny remained as

Hindus. They did not change over to Anglo Indian group, by converting to Christianity. Mr. Grifith, later left the company and moved to Ooty, and became manager of a tea estate there. The bungalow was constructed under his supervision, considering the opinion of his wife Mythili. By this time. they had two children in this wedlock. Mr. Grifith had another wife in England. She came to Ooty and found out his infidelity and asked Mythili to vacate the bungalow. She had the support of the District Collector of Nilgiris who was also an Englishman and thus Grifith was taken to England and he could not return to India again.

Mythili moved to Coorg, where Mr. Grifith had a coffee estate and this was given to her and her children. It was a big estate, covering an area of about 200 acres. Mythili, became the owner of this estate and thus her two sons Lakshmanan and Chandrasekhar grew up and both of them became doctors from Ramaiah Medical College. Chandrasekhar, later went to London, for higher studies and married an English lady and settled there.

Dr. Lakshmanan moved to Ooty and he got a job as medical officer, in their old estate and began to live in the same bungalow, where his father and family once lived. By this time, almost all Englishmen had left India and their estates came to the hands of Indians. Dr. Lakshmanan used to go to his estate at Coorg, occasionally. His mother had become old and still she was running the estate well. During one visit, he happened to see an Anglo Indian girl in their house and mother introduced her to her son. 'Lakshman, this is Brijitha, the daughter of William D'Cruz, and their estate is a short distance away from ours'. Lakshmanan liked her and wanted to marry her. Mythili was against it and she said 'I'll find out a very beautiful girl for you, from Tellichery. Although, Brigitha is a nice girl I don't know whether she'll be faithful to you, in real life.

'Mummy, I like that girl and speak to her father, at the earliest'. Lakshmanan. requested. Mythili, tried to dissuade Lakshmanan, but failed and one day, Brigitha eloped with him to Ooty. Then, Mythili went to Ooty, brought them back to Coorg and arranged their marriage, in a church first and then in temple, at Kutta, later.

'They are free to follow any religion, Christianity or Hinduism'. Said William D'Cruz after marriage.

Dr. Lakshmanan continued to be Hindu and Brijitha remained Christian. She will go to church every Sunday and sometimes, she will take Lakshmanan also with her.

Years rolled by and they have two daughters Lydia and Lucia and they are of the age 15 and 14 and they looked like European girls with very fair complexion and blonde hair. They are now studying in a boarding school, in Ooty. When his mother Mythili expired, the funeral was conducted according to the Hindu tradition and cremated in the estate compound. Dr. Chandrasekhar and family had come for the funeral and went back after completion of all the rites and functions.

Later, a manager was appointed to look after the estate. Dr. Chandrasekhar wanted his brother to sell the estate and give half the money to him. Then, Dr Lakshmanan said 'No need of selling the estate, tell me how much you require?'

'OK, not now, we can discuss it later' Dr. Chandrasekhar said at the time of going back to London.

Dr. Lakshmanan, had become part and parcel of Ooty, after staying there for over 15 years. He was member of

Flower show committee, Dog's show committee, member of SPCA, IMA, Lions and so many other committees. He is known to everybody, in the town. He is a humanitarian and donates a lot of money, every year, for the ailing and the poor. He has sponsored the education of not less than five poor students, from Tamilnadu. He has enough wealth and will donate liberally, to any charitable organisations or societies working for alleviating human misery.

In the bungalow, Brijitha had one servant maid and a gardener given by the company. There are innumerable exotic flower plants, in front of the house and the gardener is one Nachimuthu. He has a quarter attached to the bungalow and his village is near Salem and used to go there, occasionally. The maid's name is Sugandhi and she hails from Koonnur. She will visit her house once in every week.

Dr. Lakshmanan used to reach the hospital by 8 am, on all working days. Even, at that freezing cold, plenty of patients will be waiting in queue, in front of the hospital. He will take too much time, to clear each patient. For poor patients, he will give free samples of medicines and money. He is a God like figure, for the estate workers.

One day, Dr. Lakshmanan was reading newspaper after clearing all the patients. Then, the Telephone Line Man, Mr Stephen arrived there on his bike to attend the fault of the hospital phone. When he was about to leave, doctor came out and told Stephen 'Stephen my residence number is faulty for the last two days. Since flower show is coming its service is highly essential for me.'

'OK Sir, I'll create a docket now itself and attend the fault.' Stephen said.

He called the Exchange and created a docket immediately.

'Stephen, you should bring some flowers for this year's flower show.' Doctor said'

'OK Sir, I'll arrange' Said Stephen and left on his bike.

Stephen is an old friend of the doctor. For the last 15 years he has been looking after that section and for each and every thing related to telephone doctor used to approach Stephen. He is also the member of Flower show, Dog's show and also YMCA. He is really a sincere and reliable friend.

Stephen has a malayali connection. His parents came to Ooty from Palakkad and was estate labourers in another tea estate. He has married a Tamil lady and is living with his parents in the suburb of Ooty.

Stephen went straight to the bungalow of Dr. Lakshmanan. He found a bike in its stand near the gate. Stephen went to the quarters of Nachimuthu, but he was not there. Then, he came and pressed the doorbell, and waited for five minutes but no response. He pressed the bell again and again and went to the backside of the bungalow. Then, he heard footsteps of somebody descending the stairs hurriedly and something falling on the floor and a tinkling sound. Stephen waited there and looked towards the quarters of Nachimuthu.

Suddenly, the door on the backside was opened and Mr. Chengappa, Group Manager, of the estate came out stealthily and saw Stephen in front of him He was shocked and terrified on seeing him. Brijitha, came to the door and looked out with trepidation and shame. She was holding the dangling sari end by left hand and arranging the fallen hair by right hand.

'Sir, what's this, Doctor's a God like figure and this is shameful'. Stephen said. Then, Chengappa approached Stephen and said 'If you tell this to doctor, I'll commit suicide'.

Stephen was standing in a state of shock and embarrassment and then he replied.

'Sir, I'll not tell anybody, but this is a kind of treachery and it is unpardonable'.

'Stephen please come inside. We have to talk for a while'. Chengappa pulled Stephen inside the bungalow. They both sat on the sofa and Brijitha stood weeping, some distance away.

'Sorry Stephen, sorry, I'll never come here and this is certain.'

'OK then, you take an oath now itself.'

They agreed and Chengappa took the oath, in the name of Lord Krishna and Brijitha in the name of Jesus Christ.

Then, Stephen replaced the faulty instrument and both went outside, started their bikes and left. Brijitha continued weeping.

While riding on the bike, Stephen thought of Chengappa. He is a very efficient and able officer. He used to tell Stephen 'I'll not send my children to this job. They'll demand resignation letter when they give appointment order and this is company. All Officers'll kneel when they are asked to sit, but I'm not like that. If they sack me, I'll go to my estate and run it. I'll never surrender my dignity and self respect'. Everybody will envy the lifestyle of Plantation Officers, with high salary, cars, bungalow, servants and a lot of other benefits, but Mr. Chengappa says it is a job lacking freedom and self respect. Stephen was really baffled by the talk of Mr Chengappa.

Stephen remembered the charming face of Mrs Neela Chengappa. She is so beautiful and lovely and still, her husband had gone in search of another lady and cheated her. If Madam Neela came to know about this infidelity of her beloved husband, she would surely end her life.

On the way, Stephen met Nachimuthu and he was coming from shopping. He had two big bags containing provisions and vegetables. He smiled on seeing Stephen and then Stephen asked 'Nachimuthu I'd gone to the bungalow to replace the instrument. Where is your maid?'

'She had gone to her house. What is the matter?'

'I'd to convey a message to her'

'She'll come tomorrow and I'll tell her that you enquired'

They, they parted and Stephen started the bike and left.

Weeks and months passed. Stephen had gone to the flower show and met Dr. Lakshmanan and his daughters in the pavilion.

'Stephen how are you? you did not bring any pots?.'

'Sir, I was busy. My father was not well and he had to be hospitalised for two weeks. Then, wife fell ill and a lot of problems.'

Then doctor said 'Stephen, my wife is not well. She is completely bedridden. I took her to medical college, Coimbatore and met the Medicine Professor and he says It is due to rheumatoid arthritis. She is taking medicines but no relief'. Doctor said in a dejected tone.

'Sir, everything'll be alright. I'll pray for her early recovery'.

Stephen left after some time. He thought to himself 'Poor man, let God help him'

After one month, Stephen met doctor in a medical shop and then enquired 'Sir, how is madam?'

'She is still in bed. I am completely heartbroken. She is my strength and courage. If she is with me, I' ll take any risk. She is very bold and faithful. If anything happens to her, I'm gone". Doctor's eyes became wet.

'Sir, better you arrange physiotherapy, after meeting an ayurvedic physician. Don't worry, she will be alright soon.' Stephen said in a soothing tone.

'On the advice of the professor, I have applied for a transfer to Wynad'

'Ok Sir, I'll pray for her'.

'Thank you'.

Stephen started the bike and went away.

Stephen was on leave for one week to take his wife to Medical College, Coimbatore. There, he met doctor Lakshmanan, standing outside the cabin of the professor and his wife was sitting on a chair.

'Sir, how's madam?'

'No change, by the by we are going to Gudalur shortly. There is no vacancy in Wynad and hence they gave me Gudalur. I'm very much depressed. How can I leave Ooty? My father was here, my mother lived here so many years and I have completed long 15 years. But, for the sake of my wife, I'll bear anything. She's the mother of my two children. She's my companion, my guide and what not.' He began to sob.

'Doctor, don't worry. Her health is important than anything else. So, you please prepare to leave our Ooty. When she is alright, you can come back. I will pray for you'

After two weeks, he got a call from doctor to come to his bungalow. He went and there he met Group Manager Chengappa and his wife. They had come to see off doctor and family.

'Stephen let me give you a peg of brandy. This is the saddest day in my career.'

'Sorry Sir, I'm on duty'.

'OK, thank you for your love and friendship. I'll come back after some time".

Chengappa thanked Stephen for remaining tight lipped so far and thus saving the dignity and peace of two families.

The entire furniture and other items had been loaded in a truck and the same started its journey to Gudalur. Dr. Lakshmanan, his wife and children got into the car and they said goodbye to all and left. Then, Chengappa embraced Stephen and cried aloud like an insane person and Mrs Neela Chengappa and children looked at them in wonder and amazement.

********* END *********

A PRODIGAL SON

It was a sunday. The sky was cloudy, and was drizzling outside. Balagopal was scanning the newspaper, and then the clock struck 8 am. Suddenly, the Phone rang, and Balagopal took the receiver. It was Rajagopal on the other side. He spoke in a depressed tone. 'Balan our Parameswaran is gone'

'When?'

'Today morning, 5 am'.

'When's the cremation?'

'They're waiting for his brother Nandan Menon to arrive from Mumbai'

'OK Rajan, I'll be there within half an hour'

Balagopal spoke to his wife Nina about the demise, changed his dress, and moved to the house of Parameswaran. He was staying at his tharavadu at Kuttumuck, Thrissur, after estrangement with his wife, about a decade back. His mother is still alive, and is about ninety years old. His eldest brother P. S. Menon and family are also living in this house, after retirement as Technical Education Director. They are waiting for his younger brother, Nandan Menon, who is Customs Collector in Mumbai.

When Balagopal reached the house, there was a lot of people in the road, and compound. He saw many of his friends already in the house. He met P. S. Menon and expressed his condolences and then enquired 'Did Parameswaran's wife and children reach?'

'No, they won't come.' Menon replied.

'Have they been informed?'

'Yes, but they won't come. They did not come to see Parameswaran, despite repeated requests when he was lying in the hospital. He was in a critical condition for over a week in a hospital, at Ernakulam and he wanted to see his children, but they refused to come even though their house was only a few kilometres away from the hospital. After demise, what is the use of coming and seeing the body?' Menon wiped his tears.

Then Balagopal moved to his friends, who were in the crowd. Rajagopal, Syriac John, Ravikumar, Govindankutty, Sreedharan and Mathew. They were the college mates of Mr. Parameswaran, when, he was studying at Kerala Varma College, Thrissur. All of them were so close to one another, and even after three decades, they maintain intimate friendship, even now.

'Paramu's life was a tragedy. We could not do anything to help him'. Syriac John said.

'He became an addict to liquor and drug, after estrangement with his wife. He has done a lot of mistakes. If his wife has deserted him and went to her house with children, and refused to come back, it is due to his fault. During the long ten years, many people tried for reconciliation, but his father in law was very adamant' Sreedharan said.

'It was beyond reconciliation.' Govindakutty said with great remorse and mental agony.

The local MLA and MP came and paid homage and went back. After some time, a car came and stopped at the gate, and a young man and his family got down from the car, and moved to the house. When they entered the house a loud lament arose from the house, and it subsided within minute, and they presumed that it must be his brother Nandan Menon and family. After some time the body was taken out for funeral rites, and cremated at the southern side of the tharavad compound. Thus that chapter is closed.

Many people came to attend the funeral, but his wife and children did not come, despite proper intimation of the death. It remained a mystery, and question mark, in the minds of people, who gathered there. There may be rubs and frictions, quarrels and separation, in family life but nobody will skip the funeral ceremony, if either husband or wife dies.

'Why they stayed away from the funeral?' Many friends and relatives asked this question, and some of them approached Balagopal for clarification, who was very close to Parameswaran.

Balagopal is now senior Manager of a nationalised bank in the town. For many years, he was in Mumbai. After graduation, he went to Mumbai, and got job in a pharmaceutical firm, Later he joined Punjab National Bank as clerk, and after many years became Officer. After becoming Senior Manager, he tried for a transfer to Kerala, joined at Kalpetta, and later transferred to Thrissur.

Parameswaran hails from the famous Puthiyedath family, and he was the youngest son. They had about 40 acres of coconut groves and 50 acres of paddy fields. The entire paddy fields were given out for lease to about twenty families. When the land reform act came into effect they could retain only 30 acres of coconut groves in the name of two families and the remaining property were declared as excess land and as per land tribunal verdict were given to the people who had taken them on lease. Some families got 3 to 4 acres of land by this act. The excess coconut groves were taken over by the government and given to landless tenants at the rate of 10 cents each. Parameswaran's sister Subhadra Amm's family were living separately and hence she got 15 acres of land and the three sons and mother got 15 acres since they were living together in the ancestral house They did not regret in the loss of land, since they had so many other sources of income, like rent of shop buildings, and houses, and partnership in some business. There was enough wealth in the tharavadu, for living happily and comfortably, for all the three brothers and mother.

Balgopal and Parameswaran studied in the same school, in the village from 1 to 10th and college studies at Kerala Varma college. Balagopal was from a middle class family, and he did not waste time for unnecessary company, and union activities, and he passed the degree in first class. But Parameswaran was a pampered boy, and spent a lot of money, for company, and unnecessary activities, which spoiled his studies, and future life. One day, he came to the class of Prof. Regupathy with a live butterfly on his shirt. On seeing this, Regupathy Sir, became angry and said' 'Parameswaran you are in the final year, if you repeat this your future will be spoiled'. He was very kind and sympathetic towards all his students especially to Parameswaran, since he was staying in a rented building of his family. Next day, he repeated the same mischief, in the class of Johnson master. He became very angry and asked Parameswaran to get out of his class, and threw his books out of the class, in a fit of anger.

This incident was a great setback to Parameswaran, who was living like a prince in the campus. He was not allowed to attend the class of Johnson Sir, since he refused to apologise to him for the mistake. Many friends advised him to apologise to Johnson master, but he did not budge. He had to complete a lot of lab works, and the record book was incomplete. It was the end of final year. He tried to obtain the record book of a senior student, but it did not succeed. In short he could not write the final examination. All his friends passed the examination with good marks, and secured good jobs at different parts of India, and Gulf, but Parameswaran could not complete his degree, and sat idle in his house, after college days. His brother, Nandan Menon passed his MSc in Physics, and went to New Delhi for IAS coaching. In the second attempt he got IRS, and posted in Customs and Central Excise dept. During probation, he was Customs Superintendent and then Asst Collector and after many years became Customs Collector.

With the persuasion of his mother and brother P. S. Menon, who was then Professor in the Thrissur Engineering College, Parameswaran went to Gulf, with the help of a friend, and was in a good position for about 15 years. During this period, he married the daughter of a famous advocate at Ernakulam. The lady's name was Sangeetha and she was a postgraduate in English literature. Parameswaran took her to Dubai, and lived with family for long 15 years there. He had two children, elder girl and younger boy, and the children were admitted to an Indian School there, and Sangeetha also got a teaching job, in the same school. He had a lavish lifestyle, and could not save much during this period. The company was running on loss for a long time, and hence some people were retrenched, and Parameswaran was one among them. His visa was cancelled and he had to leave the country with family. His attempt to get another job did not materialise. After coming back, he took a rented house in Thrissur town and admitted the children in the NSS English medium school there. Sangeetha got a job in the same school, with a small salary. Parameswaran decided to start some business there. He took agency of a detergents company, and started distribution of their products. A lot of money was spent for taking agency, purchasing a vehicle for distribution of the products, construction of a godown, for stocking the items, office, telephone etc. He employed some people as driver, salesman, assistant salesman, helper and office assistant. There was tough competition in this field and the agency was running on loss for two years. When the agency gradually picked up business, he had to face another problem. The salesman was unfaithful. On a surprise check by Parameswaran, it was found that the salesman was maintaining two accounts. The products were given on credi, and the amount received from shops were not accounted fully, and the balance went to his pocket. He had to stop the distribution immediately, since there was huge disparity in accounts.

Parameswaran sustained huge loss. About 6.5 lakhs were shown as outstanding in the field, but on actual verification, there was roughly only 2 lakhs as outstanding in the field, and the balance of 4.5 lakhs was stolen by the salesman.

He immediately sacked the salesman and tried to collect the balance amount from the shops, with the help of driver and assistant salesman. But, it did not work and he did not get anything from the shops. Once, the distribution was stopped, they won't give the outstanding amount. He tried to restart the sale, but did not succeed. Finally, he had to wind up the business, and he incurred a loss of about 15 lakhs including the depreciation of the vehicle.

Parameswaran then started another agency of perfumes. It did not require a vehicle for sale, and hence he sold the sale vehicle at a depreciation of 30%. The perfume sale was undertaken by Parameswaran himself. He worked hard, and the sale was pushed up on credit, but sale decreased day by day, and he had to stop this business also. About 2 lakhs were lost in this business, and he could not recover the outstanding amount from shops. He was in great disappointment and took to drinking and drugs to get peace of mind. In a short time his entire savings were depleted. He approached his mother for help, but he got only small amounts on two occasions. He was too much worried, and became a real drunkard. He did not tell the truth to his wife. He had no money even to pay the rent, and approached his friends and relatives for help. At this time, he was trapped by some agents of narcotic business.

Without any investment, they supplied the goods - drugs to Parameswaran and he himself took up the sale. He lost one consignment, somewhere during his trips and he could not pay its price to the agents. They thought that, he has taken the money, and tried to terrorise him. Since they did not succeed in their tactics, they began to pester his family continuously. Sangeetha knew that she was in danger, and one day she closed the house, and left secretly with her children, without informing anybody. Parameswaran became terrified, and ran to his friend Sabu, who was a camp clerk in the police department. He feared that, the criminals have abducted his wife and children. Sabu consoled him and contacted his wife house immediately, before advising him to give a police complaint. Sangeetha and children had reached there by that time, but she refused to speak to Parameswaran. From that moment onwards, he became a full time drunkard. For money, he began to pester his friends and relatives.

This news reached the ear of Padmavathy Amma, his mother and she sent some people to bring him by force to the tharavadu. She fired him and asked him to stay with her. He asked him to look after the household properties, and she assured that, some money will be paid to him every month, to meet his personal expenses. She also asked her son P. S. Menon to meet Sangeetha and bring her and her children to the tharavadu. He went to Ernakulam and met Sangeetha and her parents. Sangeetha's father Adv. Prabhakaran Nair spoke very rudely to P. S. Menon. He said emphatically.

'I'll never permit Sangeetha to go and live with Parameswaran. He is an addict to liquor and drug. How can such an irresponsible fellow look after my daughter. She has escaped narrowly from those anti social elements. I don't want to explain the harrowing tale of my daughter at his hands.' Menon returned to tharavadu in great despair and mental agony. He was then Principal of Trivandrum Engineering College and two of his sons were doing medicine. Really Menon was humiliated by Sangeetha's father.

But, Adv. Prabhakaran Nair did not approach family court for divorce. He looked after them well. The children were studying for post graduation in a famous college in Chennai, but Sangeetha did not go for any job. Adv. Prabhakaran Nair asked his daughter to join Law College but she declined and spent time in reading and gardening.

One day, Parameswaran sent a messenger to the bank of Balagopal with a letter, requesting for a loan of Rs 500/-. When questioned, the messenger said that, Parameswaran had been detained in a bar hotel, for not paying the bill. Balagopal, immediately went to the bar hotel and released him. Balagopal advised him to avoid such things, because it is a disgrace, and shame, to his house and his brothers, who are in high positions. But, he continued begging for money from his friends, and people began to hide, on seeing Parameswaran.

In front of his mother, Parameswaran was an obedient son without any bad habits, but he continued his old habits. One day, he went to the house of Sangeetha, but he was not permitted to meet his wife or children. He, then went to the park on the side of the harbour. In bitter despair, he cried like a child and jumped into the water. People in the park saw this and rushed to the spot and rescued him. A leading newspaper reported this incident, with photo of the rescue operation.

Nandan Menon wrote to his brother, that he would arrange a job for him in Mumbai, if he stopped his drinking habits. Parameswaran was not willing to go to Mumbai. His sister, Subhadra Amma came forward to help him with a job in their wholesale medical shop, but he refused.

After a few months, Parameswaran fell ill with stomach pain and admitted to Mother Hospital.

The famous gastro- enterologist of that hospital, diagnosed his illness as acute cirhosis of liver and both lobes are in very bad shape. He was in the hospital for about two weeks, and despite the best treatment, his condition remained the same, and so he was discharged, with instruction to continue the treatment, at home. But after a few days his condition became critical and was taken to Amritha hospital at Ernakulam and he breathed his last there.

After the cremation, Balagopal gave a lift to his friend Mathew to the swaraj rounds. On the way Mathew told another story to Balagopal- the story of Prof. P. K. Menon'. Menon Sir's wife died some time back. She had immolated herself due to the drinking habits of Menon. During college days, students will throng the auditorium to hear his speech, since he was such a big orator and his ability to speak on any subject under the sun is well known. Dr. Varma and Prof. Natarajan were the other orators of those days After retirement, Prof. Menon became an addict to liquor and this ruined his family life. He is roaming like a lunatic after his wife's demise and demanding money from his old students.'

'Do you know anything about the whereabouts of our Dr Varma and Prof Natarajan?'. Balagopal enquired.

'Dr. Varma's now in US and Prof Natarajan in Chennai'

Mathew wanted to alight near Banerjee club and Balagopal parked the car near Bini Tourist Home and got down and invited his friend for a cup of a tea.

********* END *********

A REUNION OF TWO SOULS

Kodaicanal lay under the blanket of fog, and the sun is not visible even at 8 AM. Dr. Antony started the car, and moved forward, through the deserted road, for about 30 minutes, and reached an old building. The watchman came and opened the gate, and he took the car insid, and parked in the garage. It was his dispensary for the last ten years.

Some patients were waiting for him even at that chilly morning. Most of them were wearing woollen sweaters, shawls and mufflers to protect from the extreme cold. Dr. Antony went straight to the pharmacy. Compounder Selvaraj had come but pharmacist Mary not yet reached.

'Selvaraj good morning. How're you?' Doctor said.

'Fine Sir, madam has not come. I don't know what happened to her'.

'You look sleepy what is the problem?'

'Sir, I'd a house call yesterday night in a remote cardamom estate and could not sleep even a wink.'

'When Mary comes you can take rest'.

Doctor patted his shoulder and walked to his consulting room.

Doctor examined patients one by one. Most of the patients were poor estate workers or daily wage labourers. While examining a patient Dr. Antony will ask a lot of questions regarding their family, work, children, income, so on and so forth.

The first patient was one Manickan, a labourer in a vegetable farm. He is having breathing complaints, lack of sleep and fatigue. Doctor examined him and said.'You are inhaling too much pesticides and no proper food. Apply for one week leave and take this medicine. He gave him some tablets and a tonic. and did not accept any fees. Manickan left the consulting room wiping his tears.

Upto 2 PM, he examined the patients one after another and he left the consulting room after examining the last patient. It was a lady aged 25. She started weeping when doctor asked about her family.

'Sukanya how many children have you got?'

'Only one.'

'Boy or girl?'

'Girl'.

'How's your husband?'

'He's a drunkard'.

'Are you doing anything?'

'Daily wage job in a chicken farm"

'Is your husband working?'

'No.'

'Then, what's his job?'

'He was a vegetable vendor, but nowadays h's not going for sale'.

'What's your illness?'

'Unnecessary worry, fear, lack of sleep, giddiness etc.'

He checked her BP, pulse and then examined her ears and asked 'Is there any whistling sound in your ears?'

'No sir.'

'BP has gone up. It may be due to worry. Do you feel any womiting sensation?'

'No sir.'

'Then, it's not due to ear balance problem. You're too much worried because of your husband.

I don't prescribe any medicine for BP now. Ask your husband to come and meet me. For you no medicine is required. If your husband becomes OK, then you also will become OK. I will give you some tablets for acidity and you take it in the morning and night, two tablets at a time after meals'. Dr. Antony said and gave her some antacid tablets.

The lady tried to give fees, but he did not accept and said 'I don't want anything now'.

Sukanya touched his feet and left.

Then, doctor went up to Selvaraj and said 'Mary's on leave today, but she didn't call me. She may be ill, or something happened at home. Please close the dispensary, I'm going'.

Doctor started the car and left for home. He is doing a service to the people. The income from the practice is hardly sufficient to pay the salary of his staff, but it gives him great pleasure, satisfaction and peace of mind.

While driving the car to his residence, his thoughts were wandering in the Himalayas-Nainital, Manali, Dehradun and Kulu valley. The snow capped mountains loomed large in front of him. He also recollected some of his college mates in the Patna Medical College, Nandita, Rehana, Khusboo, Sanjay Singh, Siddique Ansary, Rahim Khan, Anil Jha, and Gopal Choubey etc.

Those good old days at Patna Medical College flashed through his mind. Then he thought of his wife Stella for a moment, and suddenly, his mind became cloudy and turbulent.

The car reached his residence standing on a hillock with oak trees lining the boundary. He has one acre of land there. He has cultivated all varieties of vegetables, for domestic use, such as ladies finger, brinjal, lettuce, bitter gourd, snake gourd, green peas, pumpkin, yam etc. In addition to this there is a small garden of flower plants in front of his house, different varieties of rose, marigold, dahlia, daffodils, hyacinth, tulips, lily and orchids. Dr. Antony has no reading habit except newspaper. So he will utilise his liesure time for gardening and and cultivation of vegetables and fruit trees. The fruit trees in his orchard consist of pomigranate, mango, supporta, plum, sabarjil and guva. The watchman will do all the manuring, watering, pruning and spraying pesticides etc

Dr. Antony got down from the car and went directly to the dining room. The lunch had been kept on the dining table. It consisted of rice, vegetable curry and curd. Doctor will take nonvegetarian food only on Sundays. On Saturday, he will take only wheat gruel for morning and night and no lunch. That day, after lunch he lay in bed for sometime and then slipped into slumber in which he saw his past life flashing through the screen of his mind. He was born and brought up at Ranchi. Dr Antony took his MBBS from Patna Medical College. His father was running a hotel there.

Antony was the only son. He had one sister named Celina, who was given in marriage to an employee, in a contracting firm at Dhanbad From morning till night his parents were working hard, and Antony used to help them after school hours. When workers are on leave he used to clean the vessels, utensils etc and sweep the floor. After Antony went to Patna, the hotel was sold to a bengali, and they purchased 50 acres of land, in a far away hamlet and started cultivation of wheat and paddy. There was no shortage of labou, and they got plenty of adivasi men and women and they had to pay only a pittance as wages. They constructed a thatched hut in the middle of the farm and began to live there. On holidays and vacation Antony used to go to that village, and stay with his parents, in that hut. They were getting good profit out of their cultivation, and for the education of Antony there was no dearth of money. Occasionally, some extremists used to come there, and collect money from them but there was no threat, or attack from them.

Dr. Antony completed his MBBS and then got a job in a private hospital in Delhi, along with his friend Anil Jha. They worked there for about one year, and then got selected to the Libyan health service. He had heard about Gaddafi and was afraid to go there. But he was encouraged by his friends to accept the offer. The pay offered for the job was very high and hence he readily accepted the job. He flew to Tripoli and joined duty at the government hospital there. Most of the doctors were from different parts of the world. He got a bachelor accommodation near the hospital. The life was very happy and comfortable there.

One day, he met a lady doctor from Ireland and her name was Stella. She was a gynaecologist.

and had a special charm in her words and gait.

'You're Mr. Antony from India?' She asked.

'Yes, may I know your good name?' Dr. Antony enquired.

'I'm Stella John from Ireland.'

'Glad to meet you'.

'You're a Christian?, are you Catholic?'. Stella asked.

'I'm Christian, but not Catholic'. Antony replied.

Then she smiled and it was very heartening smile.

They talked about the hospital, its patients and the equipments used for diagnosing various problems etc and she left after giving a shakehand.

Dr. Antony learned Arabic within a short time. He can now communicate with patients without interpreter. The government is doing too much for the people but the only problem is that it is a dictatorship and individual freedom has been restricted.

After three weeks, Dr. Antony met Dr. Stella again and he asked 'Stella how is your duty here?'.

'Comfortable, there are three doctors in the labour room including me, The other doctors are Deepa Bhat, and Supriya. Both of them are highly experienced with post graduate qualification.'.

'How's your food?, are you preparing it yourself.?'

'I don't know how to prepare food. I'll purchase bread and cheese and that is my main food.

My roommates are from india and they make chapattis and curry daily.'

'Have you got independent quarter?'

'Three of us are living in the same quarter. To live alone is horrible. If somebody else is living with us we can communicate with them and discuss problems and find remedy.'

They used to meet occasionally and she will enquire about Christians in India and Dr Antony in turn will enquire about the Catholic protestant rift in their country.

'I'm Catholic. The people of Ireland 're mainly Catholic, but Scottish people are mostly protestants. We hate protestants and they in turn hate Catholics'.

'In India all Christians are living in peace and harmony and there is no problem as in Britain.

A Catholic can marry a protestant and vice versa and no problems between different churches'

One day, she asked Antony 'Have you heard of IRA?'

'Yes, I've heard about IRA terrorists. They've killed our Lord Mountbatten. What for they are fighting?'

'They're fighting for the freedom of Ireland from the shackles of Scotland. We want a homeland for Catholics. We don't want to live in the subjugation of Scottish people'.

It was a new knowledge for Antony, about the rift between Catholics and Protestants. Every community want a homeland for themselves. When a homeland was given to the muslims by creating Pakistan, millions of innocent people were killed, maimed or reported missing. The colour of river Sindhu and Brahmaputra became red and still people fight for homelands. When a homeland was created for Jews in the middle east the same thing happened there also. People do not know, how to coexist with one another, and live peacefully, forgetting the differences of religion, caste and ethnic problems. Antony hated religious fundamentalism and fanaticism and the atrocities in the name of religion and ethnic differences

Antony used to meet Stella frequently and one day he asked 'Stella I am a protestant by birth and I want to marry a Catholic. What's your opinion?'

'OK, good idea'.

'Are you prepared for that?'

'Of course'.

Thus, one day they went to Bombay and got married in a Catholic church there and returned to Tripoli after two days. Other than the Vicar, there was no body in the church to witness the marriage.

They applied for a family quarter and they got it, and started a family life. Deepa Bhat and Supriya wished them best wishes for happy and harmonious life. They came with some costly gifts to the quarter of Stella and Antony. Some of Antony's friends also came and wished them happy married life. After marriage, Antony wrote to his parents, and sister, regarding the marriage. But, they were sceptical about the future of the wedlock.

Many weeks and months rolled by, and Stella became pregnant, and gave birth to two baby girls. They were identical twins and was difficult to distinguish each other. To look after the kids, they got an Ayah from Calicut, named Nabeesa. She was very able and she can look after the kids singlehandedly and perform the domestic chores except cooking. Stella and Antony will do cooking in Indian and European style. Stella learned to prepare Indian food.

Nabeesa had a daughter and she was living with her grandmother. Nabeesa's husband quarrelled with her on a trivial issue and left the house. Since there was no other means for livelihood, she took a passport, arranged visa through a travel agency and reached Libya. Her daughter has started going to the school. Nabees will send a portion of the salary every month to her mother, and she will keep the remaining money in her suitcase. For her life was comfortable and secure under Stella and Antony. The kids grew up quickly and they are now three years old, and started to go to play school. They have started speaking in English.

One day, they had an unusual visitor one Dr. Graham Stone from Canada, and Stella introduced him to Dr. Antony.'This's my old companion in the medical college in Ireland He's working with the WHO and worked at different parts of the world and now in Canada. He'll stay here for two days and leave for Ottawa'. He stayed in their house for two days and left. Stella had taken him to the Airport.

After Graham left Stella was in a worried and disturbed state of mind. Dr. Antony noticed this change in Stella and asked 'What happened to you Stella?'

'Nothing, nothing, there is a pestering headache'

Antony realized that something is troubling Stella's mind after the departure of Mr Graham Stone.

She disregarded the kids, and was in a peculiar state of mind. She was always in a pensive mood and did not care for Antony or her work. She took two days leave and remained at home even though there was heavy pressure of work at the hospital.

One day, she went to the hospital and did not return. Dr Antony was aghast and immediately contacted the labour room and was informed that she did not report for duty after two days leave. He then informed police and they after thorough investigation informed him that she had left for Canada.

Antony was grief stricken. Her loss was immense and unbearable to him and his family. He was in search of an answer for the baffling question-- why did she quit?, where did she go?, and what was the motive behind it?. He looked after the children in her place, with more love and warmth and entrusted the kitchen work to Nabeesa.

After one month, he got a call from Stella from Canada and he was thrilled to hear her voice.

'Antony excuse me, I'd no other option. How's our kids?'. Stella asked.

'Kids're fine, where're you? why did you leave us?'.

'Antony you know nothing about me. Mr Graham was my husband. H's a member of the IRA and one day he disappeared and reappeared after many years. On enquiry he said that he was in jail and could not contact me since he had no information about me. He's now working in a medical firm in Canada. Please look after our kids well. I'll come back later. Don't ask me any further questions'.

Antony worked there for a further period of five years. During this period, two calls were received from Stella. The children were studying in 3rd standard in a European school, in Tripoli. Antony has suffered a lot in the absence of Stella. Her mysterious disappearance has really devastated his dreams, for the future. Now, Nabeesa is doing all the works in in the house, cooking, looking after childre, and other domestic chores. Antony has only two duties and that are to guide the children in their studies and purchase necessary items to the household. Antony had forgotten Stella, since there was no news from her, and he feared whether she was also in jail, along with Graham Stone. Everything is shrouded in mystery, and it is difficult to get an answer for the baffling questions. Antony made enough money with his ten years of service in Libya and wanted to return to India.

One day, he asked Nabeesa 'Nabeesa, I'm planning to resign and go to Ranchi where my parents are living. Will you come with us as nani?'.

'Certainly. I'll come with you wherever you go.'

Thus Antony resigned his job and left for Ranchi. There he took a house on rent in the city, admitted children in an english medium school, and started a dispensary in the suburb. In a short time he picked up practice. He used to visit his parents occasionally. They had become very old and was unable to continue with the agricultural work. The farmland was disposed of and the money deposited in banks in Ranchi. A portion of the money was given to his sister Celina. Antony brought his parents to Ranchi and they were happy to live with him there.

Antony's parents wanted to go to Alappey to see their relatives. Hence, he made necessary arrangements for their journey. After reaching there, they refused to come back. When Antony compelled they said 'Antony so far we have been living outside Kerala and we want to spend the remaining period here.'Antony did not object and sent enough money whenever they required. They are now staying with his uncle and family, since they had no house of their own.

Once, Nabeesa wanted to go back to her village, since her mother was not well, and her daughter had appeared for SSLC. Antony was in a predicament. If she went back his children will be in difficulty, since they are too much attached to her, and Antony put a suggestion 'Nabeesa you bring your family to Ranchi and another house will be taken for your stay and your daughter can go to college here'. Nabeesa was not agreeable for this proposal.

Antony also decided to visit Kerala to see his parents. The dispensary was closed for one month. Nabeesa went to Calicut and Antony and children to Alappey.

Antony went to uncle's house and met his parents. They were very weak and ailing. Uncle and family were very helpful and Antony was very much pleased. He paid a handsome amount to uncle for the treatment and other expenses of parents, and offered to send more. During the stay at Alappey, he made a trip to Kodaicanal. He was very much impressed by the beauty and tranquility of that place. He visited Crockers walk, cascade falls, pillar rocks, suicide point, golf course and other important places there. He also visited some schools run by Christian associations and liked the place very much.

Antony returned to Ranchi after one month, but the old rush of patients was not there. One or two big hospitals have sprung up in the vicinity and hence he decided to close the dispensary and go to Kodaicanal. By this time, Nabeesa had returned to Ranchi. Nabeesa's daughter had passed SSLC in I class and she is to be admitted to college. Then Antony put another suggestion to her. 'Nabeesa you bring your mother and daughter to Kodaicanal and I'll take a house for you. Noorjahan can join for +1 there and you are free to stay with them in the new house.'. Nabeesa agreed to the new suggestion.

Antony went to Kodaicanal. Nabeesa went to Calicut closed her house and brought mother and daughter to Kodaicanal. Antony admitted his children in a famous convent school in V std and Noorjahan daughter of Nabeesa was admitted for +1 in a higher secondary school there. Thus their life again settled in the new environment. Antony studied the hillstation thoroughly and took a house for rent in the suburb, to start the dispensary. Later, Antony purchased these two places for a reasonable price and then renovated.

Dr. Antony started his practice in the new building. In the initial stages, there was no patients but picked up practice gradually since there was no other doctors in the vicinity. Dr. Antony was very friendly and sympathetic to the patients and strived hard to alleviate their sufferings. Even though, the fees he received were very less, he managed to run the dispensary as a service. He started a small lab there and appointed a lady named Mary as pharmacist and a youth from the locality named Selvaraj was appointed as the compounder. A watchman named Chellam was also appointed at the dispensary to manage the patients and giving them tokens. At the house, a gardener was appointed for looking after the compound and maintaining the garden. His name was Palaniswamy.

Years rolled by. Noorjahan passed +2 in I class and admitted to an Engineering College at Coimbatore. In the meanwhile Nabeesa arranged to sell her house and property in vellayil and deposited the amount in two banks at Calicut.

Dr. Antony used to go to Alappey and meet his parents. They are now in better health and spirit than before. For them life was very pleasant and without worries. Their daughter

Celina had come to see them recently. Her husband has been transferred to Bokaro and they have shifted residence to that place and children transferred to a good school there.

Much water has flown through Viga river and Antony's daughters Priya and Princy passed +2 and joined for medicine in Chennai. Nabeesa's daughter passed engineering with distinction and got a job in Chennai. Through matrimonial column a proposal came for her from Palakkad. The boy is also an IT Engineer by name Noushad and the marriage was conducted in an auditorium, in Palakkad town. They took a rented house in Chennai and began to live there happily.

Dr. Antony was only 47, but he looked very old, and most of his hair had greyed, due to tension and worry. Although he was financially well off, he was very much worried because of Stella.

He has strived hard to bring up his daughters to grown up women. They are going to become doctors but he had no peace of mind.

One day, Dr. Antony was sitting in his consulting room of the dispensary. He had cleared all the patients and was relaxing in his chair. Then a middle aged European lady came to see him. She waited outside till all patients had left and then she was allowed into the room by Chellam.

She came into the room, sat in front of the doctor and asked 'Dr. Antony how're you?'

Dr. Antony was startled, because that voice was very familiar to him. He looked at that lady with the spectacle sharply. Time had made many changes in her and still he could recognise her. He jumped up from his chair and wailed 'Oh! Stella, my Stella, my darling'.

In a sudden fit of excitement he ran to her and hugged her. She began to weep and asked him in that excitement and ecstasy. 'I want to see my daughters?'

For some time, Dr. Antony could not speak and words were stuck in his throat.

'They have grown up and are studying for medicine at Chennai'.

'Let us go. I want to see them now itself' She said

Dr. Antony started the car and moved towards Chennai.

'Where's your husband?'

'Oh!, he's no more. He was suffering from cancer for a long time and died a couple of weeks back. He was a patient when he came to our house and there was nobody to nurse him. I thought it my duty to take him to a good hospital in US and treat him but I could not save his life. After his demise, I went in search of you. I went to Tripoli, then to Ranchi, Alappey, and then to Kodaicanal.

'Will you again desert us?'

'No darling, never"

Dr. Antony was flying at top speed in his car and reached Chennai by evening. They did not take lunch since they had forgot hunger and thirst in that excitement and ecstasy.

They faced Priya and Princy in the portico of the College.

'Who's this lady papa?' They asked.

'This's your Mummy Stella John of Ireland'

They embraced mummy and cried.

Both of them took two days leave and returned to Kodaicanal with their parents.

********* END *********

THE ORDEAL OF A BRAHMIN FAMILY

Dr. Subramaniam, was a rich man in Rangoon upto 1975. He had a clinic, wholesale medical agency, a retail medical shop and a laboratory. In addition to this, he had a tea estate of area 800 acres. Natives and foreigners envied him, for his rise and accumulation of wealth. But, everything turned topsy turvy, with a government order. The assets of the foreigners were nationalised and they were arrested and expelled from the country. Those who challenged the president's order in court or those who were involved in protests and violence were arrested, tried and sent to jail.

It was a bolt from the blue. Dr. Subramaniam had some misgivings, when army captured power, and the Army Chief became President in 1965. He hated foreigners and used to say that everything is in the hands of foreigners and the economy is controlled by them. By the word foreigners, he meant Europeans, Indians and Chinese. Rumour began to circulate that all the properties of foreigners will be nationalised by the military junta. One leading advocate told Dr Subramaniam to be careful, since he is the proprietor of a vast empire. Hence, he decided to send his family to India. His family included his mother Sakuntala Devi aged 70, wife named Krithika, aged 30 and daughter Vani aged 10 years. One day, he directed his manager Lee Ping to book three tickets in a ship from Rangoon to Madras. He took them to the port and helped them to board the ship safely. Within two days, the ship started sailing towards Madras. When they started, he sent two telegrams to Mr Sundaran his nephew to take them safely from the port to his home at Vadapalani.

Ramanatha Iyer was an advocate in Rangoon. One day, he happened to meet an Englishman who had a small tea estate in Burma. Thus, Iyer got the estate of area 800 acres for a nominal amount. Iyer, shifted his residence to the estate after the transaction and started to run the estate. At that time, his son Subramaniam was studying for MBBS at Madras Medical College. After completion of the course he was sent to Delhi for higher studies. Dr Subramaniam joined his father Ramanatha Iyer at Rangoon after completing his MD.

At the insistence of Iyer, Dr Subramaniam started a clinic in the name of his mother, Sakuntala Devi, in the city. There was heavy rush to get his appointment and later he started the medical agency, retail medical shops and lab. Majority of the workers were natives and the remaining staff Indian and Chinese. Iyer had a friend called Ramaswamy in Rangoon and he was a retired Professor. He was living with his only daughter, since his wife had died a few years back. He had a daughter, called Krithika and she was doing her degree, in the university. One day, Ramanatha Iyer called his son and said 'Mony, I've a friend here called Ramaswamy. You go and see his daughter Krithika. She' s a very pretty girl and you'll like her' Dr. Subramaniam met Krithika and liked her very much and married her within a couple of months.

Krithika's father Ramaswamy passed away, following a minor illness before the first marriage anniversary of Dr. Subramaniam and Krithika. Thus, Krithika became lonely in her house. She discontinued her studies and moved to the house of Dr. Subramaniam, after disposing of her properties. The money was deposited in bank. By this time, Krithika became pregnant and gave birth to a baby girl. She was named Vani. When Vani became three years old, Ramanatha Iyer had a severe attack and he died instantly. Although his son reached the spot, he could not do anything. Iyer had passed away before his arrival. Thus the burden of the tea estate also fell on his shoulder.

Dr. Subramaniam had enough staff, but there was no labour problem. Years rolled by and Dr Subramaniam is the President of Tea Estate Owners Association and President of Private Hospital Association. After sending his family to Madras, Dr. Subramaniam was very much worried, till he got a telegram from Sundaram that his family had reached Madras port safely and taken to his house at Vadapalani.

After the receipt of the telegram, a police jeep came to his office and he was arrested and taken to jail. He tried to challenge the arrest through a writ petition, but it was dismissed. The entire property of the doctor was taken over by the government and many charges were framed against him including the death of a native patient in the hospital. It was treated as a death due to negligence and was treated as murder. He had a lot of friends there, but nobody came forward to help him. The case proceeded for some time and he was convicted for a period of 10 years and expulsion from the country after expiry of the jail term. Sakuntala Devi and Krithika had sent letters to Dr. Subramaniam but he did not get them.

Sakuntala Devi read in news papers, that all properties of foreign nationals were confiscated and the owners were arrested and expelled from the country and their bank accounts frozen. She thought that her son will be safe there, since he was a famous doctor. Days, months and years passed, but nothing heard about Dr. Subramaniam. They sent many letters to his hospital and tea estate but no reply received.

Sakuntala Devi, Krithika and Vani have completed three months in the house of Sundaram.

Sundaram, who is a nephew of Dr. Subramaniam is a businessman, at Anna Nagar. He had mother, wife and two children. During the initial two weeks, they showed some love and sympathy towards their guests. Now the relation is very strained. They are given meals by the hosts but show hostility openly. Sundaram goes to his shop in the morning and his family remain closed in their room. They do not talk with either Krithika, or Sakuntala Devi. Now, they stopped serving food to the guests. So, Krithika will go to the kitchen and collect food in a steel vessel. They do not smile even with the child Vani.

One day, Krithika told mother 'Amma they're hating us. Let us move to some other place.

'Where can we go?. Even though there are plenty of relatives here, we'll not get refuge for more than two days.'

'My sister's here, but they're very selfish type and hence we can't expect anything from them'

Sakuntala Devi said in despair.

'My father's brother is there at Trichy. I've heard that they're well off. We can go there and find out uncle's house.' Krithika said with some hope on her face.

One day, Sakuntala Devi spoke to Sundaram 'Sundaram we've been living here for the last three months it's not proper to trouble you further. We're thankful for your love and care. Please permit us to go to my sister's house at Mylapore.'

'Dr. Subramaniam's my friend and relative, It's my duty to help you. No need of going anywhere. There's big crisis in Burma. The assets of foreign nationals have been taken over by the governmet, and the people have been arrested and expelled from the country.' Sundaram said.

'There's no news from Rangoon. I'd sent so many letters but no reply received. He may be in prison I'm afraid. If he's out 'll definitely respond either by letter or telegram'

Sakuntala Devi said in a depressed tone.

'Dr. Mony will come out, since he's a famous doctor. The locals need his service and the General can't do any harm to him.' Sundaram said to pacify Sakuntala Devi and daughter.

'Anyway, I'm not optimistic. A lot of money was spent for hospitals, medical agency, lab etc. The entire deposits of Mony's father was withdrawn for this purpose and there's not much money in the bank. Krithika had a lot of money in bank, but that also would have been frozen or attached.'

'Aunty don't worry unnecessarily. Everything'll have a happy ending. Dr. Mony'll come without much delay.'

'One more week, we'll stay here and then move to Mylapore.'

Mr Sundaran is a nice man, and he didn't want to trouble Dr. Mony's family. But his mother, Pattamal and wife Krishnaveni are very aggressive. So, after one week, they left that house and moved to the house of Ramachandra Iyer at Mylapore. This house belonged to the younger sister of Sakuntala Devi. Ramachandra Iyer is a very big landlord. He had a lot of properties and houses there. From rent of the houses, he gets a huge amount every month. Sakuntala Devi's sister Seethalakshmy is a pious lady and will visit at least two temples every day. Her son Deepak is doing his MD in Bangalore. Daughter parvathy has been given in marriage to a chartered accountant at Coimbatore.

Sakuntala Devi had that address with her, and reached the place without any difficulty and they were received with great love and warmth.

'Who's this? Do you still remember me. You and your husband had come to see us some ten years ago and after that no news from you.' Seethalakshmy said.

'Seetha, we're in great trouble. There's problems in Burma and all foreigners have been driven out and their properties confiscated. We returned to Madras when the trouble started. Now there is no news from Burma. Where can we go?. No news about the bread winner'. Sakuntala Devi said in a voice choked with emotion.

'Akka, don't worry. We're here to help you. Till Mony's return, we'll look after you. Mony used to visit us, when he was studying for MBBS. Later, I heard that he had gone to Delhi to take MD. We'd received a telegram when your husband passsed away. By the by, who is this lady?'Seethalakshmy asked pointing towards Krithika.

She's my daughter in law Krithika and grand daughter Vani'

Seethalakshmy embraced Krithika and Vani and kissed their cheeks.

'We were not invited to Dr. Mony 's marriage. Where's her house? Is she brahmin?'.

'Yes, she's very much brahmin. She's the only daughter of Prof. Ramaswamy of Rangoon. Her father was very famous professor, but he's no more. Mother died, when she was a child. She was doing degree, but could not complete it. Marriage was a simple function and hence no invitation was sent outside Burma After this marriage, his father expired and my husband also departed to heaven'

Thus, they began to live as their guests. For the first month, there was no problem. But, after that, problems cropped up. Seethalakshmy began to ignore them. She won't give food in time, the food served were either stale or unpalatable. One day, Vani vomited after eating Idly and sambar. On seeing this Seethalakshy said 'The sambar's a bit old. Don't worry I'll prepare new sambar and give it you'

Seethalakshmy began to nag them saying 'Akka we're poor and not like you. We're living with the income from rent. Many house are lying vacant. If you want, you can move to any of them.

You can choose the best house and give me only five hundred rupees per month. and not more. The house is very convenient and comfortable.

'OK Seetha, we can find out the whereabouts of her uncle at Trichy.'

'Thank you akka. You know our difficulties'

Sakuntala Devi went and examined the houses. It is agraharam type houses without independent rooms.

'No independent rooms and hence rupees five hundred is in excess' Sakuntala Devi said.

'Then reduce it by hundred rupees and give me four hundred per month' Seethalakshmy said with a frown.

'Will you provide a stove and kerosene'

'If you give me money in advance, I'll arrange it'

Sakuntala knew that her sister is very greedy and it is difficult to adjust with her. She is trying to drive them out.

They started living in the rented accommodation. Purchased rice and vegetable and prepared food. They despised their fate. In the time of need there is nobody to help and console. There are plenty of relatives, but all are greedy and selfish. The family of a multi millionaire is living in this pitiable condition, without anybody to give a helping hand. Sakuntala Devi decided to fight for a living, and not to surrender or beg for mercy.

One night, Sakuntala Devi had a nightmare. She heard gunshots and some people lying dead in the Rangoon streets. She suddenly awoke from the sleep, and began to cry. Krithika and daughter were sleeping peacefully. She then thought of her Rangoon life. The bungalow had six bedrooms with marble flooring, two house maids, three cars with four drivers and gardener.

Sakuntala Devi closed her eyes and prayed for some time. 'Krishna be merciful to us and save my son from the hands of the army junta.' She felt somebody coming and caressing her, and a faint chime of temple bell. She then opened her eyes and searched every where, but did not see any sign of a divine hand or object anywhere in the house. She again lay in the bed, and went to sleep slowly.

One day, Sakuntala Devi took out a bundle of clothes from the luggage. She removed the covering one after the other and from the inside took out a small cover and opened it. It contained thirty bangles of gold. She took out five bangles and the remaining were kept in the same bundle unnoticed by anybody else. They went to a jewellery shop and sold it. At that time the value of one sovereign was Rs 400/'-. and she got an amount of Rs 3500/- for 10 sovereign. She thought they can survive a few months with this money.

After a couple of days, they happened to meet an old man from Thrssur, working as grocery agent He travels frequently from Thrissur to Madras and back, collects orders from shops, and sends the items to them. He gets commision on the items despatched. His name was Krishna Moorthy and was staying in the adjacent house. Sakuntala Devi told him their poignant story. He heard their story patiently and came forward to help them.

'Sister, this's a vicious circle. You can't trust anybody here. All're cut throats and will cheat anybody with impunity, and without any kind of compunction. You cannot survive here, unless you have a regular income. You come with me to Thrissur. It's a modest town with a sizeable population of brahmin community. Then, you can admit your granddaughter in a good school there. In my relation there is an old lady leading a lonely life in her house. Her sons are in high positions in Delhi Secretariat. They tried to take their mother with them but she refused. She want to go to temple every day and live in a brahmin locality as ours. Since my family is there, she is living without fear. Her eyesight has become dim and requires the help of somebody. If you come it'll be a help for her and a boon for you. If you're agreeable you can come with me to Trichur. Sakuntala Devi liked the idea and they went to Trichur along with Krishna Moorthy after one week.

Sedhulakshmy Ammal, received them with a motherly love and affection.

'This's your house and you can stay here without any problem. This's a big house with four bedrooms with all modern amenities and facilities'. Krishna Moorthy said after meeting Sedhulakshmy Ammal.

Krishna Moorthy had spoken to her elder son Bhadran and he was very happy in that arrangement. He also promised to send Rs 200/- per month for their service. Thus, after many months of worry and tension peace prevailed in their life. Krithika will do cooking and all the domestic chores and Sakuntala will take care of Sethu patti. (brahmin lady) Every day, before sunrise Sakunthala will complete the bath and other daily routines of patti and then take her to Tiruvampadi temple. After coming back, she will be given breakfast. If patti wanted to go to neighbouring houses, she will accompany her. At 1 pm lunch will be given, and after that patti will sleep up to 5 pm. After waking up, she will be given tea and snacks and then taken to Paremakkav or Vadakkumnathan temple. At 7.30 pm she will be given dinner and then sleep.

Days and months passed and school reopening time arrived. Krithika met the Headmaster of the Vivekodayam school and told him the whole story. They had no TC or other documents. The HM conducted a written test for Vani to know her knowledge and asked a lot of questions in the interview. Vani is very fluent in english and had vast knowledge about all subjects. Considering all the factors the HM agreed to admit her to Vth standard since she was studying in that class in Rangoon. After Vani's admission, Krithika started a tuition class for girl students and she could earn some money, every month. She started a bank account in Dhanalakshmy bank and began to deposit her savings. She tried to get a job, but in vain, since she had no certificates with her. God is merciful, and they found a refuge from the world of hatred, mistrust and ill treatment.

Sedhulakshmy patti's son Bhadran and family had come at the time of Thrissur pooram and they stayed in their house happily for one month and went back to Delhi. He asked a lot of questions about Krithika's life in Rangoon and about her husband Dr. Subramaniam. After hearing their traumatic story, Bhadran became very sympathetic towards them. He said to Krithika 'Your story's really touching and heart breaking. I'm very much worried about my mother who was leading a lonely life here. After your arrival, I'm very happy and satisfied. Now, she's happy in your presence and I'm relieved of the worry and tension. After going back, he contacted the Ministry of External Affairs and wanted to enquire about Dr. Subramaniam. After some time, he got a reply saying that Dr. Subramaniam is undergoing a jail term and he can come out only after long ten years. Bhadran wrote a letter to Krithika regarding the information he received through MEA.

Many years rolled by, and Vani passed SSLC with 6th rank. and joined St Mary's College. For Pre degree she got distinction and joined BSc (Physics). While studying for degree she had appeared for a Bank test to the cadre of clerks and she got selected. She discontinued her udies and joined State Bank of Travancore Thrissur. Since Vani was getting a regular income it was a big support to Krithika. She told Vani.' You deposit your salary in your account from next month onwards. We require huge amount for your marriage'. Vani has completed four years service in the bank and appeared for the Probationary Officer test but she did not get it.

Sedhulakshmy patti is not well. She is laid up with giddiness and fatigue. She was taken to Mission hospital and doctors advised her complete rest and hence she was confined to bed. The temple visit was avoided. Occasionally, Krithika will visit either Paremakav temple or Thiruvambadi. temple. She has now found a refuge in the worship of God, and she is getting peace of mind through the temple visits and prayers.

The illness of patti became aggravated and she was admitted to the government hospital. Krithika was the bystander, till she was discharged from the hospital. On hearing the news of mother's hospitalisation, Sivaraman and Bhadran arrived from Delhi. There was no relief to the illness of patti and hence she was shifted to Mission Hospital. She had all types of illness like sugar, BP renal and heart complaint. She was in the hospital for about one month and still there was no relief and one day she fainted and remained in coma for two days and died. She was cremated in the Brahmin crematorium, MG Road. Bhadran and his brother performed all the rites and rituals in connection with funeral and for other rituals and poojas the services of Vadhyar (brahmin priest)was sought.

Bhadran is now Joint Secretary in the Ministry of Health. While going back to Delhi Bhadran said 'I don't get words to thamk you. My mother'd a peaceful death and you've done great service in nursing and attending to her needs. You can stay here, without rent, any longer you require. If you want this house, please tell me and we'll give it for a reasonable amount, far less than the market value'.

At the time of their departure, Krithika gave a list of the properties taken over by the government. Also, she gave an application for making necessary investigation regarding he husband. After three months she received a letter from the ministry that enquiries have been made regarding Dr. Subramaniam, and it is stated that he had developed dementia in jail, and was released after expiry of his term. They do not know anything about his whereabouts. Then Bhadran personally met a Senior Officer in the foreign ministry and presented the case of Dr Subramaniam and requested to take up the case with Burmese authorities, for tracing out the doctor. The external affairs ministry directed Indian embassy officials in Rangoon to trace out the missing doctor. They took urgent necessary action and traced out the doctor. He was roaming in the port area as a beggar, with long beard and tattered clothes. He was brought to Delhi after completing legal formalities by embassy officials. Bhadran gave him a bath and dressed him in new clothes and brought him to Thrissur, by flight.

On seeing Dr. Subramaniam, Sakuntala Devi could not recognise him because he was looking haggard with long hair and beard. Krithika embraced her husband and wept profusely. He had lost his memory and he looked at them with fear and anxiety. His long hair and beard were cut and given a thorough bath. Now there is some sparkle in his eyes but memory is completely gone.

Bhadran returned to Delhi the next day itself. While going back Krithika thanked him for the invaluable help rendered in tracing out her husband and bringing him to their house. Dr. Subramanium was taken to a famous psychiatrist and he opined that such amnesia coupled with insanity is difficult to be cured. Doctor Subramaniam will sit idle looking outside with vacant eyes. He was treated for long two years but there was no change in his condition.

At this time, a proposal came for Vani. The boy's name is Ragesh and is a clerk in the Income Tax department He is tall and handsome and a graduate. Vani, and others liked the boy and the marriage was fixed. Krithika was afraid and anxious about the expenditure. Then Sakuntala Devi told Krithika not to worry. She went inside and took out her cloth bundles and fished out from inside 25 bangles and 3 necklaces which are enough for the marriage.

The marriage was conducted in the Samoohamadam hall. There were a number of priests to conduct the rituals of the marriage. Dr. Subramaniam had been taken to the hall but he did not sit there and went out and was simply walking outside the hall and hence kanyadanam was done by Krithika. Bhadran had come for the marriage and he returned immediately after the marriage. Sundaram and Seethalakshmy had been invited but they did not come but sent greetings.

After all the rituals and functions, Vani was taken to the house of Ragesh. At the time of leaving, Vani touched the feet of her father. Dr. Subramaniam simply looked at her with vacant eyes. Krithika and Sakuntala wept torrentially and hugged Vani and sent her with Ragesh.

A couple of days had passed, after parting with Vani Dr. Subramaniam was found in a thoughtful mood. He did not eat anything on that day and was simply walking in the verandah. Krithika was engrossed in domestic work and Sakuntala Devi sleeping in the bed. After sometime he was found missing. Krithika made a hue and cry and the neighbours rushed to the house. They sent messengers to different parts of the town but he was not found out. A complaint was lodged in the police station. Police conducted a thorough search in the town, bus stand and Railway station, but he was not traced out. On hearing the news Vani and husband came to the house.

Next day dawned, with a terrible news. A mutilated body of the doctor was found in the Railway track,. near the Trichur Railway station. Krithika identified the body and after postmortem the body was cremated in the MG Road crematorium. Krithika, and Sakuntala were lying in a dazed condition and Vani was working in the kitchen and Ragesh reading news paper. Then, they heard a scream. Vani and Ragesh rushed to the room where mother and grandma were lying. They were shocked to see Krithika in a devilish form grisly hair and staring eyes. She was making devilish sounds and gestures. Immediately, she was taken to the hospital and was brought to normalcy by one injection.

Next morning, Vani woke up and went to the room of mother. She was shocked to see her mother sitting as a statue in white sari and shortened hair and cried "Amma, amma, we have nobody in this world. Papa gone and amma in this condition, Oh! God, why did you behave in such a cruel way to this innocent girl?' She continued her lament and then Ragesh came and caressed Vani.

Then, Krithika raised her head and said 'Vani, I'm a widow, I'm a widow. Please arrange to tonsure my hair.' Vani embraced her mother and broke into tears again.

********* END *********

VINITHA'S AGONY

During hot summer, the rubber trees will shed their leaves and stand naked, looking at the sky. After pre monsoon rains, they will flourish again with abundant green leaves. When they are bare, larks used to come and sit on their branches and sing melodious songs. Woodpecker will come and make holes in it's trunk and lay eggs. In the dry leaves on the ground, snakes will roam freely undetected and climb the trees and eat woodpecker's eggs. Beetle and cricket will compete each other to show their excellence with their undulating high pitch songs and the estate will become a place of various types of rhapsody.

Kochunny warrier stopped tapping, when leaves started falling and the land became very dry and arid. He then, told the tapper 'Thankappan you come after pre monsoon rains and till that time no tapping'.

'OK Sir, I'm going' Thankappan said while going home.

After a couple of weeks, there was heavy rains followed by thunder and lightning. After this, the estate became very noisy with the songs of birds, frogs, beetle and cricket and buds began to appear on all the rubber trees and within a few days, the estate was covered with a blanket of green again. Then, one day Thankappan appeared and he went out with his pots and knife to commence tapping again. Kochunny warrier accompanied him to supervise the work.

Vineeta, the granddaughter of Kochunny warrier is leading a monotonous life, after her college days. After 3 years of hostel life, she is leading a boring life without any friends, newspaper and TV. She had distinction in SSLC and +2, but could secure only 62 % marks in BSc (Chemistry). She applied for MSc and BEd in several colleges, but did not get selection. Tried for PSC test and her name is in the rank list, but was not sure whether she will be called or not. One day, she met her friend Gopika and she said 'No need of waiting, they won't issue posting orders, till the result of the next test is released, and then this list will be cancelled'.

'What can we do in this case?' Vineetha asked.

'Some agents are collecting money, but my father didn't give anything saying that PSC is corruption free, and the deserving candidates will get selection without paying anything'

Vineeta was in great despair, after college days. The life at Kerala Varma College was really eventful and unforgettable. The college campus is extensive, like Vrindavan, with full of various types of flowering trees and exotic medicinal plants. The ladies hostel is situated, behind the chemistry block. During evening, she will roam in the campus with her friends, and sit under the gulmohar trees, and collect it's flowers and discuss various topics under the sun. She is very nostalgic about it. Her life during the last two years was boring, without any friends and any means to kill time.

Grandpa will go with Thankappan, the tapper, grandma is always engrossed in domestic chores and mother will go to her school by 8.30 am, and will be back by 5 pm. Vineetha will sit in her room alone, looking outside at the rubber trees, and the birds, resting on it's branches. The birds will not sit idle, and will make noise always, by chirping, flitting and hopping and fighting one another.

Long two years have rolled by, after her college days and she could not find out a solution for her boredom. One day, she exploded to her mother Kamala. 'Amma I am really fed up with this life. Why don't you tell uncle, to arrange a seat for BEd in the management quota. I don't know, where my papa is hiding. If he is here, he would have managed a seat for me for BEd. There is no TV, no newspaper and this house looks like a bhargavinilayam.(haunted house). It is in a dilapidated condition. Uncle's house is newly constructed and it is lying vacant. Why can't we move to that mansion from this old house?.'

Kamala became angry and said 'Your grandpa is 75 years old and still he's working hard. He's earning money for your marriage. Since your father has run away, it's his duty to give you in marriage to a good boy. Don't say anything against grandpa'

'Amma, grandpa has driven away my father and he's taking your salary also. He has given one acre of land and a lot of money to uncle, for constructing a beautiful house. It really belongs to grandpa and not uncle. Amma is so afraid, and obedient, and did not ask grandpa to bring back our father. When he is very much alive, we are living here like orphans and amma has no complaints'.

Kamala began to cry. She knew that her father had used rough language to his son in law, and did not come forward to help him, when he was in financial trouble, but he gave lakhs to his son to build a house. Now the children are demanding her to bring their father back.

'The paint has peeled off in almost all rooms, and there is no furniture to sit or dine. Ask grandpa to demolish this house and construct a new one here with his money in the bank. My marriage can be conducted only after that and not now.' said Vineetha in anguish.

'Vineetha don't repeat the same thing over and over again. That house belong to my brother, if you want a new house, we can ask grandpa to demolish this house, and construct a new one here.'

'Grandpa is not prepared to repair this house. I don't think he'll build a new house here.'

'Don't say loudly, if this reaches his ear, we'll be expelled from this house.'

'Then, my brother and I'll sit in satyagraha against this injustice'

'No, beti he's not such a person. He's prepared to send you for BEd or MSc, if you get a seat, stop blaming grandpa.'

'Will he spend money for my further studies?'

'Surely, he'll do anything for you. We should find out a seat.'

'Hurrah!, Vineetha jumped up and embraced mother.

When Dr. Pushkaran and family came next week, Kamala fired him for his indifference in the case of Vineetha

'Pushkaran, why don't you arrange a BEd seat for Vineetha?. She is in great disappointment.'

'Chechi, I'm helpless. I'm only a veterinary doctor and no connection with BEd colleges' Replied Pushkaran.

'Vineetha says you have friends in all departments. You're deliberately avoiding her. Have you friends in PSC. Her name's in the rank list.?'

'Sorry chechi, I'm really helpless. People'll say this and that and 's not true. A veterinary doctor's nobody in our society even though I've gazetted status.'

Kamala dropped that subject. Then Kochunny warrier returned to the house from the estate.

'Papa, I'm going to rent out the house. My belongings should be kept in a room under lock and key and the other portion can be rented out. The cot, chair, diningtable etc. may be given to the tenant and a receipt obtained from him and additioal rent charged for the furniture given for tenant's use.

'OK, that's good, otherwise the house will be spoiled after some time'.

'One Gopakumar, government contractor had approached me. Collect a rent of Rs 7000/- and this is the key.'

Pushkaran and family went back to Chittoor that evening.

Next day, the new tenant came to meet Kochunny warrier. He was offered a chair in the sitout and warrier sat on a stool.

'I'm Pushkaran's father Kochunny warrier. What's your name?"

'Glad to meet you, I'm Gopakumar, government. contractor doing construction and maintenance work of schools, offices etc.'

'Are you married?'

'Yes, I'm married and have two children'

'So, will you bring your family?'

'My family will come occasionally. My children are studying there and they'll come during holidays.'

'You're going to stay here alone?'

'I'm not alone. My supervisors named Paul and Govindan will be here, with me. When they go home, my family will come' said Gopakumar.

'We won't give house to married bachelors. Since you have already spoken to Pushkaran you can occupy the house. The rent's seven thousand rupees.'

'OK, agreed"

'Pushkaran is the owner and I'm only custodian. Cot, chairs, dining table etc. will be given to you, for your use and you should give me a receipt for the same'

'OK, I'll give it in my letter pad.'

At this time Kamala came to the sitout, with one cup of tea and gave it to Gopakumar and then Kochunny warrier introduced her. 'Gopakumar, this is my daughter Kamala. She is a teacher in a primary school here.'

'OK, good.'

'Contractor sir, my daughter has passed BSc and she wants to join for BEd. Do you know anybody in BEd colleges, there at Thrissur?' Kamala said. Vineetha came and stood behind her.

'There are many BEd colleges there. Only thing's that they'll demand a small amount as donation for management seat.'

'OK, we're prepared to give it. How much is donation?'.

'Rs 30000/- has to be paid in the office in addition to usual fees. If agreed she can join tomorrow itself' Gopakumar said.

Next day, Mr. Gopakumar took Kochunny warrier and Vineetha in his car to the BEd College at Moothakunnam, North Paravoor, where he had arranged a seat. After paying necessary fees etc Vineetha was taken to the hostel and Gopakumar and Warrier returned to Wadakkanchery in the evening.

After reaching home, Warrier said to Kamala 'Gopakumar is really a gentleman. He has met the entire expense for our journey. How, easy was it for him to arrange a seat. Vineetha has lost two years.'

Vineetha was happy at the college. Some of her college mates were also there in the same class.

The college was on the bank of a river, and they could see boats passing through the river from the class. The higher secondary school is in the adjacent compound of the college. Except day scholars, all other girl students were in the hostel. and the matron was one Prabha Devi. The students from their Arts college were also in the hostel. Vineetha's roommates were one Sulekha and Sherina from. Ernakulam.

Vineetha used to visit her house once in a month. There was one student from Nenmara, her father's place and her name was Praseetha. Vineetha befriended with Preseetha and learned more about her grandma and papa. Vineetha has not seen her father, and grandmother, for about 12 years. But, their faces are still vivid in her memory. When she was a child, her father used to take her to his ancestral house, at Nenmara. The grandmother was a very graceful lady, and used to take her to the Nemara templ, daily. She had a lot of cousins there and used to play with them. From Praseetha, Vineetha came to know, that her grandma is still in good health, and her father is now working in a coffee estate in Coorg.

Vineetha's mother did not like to go to Nenmara, and avoided going there, on the flimsy excuse of school job, and looking after aged parents. Her father was running a telephone booth at Wadakkanchery and he stayed in mother's house, since it was difficult for him to reach Nenmara, after closing the booth. Hence, father did not compel mother to move to Nenmara house. In those days, papa had a good income from his booth and hence he did not even demand mother's salary. She was giving the salary to grandpa, ever since she got the job, and papa did not object, since he was also living there. Papa used to bring provisions, vegetables and fruits from market, occasionally. But after the birth of her brother Sandeep his cordial relations with grandpa became strained and finally snapped.

When papa had a good income from booth, grandpa used to praise him for running it singlehandedly. With the advent of mobile phones, the collection in the booth dwindled and finally, he had to close it down, since the income was insufficient even to pay the rent. One day, papa came to the house and told grandpa, that he had closed the booth and handed over the key to the shop owner. Then Grandpa became very rude and asked him, why he had not consulted him before returning the key to the owner. He said that, he would have financed him to start a stationary shop with photcopy machine. Father admitted his mistake, and requested grandpa to finance some two lakhs for starting a hardware or electrcal shop, but he did not agree and suggested a dairy near Kuthiran. Since he had no experience in that field, he refused. Grandpa said that he was lazy and on a minor issue he got enraged, and quarrelled with father, and in a sudden fit of anger, asked him to get out of his house. Father left the house immediately, and never returned. Nobody tried for any reconciliation. Mother could have sent letters to him, to maintain the relation, but she did not. Grandpa used to tell mother, that he was very idle and unable to look after his wife and children. Fearing grandpa's anger she did not even send a letter to him, or ask grandpa to send somebody for reconciliation.

Kochunny warrier belonged to Ottapalam, and he was village officer at Wadakkanchery for along time, and during this period, he purchased this four acres of land for a small amount. He then planted rubber saplings, knowing that the price of rubber will shoot up, after some time. He is earning a very good income from his rubber plantation every month, and has deposited huge amounts in the bank.

Vineetha, when she was in SSLC class wanted to meet her father. She said 'I should get blessings from my father and grandmother for writing the examination'. Amma refused and said 'You are a fool, and your father is a bigger fool. He fought with his father in law, and left without taking us with him, He could have taken us to his ancestral house at Nenmara, or to a rented house here, or somewhere else. In that case, I would have given him my salary, and he could have worked somewher, as clerk or helper. He treated all of us as enemy, and ran away from here. From enquiries made, I have learned that he is working in a coffee estate in Coorg.' Kamala began to cry saying this much and then Vineetha said 'Don't cry, amma, I don't want to see father. I want only you, grandpa and grandma. I have withdrawn what I said.'.

From that day onwards, Vineetha never wanted to see father and was happy in mother's house. After befriending Praseetha, her desire to see her father grew stronger and stronger. At this time, a proposal came for Vineetha from Ollur. The boy is a graduate teacher in an aided high school. He had applied for PSC, and got selected as High School Assistant. He wanted a bride with BEd qualification, so that when he resigns, she will get that aided school job. Grandpa, Vineetha and mother liked the boy. One day, Grandpa, and Kamala went to the boy's house and they liked the proposal very much, and agreed for the marriage.

The engagement was conducted in a grand style. A big pandal(shamiana) was erected in the courtyard and all friends and relatives invited for the function. But the Nenmara tharavadu and Achutha warrier were not invited for the function. Vineetha had great mental agony for not inviting her father and his relatives, but she did not protest. Gopakumar, his wife Lishi and daughter Lovna had come for the engagement. Many hostel inmates and matron attended the function. Dr. Pushkaran and family had come for the engagement and returned to Chittoor in the evening. In the function it was decided to conduct the marriage after the BEd examinations.

Vineetha prepared well for the examination and her performance was excellent. She left the hostel with all her belongings along with Praseetha in a taxi arranged by Praseetha's father. They dropped Vineetha at her house and left for Nenmara. Vineetha offered to meet half the taxi fare but they did not accept.

The groom's uncle came one day to discuss the date of the marriage but Vineetha wanted some more time for the marriage and hence the groom's uncle went back giving his phone number.

By the time the result of BEd examination was released and Vineetha secured distinction. Vineetha one day told her mother to write a letter to her father, but she refused. Then she asked grandpa 'Grandpa for engagement my father and his relatives were not invited, but for marriage they should be invited.'

Grandpa became very angry and said 'He ran away from this house twelve years ago and after that he has not enquired about you. Then why should I go in search of such an irresponsible son in law? No, I can not.'

'Grandpa this is my marriage and to conduct it without my father is not proper.'

'If you don't obey me I'll give up everything and go to Kashi (Varanasi) and never return.'

'Grandpa don't be angry. He is irresponsible, I admit but for me this is a very important function, and that day will never return to my life later. Hence, without my father's presence I can not agree for the marriage'. Vineetha was very firm in her reply.

Grandpa sat depressed in the sitou, after the talk with Vineetha.

Kamala fired Vineetha, for talking with grandpa, in an unruly manner.'He is working hard for your marriage, and you misbehave with him, on the issue of your irresponsible father and his relations'.

But Veneetha did not budge, and she was firm that she will not agree for the marriage, in the absence of father. Her brother Sandeep also blamed her, for creating unnecessary problems.

Grandpa said to Kamala after sometime 'I will invite Achuthan and his relatives,. If they do not come, don't blame me.'

'Never, if they do not come, it is their fault. I am satisfied'. Vineetha said.

After a few days, Dr. Pushkaran came with family, and then Kochunny warrier said 'Pushkaran Vineetha wants to invite her father and their relatives for the marriage. Even though, I resented it, later I thought it is correct. So, you please go to Nenmara and ask Achuthan to come one day to discuss the date of marriage.'

'No, I can't go there. They'll misbehave with me. We can send a letter and no need of going.'

Pushkaran and family went back to Chittoor, that evening.

Again, the uncle of the groom came from Ollur, to discuss the date of marriage, and this time Kochunny warrier said 'No need of coming again, I will come over there, and inform you the convenient date, within one week. This is certain.'

'OK, don't delay. It's the future of your child. Sidharth has to report for the new job in government school shortly, and Vineetha should take charge in his place'.

'No, I won't delay. It's not a matter of money, but the presence of Achuthan, my son in law in the marriage. The marriage can be arranged within one month'.

'OK, come to our house within one week'. Saying this uncle left to Ollur.

Next day, Kochunny warrior spoke to Gopakumar 'Gopan, I want your help. I am in a dilemma'.

'What is the matter?' Gopakumar enquired and Kochunny warrior told him, the family problems in detail.

'Don't worry, I'll go to Nenmara, collect his Coorg address and bring him here, within two days' Gopakumar assured Warrier.

Gopakumar scanned through the piece of paper, on which the address has been written by Warrier.

C. Achuthan, Edaguni warriam, Near Nenmara temple, Nenmara.

Gopakumar and his supervisor Paul left for Nenmara next day morning. He had visited Nenmara in connection with the Nenmara Vallanky festival, and he knew the place well. Near the temple they enquired to a shop owner and he came with them and showed the house.

On ringing the doorbell, an old lady came and opened the door and asked 'What do you want?'.

'I'm a government contractor, where's Achutha warrier?'.

'I'm his mother, Ambujam. He's now working in a coffee estate in Coorg'.

'Can you give me his present address?'

She, then went inside and brought a cover and his address was there, on the back side. C. Achuthan, Gokulam Estate, Kutta, Coorg.

'Is there any phone number?'

'No phone number with me. He used to come once in a month. If you want the phone number please meet his brother Parameswaran working in the post office.'

'No, not required. We'll find out'

'It's related to the marriage of Vineetha, daughter of Achutha warrier'.

'Oh!, my grand daughter.' Her face brightened for a moment and became gloomy again.

'Do you know her?'Tell her, I'm still alive.'

They went to Kutta through the Wynad route touching Palakkad, Manathavady, Tholpetti and then Kutta.

At Kutt, they made enquiries at many places, but had no idea. Then, went to the post office and on enquiry the postman asked them to go back, along the same road for about one kilometre and turn left, when they see Nizar coffee curing works. If they go about 500 M, in that road they will see a steel gate, and that is Gokulam Estate.

At the gate of the estate, they were stopped by the watchman and they mentioned the name of Achuthan and they were permitted to go inside. They had to go a further distance of 1 KM to reach the office.

A tall and sturdy man stood in front of the office, and he asked 'Who are you? where do you come from?'

'Coming from Trichur, want to meet Mr Achuthan' Gopakumar said.

'Wait here, I'll call him' saying this he went inside.

Within ten minutes, Achuthan came out and shook hands with Kesavan and Antony. He was a tall, handsome figure with a thin mustache.'I am Gopakumar government contractor coming from Wadakkanchery. I was sent by Kochunny warrier. Vineetha's marriage has been settled and your presence is required for fixing the date and follow up functions.

'The groom is a high school teacher.'

'They were silent for 12 long years, and now why did they send for me.?Kochunny warrior has used very harsh words, and sent me out of their house, and now, I am wanted for Vineetha's marriage. Why can't they conduct it without my presence.?' Achuthan's eyes became wet and he wiped it with his towel.

'Kochunny warrior has realised his mistakes, and has regretted for what he has said and done. Your daughter is in need of your presence. It is your duty to come and make necessary arrangements for the marriage. Without you, marriage will not take place.'Gopakumar said.

Achuthan thought for a moment and said 'I love my daughter. If she wants my presence I will come.'

'OK, come with us in this car'.

Achuthan hesitated for a moment and said 'My boss is one Devaiyah. He is a good man and I have to get leave and an advance.'

Achuthan again went inside, and came out after some time, and told Gopakumar. 'I have got one week leave. Let us proceed now itself. They got into the car and the car sped up, along the same road through which they had come, and stopped at Harithagiri Hotel, Kalpetta and stayed that night there. Next day morning, they started in the early morning and reached Wadakkanchery by 2pm. The car was taken to the courtyard of the house and stopped. The door was opened and Achuthan got down from the car along with Gopakumar. Vineetha saw them and ran up to the car and embraced father. Kamala, and Kochunny warrior, came running to the spot. Kamala broke into tears and Kochunny warrior looked in wonder and amazement.

'Papa, where were you, during this twelve years. How we longed to see you. You treated us as your enemy and did not send even a letter. We have suffered a lot for no fault of ours. Papa, we will not allow you to go back again.... Papa, papa.' Vineetha lamented.

Kochunny warrier came and embraced Achuthan and said 'Sorry for my mistake, excuse me let us forget and forgive. Sorry sorry for what happened earlier'.

Achuthan broke into tears and touched the feet of Kochunny warrier and said 'I am also sorry, for what happened earlier. I must thank you for looking after my wife and children for long twelve years '.

By this time, a huge crowd had gathered there and the entire people were glad on seeing the happy ending of things. Kochunny warrier took Achuthan inside and Janaki warassiar had prepared tea and brought a cup to Achuthan. Kochunny warrier looked for Gopakumar and Paul, but by that time they had left the place to visit their worksite.

Kochunny warrier and Achuthan went together to Ollur, to fix the date of marriage. An astrologer was called to their house and a suitable date was arrived at. It was a wednesday after three weeks.

Invitation cards were printed, and started sending them, to distant relatives and friends. All near relatives were invited personally by Kochunny warrier, Achuthan and Kamala. Achuthan promised an amount of Rs. Five lakhs towards Vineetha's marriage and Kochunny warrier agreed to take the balance amount.

Gopakumar vacated the house for a period of two weeks for the convenience of Dr. Pushkaran and family and other relatives. Dr. Pushkaran came on the previous day of the marriage and was active in all arrangements. The marriage was in an auditorium in the Wadakkanchery town.

Achuthan went back after one week and returned one week before the marriage. The entire people from Nenmara tharavad had come to see the bride with various types of gifts. Vineetha's grandma gave a necklace as gift and Parameswaran uncle one bangle and aunty Suseela an ear ring. Achuthan and Kochunny warrier had purchased three necklaces, two chains and twenty bangles. The marriage was conducted on a grand scale. A lot of people had participated in that marriage, including Mr Devaiyah and family and Gopakumar and family.

After marriage, Vineetha was taken to the house of Sidharth after one week. Sidharth resigned from his present school and joined the government school at Kodungallur and Vineetha joined in his place. Achuthan went back to Kutta and Gopakumar came back to his house, when all the guests left the house. One day, he was reading the newspaper and then a car came and stopped in front of his house and a couple came out and walked direct to his house. It was Vineetha and Siddarth. Both of them folded their hands and said 'Sir, you have saved our lives. Thank you very much for your selfless service'

'It's our duty to mitigate the sufferings of fellow human beings. I've done my duty as a citizen, and no need of any thanks.'

They went back to the car, and the car moved towards the house of Kochunny warrier.

********* END *********

Noorjahan Villa

Pradeep Kadalundi, was a novelist and short story writer, in Malayalam. Many of his books have been published. He has been working as a teacher at Manjeswaram, in Kasargod District, for long five years From the date of joining, he has been trying for a transfer to Calicut, but, the same was not considered for want of vacancy at Calicut. His name was considered against a vacancy in Sultans Bathery and he accepted the same and joined duty, without any second thought, since he liked Wynad for its natural beauty and pleasant climate.

After joining duty, at the new school at Sultans Bathery, Pradeep master stayed in a hotel for about one week since lodge accommodation was not readily available. On a Saturday, he decided to go out in search of accommodation and requested his friend Paul master to accompany him. He liked Pradeep very much for his soft spoken attitude amiable nature and agreed with pleasure. He was a resident of that area and knew every nook and corner of the town.

They visited many lodges, but there was no vacancy anywhere and finally Paul master took him to the house of his sister Santha James. After tea, Paul master told his brother in law James to arrange a room in his outhouse to Pradeep master. He was fully willing to comply with the request but one condition that he should get it back at the time of coffee plucking. His workers for coffee plucking are brought from Guntelpet area and they will stay in the estate premises in temporary sheds and the outhouse will be given to them, for keeping their personal belongings. Pradeep promised that he will vacate it, within three months and thus the outhouse was allotted to him that day itself, without any documentary support.

Pradeep shifted his luggage to the outhouse that evening itself. It was a tranquil place without anybody in the surrounding area, since both sides of the road were full of coffee plantations. The day was calm and quiet but night was horrible with a whistling sound of the beetle and cricket. James had about 20 acres of coffee estate and his house is situated in the middle of the estate, but the outhouse is near the gate. Pradeep liked the place very much, for the beauty and serenity of the landscape. There was a small kitchen inside the outhouse and he began to prepare food in the morning and evening. There is about 2 KMs to the school and he will walk that distance to the school in the morning as well as in the evening. Pradeep felt a new energy and enthusiasm, due to the self preparation of food and daily walk in the morning and evening.

One day, he noticed a big uninhabited bungalow with the name 'Noorjahan Villa' in the middle of his route to his school. Next day, while returning home after dusk, he saw a lady in the courtyard of the villa. He clearly saw the lady, in the dim light and she was in a pink sari. After two days, he watched the building again, when he was returning home at 8 pm. There was a faint light inside, and it glared through the window panes. He thought that, it must be the glow of a candle burning inside the bungalow and did not see anybody outside.

Pradeep told this to Paul master and he then laughed and said 'It's a haunted house. Nobody's staying there. It's in closed condition for over five years'

'Where's the owner of the bungalow?' Pradeep enquired.

'It's a long story. I'll tell you everything one day.'

On many days, Pradeep master returned to his house before sunset and did not care much about the bungalow. One day, he was startled by a sudden noise while passing through the road in front of the bungalow and he turned around but did not find anything or anybody. He thought something had fallen inside the house, or somebody has hit a steel almirah or something hollow with a hammer or heavy rod. He became impatient to hear the story of the haunted house. So, he met Paul master in the morning and requested him to spare some time to tell the story. The next Saturday, Paul master came to his residence and spent the whole time there. He started telling the story.

There was a Divisional Forest Officer named Ibrahim. He was immensely rich and had many estates in various parts of Wynad, Guntelpet, Coorg and Nilgiris. He had only one son and his name was Rafeek Ahmed. He was very healthy and was about 45 years when his father expired. Rafeeq spent huge amounts for maintaining his youthful energy and vitality. His wife, Nilofer was about 40 and had two daughters aged 12 and 8. They were studying in a convent boarding school in Ooty. He had many concubines in Guntelpet and Coorg. Whenever, he visited his estate at Guntelpet his manager will bring minimum two of them to the estate bungalow. He will spend one week or two there and return to Kerala. He will make occasional visit to Coorg and there also he will live lavishly, enjoying wine and women. He will give anything to his sweethearts and to the managers. But in Kerala and in Nilgiris he maintained a low profile and did not engage in any kind of revelry or pleasure hunting. His wife, Nilofer was also from a very rich family in Manjery. She somehow, came to know about the infidelity of her husband and waited for a chance to catch him red handed. He spoke to his brothers Rashid and Abdulla to help her to trap him. One day, Rafeek went to Guntelpet after informing his wife Nilofer. She and his brothers followed him in an Innova car with some goons.

When they reached the estate Rafeek was in a room with two of his sweethearts. He was caught red handed. Nilofer slapped the cheeks of the ladies and asked the manager to pack them up immediately,. Rafeek was brought to Bathery residence and given severe thrashing by the goons and the brothers of Nilofer and warned him of dire consequences if he repeated any kind of immorality in future. They also compelled him to issue a power of attorney to Nilofer in respect of his three estates in Wynad viz. the 50 acre estate at Bathery, 20 acre estate at Vaduvanchal and 35 acre estate at Kartikulam. Rasheed and Abdulla terrorised Rafeeq for three days and they left for Manjery after preparation of the power of attorney.

Rafeeq came to know that, his wife was behind his humiliation and the power of attorney, he became very furious and stabbed her in the stomach and ran away. She was immediately taken to a hospital at Bathery, and her life was saved through a major surgery. Nobody has seen Rafeek after that incident in Bathery. Police registered a case against the murder attempt on his wife Nilofer and he was arrested and let on bail. After ths, he was living in Coorg without any connection with his wife and children.

Nilofer took over the estates in Wynad and she began to tour to her estates at Vaduvanchal and Kartikulam with a driver named Safvan who was a distant relative of Nilofer. In due course she became very close with him and lived as man and wife. One day, Safvan who was only 25 was found hanging from a tree in the estate. Police enquiry and postmortem revealed that it was a suicide. But, the relatives of Safvan sent memorandum to the Chief Minister and Home Minister stating that it was a cold blooded murder planned and executed by Nilofer with the connivance of a planter named Mustapha and his goons. It was also mentioned that she had illicit relations with Mustapha and some other planters for a long time. Even though, many agencies investigated the murder no evidence was obtained to register a murder case. The relatives of Safvan, ultimately approached the Honourable High Court and pleaded to hand over the case to CBI.

The death of Safvan had been made sensational due to wide publicity by media and press.. Nilofer was very much disturbed and worried for a long time, and hence shifted residence to her estate at Kartikulam to escape from unnecessary publicity. After some two years, the house and one acre of the coffee estate at Bathery, was sold to a DySP named Abdul Salam using the power of attorney with her. The new owner spent a lot of money for the renovation of the house and began to come and stay there occasionally. He was then working at Malappuram. There was a rumour in the town that it was he who scuttled the murder probe of Safvan. But nobody could provide any proof for the same.

'Where's Rafeek now?' Pradeep asked Paul master.

'It is heard that, he is living in Coorg with a Kannadiga wife But, nobody has seen him in Bathery after that' Said Paul maser.

'This story has all the ingredients of a detective novel'

'Tell me, is it a murder or suicide'

'It's likely, that the brothers of Nilofer will be behind the murder of Safvan'

'But, where is the evidence?.

'People say, the DySP did not purchase it, and he got it as a gift'

'The truth'll come out if CBI comes to investigate the case'

'Now, It's many years and people have forgotten this case since more sensational cases have occurred after that'.

For many weeks, Pradeep master was investigating this case as a freelance detective. One day, there was another sensational news, that the DySP was found dead in the courtyard of his house at Calicut. His wife and children were out of station, when the death occurred and the dead body had a snake bite mark on the heal, from which blood was oozing. But, no snake venom was detected in the blood, during postmortem and chemical examination of viscera.

After the demise of the DySP, the house and property was purchased by one Augustine from Cheeral. He is an ex- serviceman and had enough money with him. He renovated the house again and began to live there with his family. He was very bold and did not believe in any kind of superstitions. But, he could not live there even for one month. After occupying that house he could not sleep properly, since he was disturbed by horrible nightmares. One day, he fell from the cot and sustained some injuries to the head. So, he sold it to one Noorjahan who was a widow with a grown up son. One day, after occupying the house Noorjahan brought a Musaliyar and done necessary rituals to ward off unnecessary spirits and gins(devils) from the compound. Before completing two months in that house, she was found dead in her bed. After her funeral, the son went to his uncle's house at Meppadi. Nobody has come to purchase that house after tha, and the house was in locked condition for years.

One day, Pradeep master watched the bungalow closely and found that it's lock is missing and saw a lady coming out of the house in darkness. He was startled and hid behind the boundary wall and listened and he heard human conversation from the house. After sometime, another lady came out and both the ladies were talking in malayalam. He also heard giggling and laughter. He moved to a vantage point and watched. The two ladies walked in the courtyard for some time and then went inside and closed the door. He thought somebody would have broken the lock, and entered the bungalow and it is being used for some kind of immoral or illegal activities.

Next day, Pradeep told Paul master about his investigation and findings and they both went to the police station and lodged a complaint. The Sub Inspector assured them that the case will be looked into. After a couple of weeks, the bungalow was raided in the dead of the night and a gang of three ladies and five men were arrested and after producing in cour tand remanded to police custody for a period of two weeks. They were framed under various sections of immoral traffic, stocking and distribution of narcotics, breaking the lock of the house and using the premises for unlawful activities.

After one week, there was an important news in the daily and channels that Rafeek Ahmed was convicted to a jail term for 5 years for attempting murder on his wife Nilofer. The second news was that the honourable high court has asked the State government to hand over the case of the mysterious death of Safvan, DySP Abdul Salam and Noorjahan to CBI. Pradeep got an accommodation in a men's paying guest hostel near the school and he shifted his residence to that place shortly.

Pradeep forgot the haunted house after some time, and was engrossed in his work since annual examinations were approaching. During the vacation he went to his native place at Kadalundi.

He spent the vacation with his friends in roaming along the beach and fishing in the backwaters.

He read a lot of library books and wrote a Sherlock Holms type detective story about the haunted house.

In this story, Pradeep found Nilofer as a lady of unusual sensuality with a tinge of criminality in her character. Her journey to Guntelpet estate to catch her husband is a daring attempt unheard of in the history of ordinary housewives especially among muslim ladies who were very submissive to their husbands and were perpetually in the fear of Talaq. She has managed to get power of attorney through threat and coercion. Pradeep found that she had physical relation with Safvan who was only 25 years of age. She had to meet many others, planters and traders in connection with the running of the estates and Safvan tried to blackmail her continuously for money or sex. She was fed up with him and got him finished with the help of her brothers or goons. She would have influenced the DySP for making it a suicide by offering money or gift. It is likely that the house and one acre of land was given to him as gift. The DySP was not satisfied with the gift and would have demanded more, either money or a relation with her. Then, she would have used the old goons to eleminate him without any evidence of a foul play. It is likely that he would have been finished inside the house by compelling to drink a juice mixed with sleeping pills or some other BP or epileptic drugs in overdose or mercury and to divert the attention of the police made a snake bite type injury at his heals and laid him in the courtyard. After reopening of the school, Pradeep master showed the brief crimethriller story to Paul master who agreed with him in all the points raised by Pradeep.

CBI started investigation of the case and they did not disclose any of the details of evidence to the media or press till the accused was arrested. The two maids who were working in the residence of Nilofer were grilled since Nilofer and her brothers were tight lipped and did not admit the guilt. After six months of the investigation Nilofer was arrested from her residence at Kartikulam and produced in the court and remanded to judicial custody of two weeks. The other accused were remanded to CBI custody for a period of two weeks. After the arrest, full details regarding the murder of Safvan were shared with the press and media. Full evidence of the murder was obtained from the maids and they even named the people who perpetrated the heinous crime. The murder was accomplished with the help of two of their workers Yousaf and Rehman. They were paid huge amounts ie. about fifteen lakhs were paid to them by cash by Nilofer. The maids also were paid some amount to keep it a secret from the public and police. The CBI also has found that the DySP has helped in this case to destroy evidence and make it a suicide.

Regarding the death of the DySP Abdul Salam, the CBI did not get any credible evidence and on the basis of the postmortem report the same was treated as death due to lightning or snake bite and closed it. Many people had testified that the accused in the above case were present at Bathery on the day of of the death of DySP Abdul Salam. Regarding the death of Noorjahan the CBI has reported that the death was due to natural causes. She had severe cardiac asthma and was under treatment at a missionary hospital at Bathery. The death occurred during the sleep and the son who was sleeping in the adjacent room did not hear any sound or cry.

Nilofer and the other two accused were released on bail after two weeks. The case was tried in the CBI Special court and was acquitted after one year since all the witnesses turned hostile and the money alleged to have been paid to the accused could not be traced out by CBI. The court also observed that the line between suicide and murder is very thin and without credible evidence the accused could not be convicted. It is evident that Safvan had physical relation with her and he did not like her mingling with other planters and traders and he was mentally disturbed. There is every chance for a suicide and hence the accused were let free by the court.

Pradeep master and Paul read the judgement and jumped in joy that their observations were almost correct.

'Pradeep, please write a crime thriller on the basis of this story and we can approach some film directors to make a hit film'.

'OK, let me try'. Pradeep master smiled.

********* END *********

PREETI HAS COME BACK!

Monsoon was in its full fury, in the coastal district of Calicut. There was torrential rain without any break, for a full week. All the low lying areas were inundated and the roads became water logged. Despite heavy rains, there is no appreciable reduction in the rush of customers in the City Branch, of the State Bank of India. Mrs. Preeti sat in the Teller counter No 1 and in the adjacent counter No 2 sat Mr Madhu. There was long queue in front of both the counters.

Even though, Preeti was very diligent and careful in her duty there will be shortage of small amounts every day and the same will be made good by her from her purse. One da, there was a shortage of Rupees ten thousand and the matter was immediately reported to the operation manager Mr Samuel. He wanted her to give the names of the suspected customers, to whom excess money was paid. He visited their houses and recovered the amount within a short time. One client got one bundle of hundred rupee notes in excess, and he took it home and admitted his mistake to the bank staff and returned the amount. On another occasion, Mr Madhu lost Rupees fifty thousand, but efforts made to retrieve the amount did not succeed. The entire staff of the bank had to contribute towards the loss and thus the shortage was made good. The cash counter is very risky, and hence many employees are afraid to move to that seat.

Mrs Preethi's mind was cloudy and turbulent, and still she got engrossed in her work to clear the queue at the earliest Occasionally, Madhu will put in some questions or doubts and then Preethi will raise her head from the counter and give reply spontaneously That day, a man brought a cheque without showing amount in words. It was a bearer cheque and hence it was returned. Another cheque came, without date and that also was returned. One client came with a crossed cheque, without having account in that branch and he was asked to produce the cheque in that branch where he is having account. By 1.30 pm, Preethi cleared the queue and heaved a sigh of relief.

After lunch, she came to the seat again by 2.30 pm and Madhu was already in his seat at that time. Preethi scribbled something in a piece of paper, and passed it over to Madhu. He glanced the paper, and then read it again and again and his face reflected anxiety and dread.

'Madhu will you take me to your house today. I don't want to go back to my house'- Preethi.

Madhu was startled, and some kind of fear gripped his mind but he concealed it with a smile, turned towards Preethi and said 'Yes, you are welcome'.

Preethi's face brightened.

At 6.30 pm, Madhu returned to his house on his bike with Preethi on the pillion seat. At home Bhanumathi

Amma was waiting for them with a terrified face. Preethi was warmly welcomed and taken inside and given tea and snacks.

Madhu had some fear and misgivings in his mind but he did not show it to his mother.

'If they come to take her what can we do?'Bhanumathi Amma asked Madhu.'

'If they can take her let them take but Preethi will not go with them'.

Preethi was resolute that she will not go back to her house even if the children make a hue and cry.

'Preethi, please tell me what is the real problem?' Madhu enquired.

'My husband Bose has been cheating me ever since we got married seven years ago. I thought he will improve, but in vain. I have changed three maids one after the other and then brought his mother since I told him plainly not to bring any more young maids. The maids have confessed, everything to me. They were helpless, and he was responsible for everything. He is really a deboucher and rake. I thought of suicide on many occasions but I had to retract later because of my children. Really I'm fed up with him and he is not going to improve '. Preethi said in anger and resentment.

'What is the immediate provocation for such an extreme step?'

'He had many sweet hearts at different parts of the city, mostly married women. They used to call him frequently and he comes home very late in the night fully drunk. From office he will be free by 5.30 pm. Where does he go till 10 to 11 pm. Whenever I ask him he gives evasive replies. In his mobiles there are many initiala like GK, PK, SR etc. In his absence, I have rung up these numbers and found out the real subscribers. He is a cheat, and can not be trusted. I don't want to live with him. But my Anu and Vinu are very much attached to him'.

'If he gives a police complaint how can we face it?'. Asked Madhu.

'I 've not married Madhu. I'm living here as a paying guest. Law can not do anything in this regard If he wants to get divorce he can approach family court and I am ready to give my consent.' Preethi said with a frown.

'Preethi don't worry. I'll be with you to the end whatever may be the consequences'. Madhu assured Preethi.

'Madhu, please inform my mother in law that I'm staying here as paying guest".

Madhu immediately rang up his friend John Abraham, who is staying near Preethi's house and said 'John you please go to Preethi's house and tell her mother in law that she is in my house and will not return to their house today'.

John Abraham, immediately went to the house of Preethi and conveyed the news to her mother in law.

At 10.30 pm, a car came to the house of Mr Madhu and Mr Bose and three others got down from the car. 'Madhu where is my wife? I will take her now itself. Where is she?. Send her out.' Bose shouted at the top of his voice.

Mr Bose was very furious and his friends were in fully drunken state and used many abusive and obscene words against Madhu and Preethi.

Bose shouted again 'Where is the custodian of my wife. Send her out or we will enter the house and do whatever we like.'

Madhu then rang up some of his friends in the vici, and also the police station.

A jeep full of police including SI arrived on the spot, and tried to pacify Mr Bose and his friends.

Mrs Preethi came out and spoke to the SI.'Sir, I don't want to live with my husband Mr. Bose. He is a cheat and has many concubines. and treats me very badly. I'm living here as paying guest. I'll not go with him unless and until he gives up his present habits and criminal friends'.

The SI asked Mr Bose to go back to his house.

'She has every right to live here as paying guest. If you give up your company and bad habits then she'll come back and live with you."

'You are on their side. We 'll go back now, but won't permit her to do adultery' Bose shouted at the top of his voice, boarded the car and left with his friends.

The police left after dispersing the crowd.

Bhanumathy Amma began to cry like a child' when the police left and Madhu patted her and consoled. 'Amma why do you cry, nothing has happened. I had anticipated this when I brought Preethy.'.

That night, Preethi slept with Bhanumathy Amma and Madhu slept in the adjacent room. He was terribly shaken by the incident and could not sleep properly that night Madhu and Preeti went to the bank next day on bike and nobody in the bank asked them anything about the incident on the previous night.

At 10.30 am, Preethi received a telephone call from mother in law Indira 'Preethi Anu and Vinu are crying incessantly. They did not eat anything for two days. 'Will you come and console the children?' Indira requested.

'Amma, there is long queue here and I can not come before 2 pm.' Preethi said in a worried tone.

Preethi was upset and her face became pale and depressed after talking to mother in law.

She controlled herself and faced the queue of customers and started disbursing cash unmindful of the tension and anguish in her mind.

During lunch break, Bhanumathy Amma came to the bank with children and met Preethi. Children became very happy on seeing mother. Preethi lost her control and wept hugging her children. After sometime, Bhanumathy Amma returned home with the children. Preethi's mind was crestfallen and morose when they left. She recalled what her mother in law had asked her when they met 'Why did you leave your children and husband? What is the reason for such an extreme step?' Her mother in law's words resounded in Preethi's mind and made her sick.

Preethi told her mother in law the secret which made her violent 'Amma he is misusing my sister. Once he had gone to her hostel and taken her out on the authority that he is the local guardian. How can I bear it? Her matron had telephoned me and enquired whether she had come to the house and I had lied to her that there was a function in the house and she had come to attend it He had so many other sweethearts and now he is trying to spoil my sister'

Her mother in law Indira Devi was aghast and she did not say anything further and Preethi returned to her seat after sending them home.

That night, Madhu and Preethi reached home by 7.30 pm. Bhanumathy Amma was waiting for them with a worried face and she heaved a sigh of relief on seeing them.

After dinner Bhanumathy Amma told Preethi that she had arranged a room for her and showed it to her. It was a nice room with a single coat, a chair, one tea poy and an almirah.

Bhanumathy Amma went to sleep by 10.30 pm. Madhu and Preethi were talking about various issues of the bank and slept together in the newly arranged room. Bhanumathy Amma noticed that they were living like newly married couple but did not say anything either to Madhu or Preethi.

After two weeks, Preethi got a call from mother in law and she went out during lunch break saying something to Madhu. She went straight to meet her children. The children have not taken anything that day and were crying for mother. She gave them toffee and fruits and remained with them till they slept. Indira complained to Preethi that the new housemaid stopped coming and she was hard pressed to prepare food, domestic chores and care of children.

'Preethi forget everything and return home, otherwise the children will suffer'. Indira said.

'Amma I am sorry, let him give up his bad habits and then I will return home immediately.' Said Preethi.

'Preethi I have suffered a lot at the hands of my husband, father of Bose, I tried to immolate myself by pouring kerosene on my head. Before striking the match my sister in law came and saved me by pouring cold water all over the body. I have survived those difficult days and now I am facing another problem on account of my son.' Saying this Indira Devi began to weep.

Then Bose came to the house and Preethi was taken aback. Bose's eyes were reddish and he was drunk.

'You harlot, why did you come here?' He shouted and in a violent fit of anger slapped Preethi.

She broke into tears and ran out of the house.

Days, weeks and months passed and Preethi did not visit her children despite frequent requests from mother in law.

Preethi became part and parcel of Madhu's house. She will help Bhanumathy Amma in domestic chores and upkeep of the house. Preethi's parents came to know about the rift in the married life of Preethi and Bose and they flew to Calicut from Abu Dhabi. They came to the house of Bose, met the children and Indira Devi and then went to the bank to see Preethi. She took them to Madhu's house and told them that she was staying there as paying guest. Preethi's parents did not like this arrangement and asked her to reconcile or apply for divorce.

'Papa, he's trying to spoil our Priya'. Preethi whispered to father.

'There's no pardon for him. You better break away from him through divorce. I didn't know he is such an immoral fellow.' Father said with shock and resentment.

'Nobody, except my mother in law is aware of this. Don't say anything to mother in this regard, she cannot bear it.' Said Preeti.

They stayed at Calicut for a couple of days and returned to Gulf.

'I'll bring Priya to Abu Dhabi and find a job for her.' Priya's father told her at the time of going to the departure lounge.

'OK papa, then my life will come round to normalcy and I can live with my children. Thank you very much Papa'.

Within three months, Priya flew to. Abu Dhabi. She discontinued her postgraduate studies at Providence College and left in the hope that peace will return to the life of her sister. It was a big relief to Preethi. She and Madhu had gone to the Airport to see her off and on her way back she told Madhu, 'Madhu, if Bose realizes his mistakes and becomes a good man what shall I do?'

'OK, if he becomes a good man you can go with him. I've no objection.' Madhu replied.

One night, Madhu was returning home after purchasing some grocery items from a shop nearby. Some masked men were waiting at a dimly lit part of the road, and he was attacked brutally and the assailants ran away stealthily. Madhu lay on the road bleeding for about twenty minutes.. Then, some of his friends came that way and took him to a nearby private hospital. On hearing the news, Preethi and Bhanumathy Amma rushed to the hospital. Madhu had sustained serious head injuries and he was not in a position to speak. He was transferred to the Medical College hospital. The Neurosurgeon came and examined him and he was immediately subjected to an operation. Preethi wept profusely, and remained there as bystander and Bhanumathy Amma went home and informed her daughter and son in law. They rushed to the hospital and filed a police complaint. Mr Bose and two of his friends were arrested and remanded to two weeks police custody.

Preethi was blamed by Madhu's sister and brother in law, and asked her to go to her house. She had no other go but to obey and she went to her house reluctantly. She was fired by her mother in law Indira Devi and said that she was responsible for everything. She did not get any refuge there. Her children also were in an angry mood with her. Then, she took some of her personal belongings and dress and went to the YWCA hostel. She went to attend duty next day and she had to reply to so many questions by her friends and colleagues. She was firm and bold and did not flinch.

Preethi's father arrived the next day itself, and consoled her. She applied for one month leave but it was rejected since there was acute shortage of staff in the bank. Preethi's father met Bose in the sub jail and also Madhu in the hospital even though he had to face the wrath of Madhu's relatives. After a couple of days, he returned to Abu Dhabi. Preethi met an advocate and arranged for the bail of Mr Bose and his friends. By this time, an appeal had already been filed in the court for bail by the friends of Bose and Preethi's help was not required for Mr Bose to come out of the sub jail.

Preethi was in a very difficult mental condition and she felt isolated and nobody sympathised with her. She went to the bank every day and returned to the hostel in the evening. She thought that the entire world has turned against her. She did not go to see her children nor did she go to the hospital to see Madhu.

Bose and his friends got bail after one week. Madhu continued in the hospital for over two months. There was a rumour that he was in a paralysed condition. Preethi prayed to God to save his life. After one week she got a legal notice from the advocate of Bose asking her to return to his house immediately or face divorce. She gave a reply through her advocate that she had returned to his house on hearing the news of his arrest but she was driven out by her mother in law. She also mentioned that she is willing to return to the house if he'd personally come and invite her.

Bose was intransigent, and did not come to invite her and she continued in the hostel. Bose was very adamant that she should come of her own and no question of coming to her hostel to invite her. Both sides were stubborn and Preethi was intrepid and indomitable and hence she continued in the hostel.

Madhu was discharged from hospital after two months and he had become a cripple. One side of his body had been paralysed and doctors advised him prolonged physiotherapy. Madhu had great forbearance and did not despise his fate in the tragedy which spoiled his life and career. He was confined to the bed always and still he smiled to his friends and relatives who visited him.

He was in great financial difficulties, since a lot of money had been spent for the hospital treatment and only a portion of the same was reimbursed by the bank. The bank extended some special relief to him and the association collected a good amount from the members and handed it over to him. His leave at credit has completely exhausted, and he was running on loss of pay. One day, Preethi went to his house with some money, but his mother and sister did not permit her to meet Madhu. She wept silently and despised her fate and returned to the hostel.

Bose was working in a private firm and hence there was no threat to his job. He fought the case very vigorously engaging a very famous criminal lawyer and the case continued for long two years and finally they were acquitted. Bose spent a huge amount for the case and still he was financially well off.

Bose filed a case for divorce. Preethi informed the court that she is willing for divorce on mutual consent. The court accepted their mutual request for divorce and the same was granted after a period of six months and the children were permitted to live with their father. After the divorce Preethi resigned her job and went to her parents at Abu Dhabi. Madhu was unable to work and hence proceeded on long leave without pay and ultimately resigned the job.

Bose brought a maid named Devayani from Palakkad, with a son aged 4 years. The lady was about 25 years old. Bose allotted a room near the kitchen to the maid and her son. The boy's name is Kuttan and with his arrival Anu and Vinu got a playmate, Anu, Vinu and Kuttan were admitted to an english medium nursery school near their house. For one week Bose accompanied them to the school. He also met the entire expenditure for admitting Kuttan, his dress, book etc.

The new maid was very able in kitchen work and house keeping and Indira Devi liked her very much. One day Indira asked her 'Where is your husband?'

'He is under treatment for paralysis. He fell from palmyra tree and his backbone was damaged.'.

'Who's looking after him?'

'My father and mother"

Indira Devi's mind was overflowed with love and compassion.

'Whatever you require, please tell me I'll ask Bose to provide it We'll help you financially, for the treatment of your husband.' Indira Devi said.

Bose treated the maid with a special love and compassion. He purchased new clothes for Devayani, Kuttan and his father. It was a clear sign that he was improving, Indira Devi noticed this change and thanked God, the almighty for the transformation of of her son. The old peace and tranquility returned to the house with passage of time.

On a Saturday, Bose arranged a taxi and they went to Muthalamada, Palakkad. Wherever they looked they saw palmira groves and paddy fields and they stopped in front of a thatched hut. They had to bend to get into the hut. Devayani introduced her husband who was lying in a mat on the floor. On seeing them, he smiled but was unable to move and tears streaked down from his eyes. He was able to speak and he narrated the story. One day, he climbed a palmyra tree to pluck its fruits. There was rain on the previous night, and the trunk was slippery. He had reached the top and was plucking the fruits and then slipped and fell to the rocky ground. He lost his sense and then some people saw this and, rushed to the spot and took him to a hospital at Chittoor and then to Medical College Hospital, Thrissur. He lay in hospital for about three months and then discharged. He was advised physiotherapy, for one year. He was taken to a hospital at Palakkad on two occasions for physiotherapy and then stopped, since they could not afford it due to high expenditure involved. Now, he is undergoing Ayurvedic treatment and the doctor will come occasionally and treat him and Bose offered to meet the complete expenditure...

Devayani introduced her parents, who are above 70 years old. They were farm labourers and stopped going for work some ten years back. They are getting a small amount as pension and there is no other source of income for the family. They had sent application to the Chief Minister's relief fund for treatment of the paralysed patient but nothing materialised even after one year. Bose and Indira Devi became very much aggrieved on seeing the pathetic condition of the family. Bose gave an amount of Rs 2000/- as immediate relief and he offered more after some time. The children played outside unaware of the penury and misery of that house. Indira Devi was weeping silently during their return journey to Calicut.

About two years have passed after the estrangement with Preethi and the children even now cry for their mother. Then Devayani will come and take them outside and soothe and console them by telling stories from Mahabharata and Ramayana. Then they stop crying and forget everything and become happy and cheerful. They have started calling Devayani as mummy. Whenever they become angry or naughty Devayani will come and and console them. They find solace and happiness in the presence of Devayani and Kuttan.

One day, the children came with a letter from the school in which the parents were invited to the school to discuss the progress of the children. Bose wanted his mother Indira Devi to accompany him to the school. Then, she asked Devayani also to come with them. Thus in addition to kuttan Devayani donned the role of mummy for Anu and Vinu also. Now, Indira Devi is happy since Devayani will not permit her to do anything and she herself will do all the works of rearing children, cooking food and domestic chores. Bose was happy in the peace and tranquility of the household without the presence of Preethi.

One day, Bose came and said to his mother.'Amma it is heard that Preethi has resigned her job and went to Gulf. Madhu has become a cripple and he also has resigned his job and undergoing treatment for paralysis. Because of Preethi he has lost everything. I am really sorry. He is innocent and Preethi is responsible for everything.'.

'Bose, what you did is not correct. Preethi is a good lady and she did desert you because you were very unfaithful to her. You jumped up and did everything in a fit of anger and now repent. The children have lost their mother once and for ever. One day they will go in search of their mother and you will be left alone here. She will get a job there and she may remarry somebody after some time.

Bose was in an angry mood and said with indignation 'Let her go to hell and I want a wife to look after the children and it is not advisable to remain as a divorcee till death. Let me marry Devayani. She is a nice lady and we can look after her family including her husband.'

'She'll not agree as long as her husband is alive'.

'We can simply ask her opinion"

'No, not now. You're really cruel. You don't know the mind of women.

Many years rolled by, and. Anu, Vinu and Kuttan are now in 12th class in a Higher Secondary School in the city. Anu and Vinu have forgotten.'their mother. Devayani is still working in their house. She is mother to all the three children. Her husband passed away, sometime back after lying in pathetic condition for years. Bose has spent huge amount for his treatment and lookafter of Devayani's parents. After the demise of Devayani's husband Bose brought her parents to Calicut and they are now living with them. Indira Devi is lying bedridden due to various illness. Devayani is all in all in the household, and even Bose is afraid of her.

Bose did not propose to Devayani. Now he treats her as his own sister. His youthful vigour and anger have disappeared and is very passive and considerate. He has realized that two families have suffered irreparable damage due to his high handed behaviour and now he is unable to do anything to alleviate their sufferings.

One day, Bose came with a news and told mother 'Amma did you hear. There's a pleasant news. Preethi was working in a bank in Abu Dhabi for the last ten years. She has now come back and married Madhu who is hardly able to walk with the help of a stick. It's heard that she is not going back and will spend the rest of her life by nursing Madhu.'.

'OK, it's really a very good news, but a bad news for you.' Indira Devi said in a plaintive tone.

******** END *********

A FEMALE REVENGE

It was a chilly winter morning and the Island Express slowly came to a halt in the City station of Bangalore. Rajendran alighted from the train with his bag and baggage and looked around in the platform, but no familiar face was found.

'Hello Rajendran' somebody called him from the crowd.

Rajendran turned around and saw Mr Joseph standing in front of him with a beaming smile.

'Hello Joseph, I thought you would have forgotten my call' Rajendran said in a complaining tone.

They both moved out and got into a waiting taxi. The taxi passed through the busy street for half an hour and then entered a narrow road and the taxi stopped in front of a small house with a garden in front of it.

'This's my palace' Joseph joked when they got out of the taxi. An old lady came out and greeted them.

'Rajendran this's my mother in law'

Mr Joseph is the branch manager of a nationalised bank in Bangalore city. He was a Junior Engineer in the

Telecom Dept. at Calicut when Mr. Rajendran was also working in the same office. Mr Joseph got selection as probationary offocer in the nationalised bank at Bangalore and he resigned from the department and left for Karnataka years back. Rajendran was close with Mr Joseph since their ancestral houses were in the same village in Trichur district.

Those days at Calicut were still fresh in the memory of Mr. Rajendran. The office was full of girls and had the atmosphere of a college. But after a few years the entire staff belonging to different cadres left to various places and only Rajendran was left behind.

Rajendran was sitting in a pensive mood. He was thinking of those days when both of them were staying in the same lodge at Puthiyara near Municipal stadium.

'Rajendran 're you homesick? your face looks gloomy.' Joseph sad.

At this time a graceful lady came out with two cups of tea.

'Lakshmy this's Rajendran, do you remember him?. He'd come to attend our marriage'

Rajendran smiled and she returned the smile.

Lakshmy belonged to a middle class family of Mangalore. Her father was a clerk in the Statistics department and was staying in a rented house near the house of Mr. Joseph. He liked Lakshmy and wanted to marry her. Her father was willing, but his father objected. Years rolled by and they have a daughter aged 15 years. Mr. Joseph has not taken his wife and daughter to his ancestral house so far. Joseph hails from an aristocratic Roman Catholic family and his father is still uncompromising. His father once told Rajendran 'My son has brought disgrace to our family and I will never accept her as my daughter in law. Our vicar once came with a proposal that if she is converted to christianity the problem can be solved amicably. Secondly the daughter has to be baptised. But my son is not agreeable for that.'

Mr. Rajendran tried to bring about a compromise without conversion, but failed. They are always harping on conversion to which Mr. Joseph will never agree. Hence father and son remained at loggerheads. Joseph used to visit his parents occasionally, but never brought his family with him even for the marriage of his sister.

'Rajendran where's Rajamma now?'

'No information. It's heard that she's living in a remote village in Kottayam district with her husband and children.'His face became crestfallen.

'What happened to your love?' Joseph was inquisitive.

'My eyes become wet whenever I think of her. We were hundred percent sincere and wanted to marry, but fate was against us. I had gone for a training at Ghaziabad and before I returned she had resigned and left'.

'Did she get another job?''Yes she got a more attractive job in State Electricity Board near her house and her father compelled her to resign and she obeyed.'

Joseph did not ask further questions.

After lunch they moved out to the lodge arranged for Rajendran.

Next day Rajendran joined duty in one of the satellite Exchanges of Bangalore. He has waited long 18 years for a promotion. The promotion was blocked by the court cases filed by junior members of the cadre to spoil the chances of the seniors. It took years for the final settlement of the case and when promotion came there was not sufficient vacancies in Kerala Circle to accomodate all.

Rajendran was prepared to go anywhere in India because he was fed up with the life at Calicut. His marriage and subsequent estrangement had made his life horrible.

\When promotion and subsequent transfer to Bangalore came he was very much relieved. He took it as a boon from the God Almighty. Rajendran was in charge of a large Exchange. The present Sub Divisional Engineer was one Naik and he was relieved to Mangalore. A send off party was given to Mr. Naik in the evening which was presided over by Narendran, Divisional Engineer. Rajendran was introduced to the audience by the DET.

After the send off party Rajendran went to the switch room of the Exchange and was surprised to see a girl resembling the old Rajamma. The girl got up when he saw Rajendran.

'So You're the JTO of switch room, I presume?'

'Yes sir'.

'Your good name?'.

'Rajani'.

You belong to which place?'

'Kerala'.

'Which district?'

'Ernakulam'.

'That's not enough, correct place?'

'Alwaye'.

'OK you proceed'.

Rajendran moved to the other staff. There are five other internal staff and all of them are from Karnataka namely Ganesh, Najeeb, Padmanabh, Donald and Nagamma. They were found to be very friendly, meek and amiable. The office atmosphere was very conducive. Rajani is an expert in MBM (Main Base Module) which is a higher form of C-DOT Exchange. She is postgraduate in Physics. Every day Rajani will come to the cabin of Mr. Rajendran with some problems relating to the Exchange. While talking official matters a lot of personal problems were also discussed. Her sister is studying for Nursing at Bangalore and her only brother doing BSc at UC College, Alwaye. She enquired the family details of Mr. Rajendran.

'I'm leading the life of a married bachelor'

Rajendran gave an evasive reply and did not go into details. Rajani understood the difficulties of Mr. Rajendran and did not ask further.

At the beginning Rajani appeared to be very friendly and amiable in nature. In a short time a close relationship was established between them. Every day Rajendran will go to the switch room and discuss difficult problems. Mr. Joseph used to visit the Exchange frequently and once Miss Rajani was introduced to him by Mr. Rajendran. Mr Joseph liked her very much and was invited to his house. Ond day Rajani and her sister Suman visited the house of Mr. Joseph. At that time Rajendran was also available there. Rajani liked Mrs. Lakshmy, the wife of Mr. Joseph and his daughter Sangeetha. Joseph found out during conversation with Rajani a distant relationship with her family.

'Now all of you are one and I'm out' Rajendran complained jokingly.

'We're catholics and don't interfere in our family affair' joseph shot back smilingly.

'Joseph why don't you find out a suitable match for Rajani. She is already 27.'

'Here there is dearth of catholics and we can find out a boy from some other community'

Rajani and Suman broke into peals of laughter.

Joseph invited them for a tour to Mysore.

Rajani and Suman hesitatingly agreed.

'We've to get permission from father' Rajani said.

'Ok you get it early and I'll do all arrangements for the same'. Joseph was overwhelmed with joy.

'will you invite me for the tri?.'

'Why not, you're also welcome'

One Sunday they set out in the early morning in a Tata sumo van and reached Mysore by 9 am. After breakfast and rest they visited Chamundy temple, zoo, and the palace and in the evening vrindavan. They reached back by 10.30 pm. Rajani and Suman relished the trip very much and that journey has made Sangeetha and Rajani close friends.

For a few months after joining duty there were no problems for Rajendran. Rajani was very cooperative and helpful in every respect. She will come and sit in the cabin for hours discussing and talking about various problems. There were a lot of trouble in the Exchange due to voltage fluctuation of Mains supply and lightning. Many control cards had been burned and a portion of the Exchange had failed. Rajani will handle the Exchange single handedly in the face of any crisis.

Najeeb, Technical Assistant attached to the Exchange is able but proceeds on leave frequently and Rajani does not get any help from him, but she can not provoke him because she learnt the work from him. Najeeb was a local man and was very close with the public and he obliged for provision of various facilities unauthorisedly. Rajendran stopped all kinds of unauthorised actions and hence had to face the wrath of both his subordinates and public. Rajani was straightforward in all respects. Rajendran gave due consideration to all his staff and they co-operated with him without any murmur. Rajani's presence in the Exchange was a morale booster to Rajendran and he felt a kind of restlessness if she is absent or leave.

Rajani was a hardworking girl. She will work in the switch room up to 6 pm and will come and work on all holidays and even on Sundays. Her dedication and hard work was noticed by Rajendran and asked her to entrust the works in the Test Desk, Fault repair service and power plant to Najeeb, but she was reluctant.

'I'll better do it myself than compelling him to do it'

She had no problems in the MDF section. Ganesh was lazy, but sincere. Donald was very active and so was Nagamma.

Rajendran called Najeeb to his cabin and advised to come for duty regularly and assist Rajani in the maintenance work. Najeeb heard everything patiently and agreed to comply with the instructions.

One day Rajani came to his cabin with some statements. She looked very pretty in a pink Churidar and was exactly like Rajamma. She was tall slim and fair in completion. The only difference was that valsamma had spectacles. Rajani smiled and the smile was very enchanting like that of Rajamma. Rajani was very much perplexed on seeing the penetrating glance of Rajendran.

Rajani broke the silence.

'Sir, one BM (Base Module) is having some problems. It goes out of service frequently'

'you're an expert in MBM (Main Base Module). Please check up again and if the fault is elusive we can contact the installation people'

When Rajani turned to go Rajendran said 'I am going to Always tomorrow in connection with a marriage. If your clearance is received I will visit your parents'

Rajani turned and looked at Rajendran but did not say anything.

'Ok, no problem, sorry for the trouble'

After his return from Kerala, Rajendran called Rajani to his cabin. Rajani was surprised to see a young chap sitting in the cabin talking to Rajendran.

'Rajani this's my friend Thomas, a graduate Engineer working in a construction company in White Field'

Rajani's face blushed with shyness.

Thomas asked some questions and she hesitatingly answered. After standing there for about 5 minutes she left. Next day Thomas spoke to her over phone that she liked her.

Thomas liked her very much and wanted to intimate his father before conveying the decision to Rajani. After one week Rajendran went to see Mr Thomas and was informed by his friend that he is in the hospital. Rajendran found Thomas in a serious condition. Thomas slipped and fell from the fourth floor of a building and had a narrow escape. Thomas was not in a condition to speak. Rajendran spent there for about one hour and returned to his lodge.

Rajendran was very much disturbed and could not sleep that night. He talked to Joseph over phone several times. How to tell Rajani was a big problem. He somehow informed her that Thomas liked her very much but he could not think of marriage then since he had got a chance in the Gulf. Rajani heard everything and did not show any kind of emotion. Rajendran's mind was cloudy and was afraid whether she believed what he said.

A target was fixed for the Exchange for the month of March, adding of 500 lines in one month. Rajendran called the entire staff to his cabin and requested their co-operation. But Rajani was critical about the decision.

'The overload alarm is frequent and if load is increased further there will be crisis'

'what crisis' Rajendran blurted out.

'Exchange failure' saying this Rajani went out of the cabin.

A new line module of 728 lines was installed and the same was offered for Acceptance and Testing. Usually, AT is conducted during night and the same came to an end at 4 am next day. He went to his lodge in the early morning in the jeep of the AT Team and informed Rajani about the completion of AT.

In the morning GM(Development)called Rajani and enquired about AT.

'I don't know sir'

'What!, you are in charge of the Exchange and say that you don't know anything, you're irresponsible' GM said in an agitated tone.

This case was discussed in the next development meeting convened by the GM(Development) and Rajendran could not defend her, because what she had said was not correct. He did not mention anything about this to Rajani, but she came to know about this from another SDE. She was completely upset and wept profusely for a long time.

Rajendran came to console her but shouted at him.

'I'm working hard and still I am blamed. I do not want your sympathy'

That day onwards, Rajani spoke to Rajendran only rarely and was in an angry mood. Days and months passed and Rajani continued in no mood to patch up with Rajendran.

Onam festival arrived. Rajendran wanted to go home and took 5 days leave. Rajani had applied for 7 days leave, but did not discuss anything with him regarding posting of somebody to look after the Exchange. Her leave was granted and Najeeb was asked to look after the Exchange in the absence of Rajani.

Rajendran booked a seat in the Karnataka Transport Corporation bus going to Ernakulam. The bus started at 4 PM and it stopped at Guntelpet for meals. Rajendran got out and moved to the hotel and was surprised to see Rajani coming out of the bus with another lady. He smiled at her but she did not respond and went to the family room. He was blushed and his face became pale. He had a tea and snacks and was about to go to the bus when Rajani and her friend walked back to the bus. Rajendran felt dejected and he was sure that she had seen him and purposefully avoided him.

Bus reached Thrissur at 4am next day and Rajendran got down from the bus. He looked at the seat of Rajani in the front row and she was found to be fast asleep. When Rajendran returned to Bangalore after Onam Rajani was there in the Exchange. He went to the switch room and then Rajani was working in the computer and Najeeb was standing near her.

'Hallo Najeeb is there any problem in the Exchange?' 'One BM (Base Module) goes faulty frequently.'

'Find out the fault or contact Installation people'.

Rajani went on working in the computer and did not pay any heed to Rajendran.

The relation between Rajani and Rajendran became very strained. She did everything to provoke Rajendran. He learned that she was crossing the limits and it is high time to stop it.

After a couple of days, there was a partial failure in the Exchange and hence a circuit was rerouted. Rajendran was informed about it by Installation people after many days. Rajendran took it as an affront and issued a memo to Rajani. She, immediately wrote a lengthy reply and sent it through Donald. She had admitted all charges and has regretted her actions and hence further actions were dropped.

After a few days, the Divisional Engineer received a complaint from Rajani that she is being harassed by the SDE Rajendran and requested stringent action against him. The DE forwarded the letter to the Area Manager and the AM sent it to GM. Rajendran came to know about the revengeful attitude of Rajani, but he kept quiet and did not even inform Mr. Joseph.

After a few days, the Area Manager came to the Exchange and conducted some enquiries.

During the enquiry, Rajani Told him that SDE Rajendran misbehaved with her several times and hence she is afraid to work there. Following this, there was a rumour that Rajendran is going to be suspended and Rule

14 chargesheet given for gross misconduct. But, nothing happened. Rajendran was transferred to Chikkamangalore with immediate effect and one Abdul Jaffer was posted in his place. Next day itself, charge was made over to Abdul Jaffer and Rajendran said goodbye to all his staff. Rajani was absent on that day, on the pretext of illness.

After being relieved, Rajendran went straight away to meet Mr Joseph in his Bank and apprised him about the developments.

'Why did you keep it a secret? Joseph said in a depressed tone.

'She's very revengeful and nobody can do anything in this regard.

'No my daughter would have changed her mind. They are so close and attached.'

'There's a saying that familiarity breeds contempt. In this I loved her too much as my own sister, but in return she hated me.

'Let us forget it. I don't believe that she's able to do such things. There'll be a brain behind it and she'll be only a puppet.'

'My doubt's that she liked the boy Thomas and wanted to marry him. My reply may be unconvincing to her and she would have thought that I had scuttled it.

Then Joseph took Rajendran to his house and spent hours discussing this problem.

Before shifting to Chikkamangalore, Rajendran wanted to go home in connection with a marriage. He boarded a Karnataka Corporation bus to Ernakulam, on a Friday evening. He saw Rajani and Suman sitting in the front row seat. His seat was just behind it and on seeing Rajendran Suman smiled.

'Suman is there any important function at home, both of you are going home?'

'Sir, please excuse Rajani. Some people have settled score with you and she became the tool.' Suman said in an apologetic tone.

'I don't believe it. How can she do like that?'

'Sir, my marriage has been fixed. She was hopeful that her marriage with Thomas will take place. Somebody told her that it was you who spoiled it and she believed it.'

'I'll tell you the truth. Thomas fell from 4th floor of a building under construction and his spinal cord was damaged. He is still in the hospital'. Rajendran said in an angry tone. Rajani wept loudly like a child and all passengers in the bus looked at her. 'Cool down Rajani, I have no hatred towards you. Still, I love you as my sister.' He consoled her.

Then, the driver started the bus and in that sound and noise Rajani's cry was drowned.

********* END *********

An Internet Love

Ottawa city was shivering in freezing cold. Snowfall commenced all of a sudden, and it is still continuing even after one week, and almost all trees and shrubs are draped in snowflakes. Saritha peeped through the window, and saw glittering snow all around, and nothing else was visible. She thought of her village at Kadari hills near Mangalore. It is a lovely place with many hillocks and a water fall. Many tourists used to come to that place daily. They will climb the hillocks and bathe in the springs and go back when dusk falls. This far away place Canada is alien to her. They migrated to Canada from Dubai recently and her parents are in search of jobs. Saritha had appeared for +2 at Dubai and before the result was out, they left for Canada. She was bright in her studies, but failed in mathematics. Her mother Nimmi scolded her severely, but her father Mohandas was sympathetic towards her, and asked her to appear in the lost subject again. After receipt of the CBSE marklist she flew to Mumbai. At the Airport she was received by her uncle Sunil and his wife Reena. While driving to his flat at Borivli, Sunil asked her 'In which paper did you fail?'

'Uncle only one subject, mathematics'.

'That's not an issue. I'll arrange a tuition for you in maths" Sunil said.

Saritha liked the flat. It is in the fourth floor and full of light and ventilation. If we look down from the balcony we will get a full view of the surroundings up to their clubhouse and swimming pool.

Saritha is an internet girl, and her main job is chatting with friends and relatives. She used to lock the room while chatting, but Reena did not like this and told her plainly 'Saritha there should be no secrecy. You keep the door open while chatting'.

After one week, she joined an institute there for special coaching in the failed subject- Maths.

There is a distance of four kilometres from the house to the coaching centre, and Saritha learned to go there, by bus alone. She applied for the supplementary examination, and got through with high marks.

Saritha joined for BSc in a college at Borivli west, and started going to college from uncle's flat. In a short time, she made a number of boyfriends there. She used to bring some of them to their flat occasionally, and introduce them to Reena. After some time problems cropped up between them.

'Saritha don't bring your friends here. If you go for study, study well and don't waste your future by roaming here and there with friends. This is Mumbai, if anything happens to you your parents will blame us unnecessarily.'

Saritha could not tolerate this high handed behaviour of Reena. She had a verbal duel with her and then went out of the house and did not return. Reena became panicky and informed Sunil.

He made a number of calls to his friends and relatives and also to sister Nimmi in Canada.

Mohandas called from Ottawa and said 'Avoid giving a police complaint. It will give wide publicity and make the case sensational. Two days passed and she did not return to the flat. Sunil met some of her friends and from them he learned that she had boarded a train to Mangalore. Then Sunil called the house of Mohandas at Kadari hills and learned that she had reached there safely. It was a horrible and traumatic experience for Sunil and Reena. They did not sleep or eat for two days and heaved a sigh of relief when they heard that Saritha has reached her ancestral home safely.

'No more study in Bombay, let her study at Mangalore or Ottawa. I can't take more tension'. Reena told Sunil.

Saritha did not call Sunil or Reena. She was very angry with them, for the rough treatment meted out to her by Reena,. and she made a lot of complaints to her mother, that they tried to make her a prisoner in their house in Bombay. She spent about six months there, under the care of her paternal grandparents. During this time she went to attend some special computer courses and also driving. She then approached her maternal grandpa Mr Srinivas Shenoy, who was working as Joint Secretary in the Central Secretariat, New Delhi, and on his direction she went to New Delhi.

Saritha did not join any college there, and her parents compelled her again to return to Ottawa. Her mother

Nimmi who was electrical engineer by profession got a job in the electricity department and father who was law graduate became legal assistant in a private firm. Later Saritha joined the BSc degree course in Mathematics of Ignou and dropped the idea of going back to Canada. There was an institute for imparting coaching and supplying lessons. They were staying at RK Puram, and the institute was at a distance of 5 KMs from there, and she used a scooter for going to the Institute. When the institute was closed in connection with Deepavali they went to Mangalore on a short trip. While coming back there were some North Indians in the the coach. They were returning after visiting the temples at Kollur, Dharmasthala and Udupi Three of them came and acquainted with them, and sat in the opposite seat. They consisted of an old lady, her son, and daughter, and they were going to Delh. The girl was about 20 and her brother looked 25 years old. They were very jovial and talkative and Saritha also joined them in their conversation. The boy said 'Uncle I am Rajesh and this is my sister Babitha and mother Ganga Devi. We are returning to Delhi after a pilgrimage Our father is working in the Central Secretariat. My sister is studying for MBA in JNU and myself working in a private firm named Sreeram Cosmetics at Gurgaon.'.

Srinivas Shenoy said 'I'm also working in Central Secretariat. What's the name of your father?'

'Nirmal Jha, working in the Industries department. Do you know him?' Rajesh asked.

'There're many Jhas and if I see him I can recognise. I'm working in Steel & Mines department.' Shenoy said.

'We belonged to Varanasi and our grandparents are living there. We will go to our village at the time of Deepavali and other important festivals and have a big family there with grandfather, grandmother, uncles, aunties etc. When father retires they will also return to our village. They said goodbye and left when the train reached New Delhi.

Saritha used to chat in the internet for hours, after coming back from the Institute. She used to close the door during chatting, but the grandparents did not pay any attention to her. They were aware that she had no mobile. and she used to make calls to Canada from the land phone by using BSNL card. Every friday she used to receive calls from her mother and sister. Her father is not in the habit of making calls to Saritha, They went to Mangalore during Christmas and during this journey one terrific incident occurred. After boarding from New Delhi, whenever the train stopped at stations, some people came and stared at them from the platform. It was an unusual thing and grandmother became afraid. and told Saritha 'Saritha don't go to toilet without telling me' and she agreed and slept in the upper berth. After Bombay the train was running at high speed and then slowed down and almost stopped at two places before Goa for crossing purpose. When it reached Goa station, Saritha was not in the upper berth. Grandma noticed the absence of Sarita in the train and informed grandfather.

Srinivas Shenoy searched all the bogies of the train and toilets but she was not found out. He became panicky, and the train had left the station by that time. He came to the seat and told his wife that Saritha is missing. Hearing this she began to cry.

Some people were watching her when the train stopped at various stations and I'm sure that she has been kidnapped.' Grandmother Nalini said.

'If she'd gone to the toilet she'd have returned by this time'. Shenay said. The train was running at high speed and Shenoy went in search of the TTE and told him about the mysterious disappearance of the girl. The TTE advised him to get down at the next big station and complain to the GRP(Government Railway Police) and hence he and his wife got down at Udupi station with their luggage. They had a lot of luggage and found it difficult to carry it to the station. Mrs Nalini Shenoy sat near the luggage and Shenay went to the GRP station, wrote a complaint and gave it to the Inspector. The Inspector was reluctant to receive the same and said 'You should have given the complaint to the GRP station at Goa since the missing took place within their jurisdiction. and after repeated requests he accepted the complaint on condition that it will be transferred to Goa.

Srinivasa Shenoy and family struggled to board a train going to Ernakulam, and in that melee he lost two boxes from his luggage. Somehow he reached Mangalore station, unloaded the luggage and went to his residence at Surathkal in a taxi. His brother Gopal Shenoy and family were waiting for them in their house. First he hesitated to tell the truth, and finally he said that Saritha is missing. His wife was grief stricken and told Gopal Shenoy and wife 'She was kidnapped and no need of searching for her. Her body will be lying in the Railway track, or she would have been sold to a brothel in Bombay'. She was unable to control her grief.

After two days, Srinivas Shenoy made a call to the GRP station Udupi and the Inspector said that the complaint had been forwarded to the Inspector, GRP Station, Goa. Next day he made a call to GRP station Goa, and spoke to the Inspector, there and was told that they would investigate the case on receipt of the complaint. He said 'It is likely that this will be an elopement case. Is she in love with anybody?'. Srinivasa Shenoy replied that it was not a case of love since she was staying with them at Delhi and no contact or connection with anybody outside. Then, he reminded that it can not be taken lightly, since internet love cases are reported very frequently.

Srinivas Shenay had some suspicion regarding the boy, whom they met in the train. So he called his friend Arunkumar from Varanasi to visit the house of Mr. Jha, who is the father of that boy. Arunkumar and wife went to the house of Mr. Jha and enquired, whether there was any news from Mr Rajesh. He revealed to him the disappearance of Miss Saritha, granddaughter of Srinivasa Shenoy, Joint Secretary, in the Dept. of Home. Mr. Jha, then said 'They are wrongly suspecting my son. He will not do any such thing. I have brought up my children in such a way that they will not do any wrong'. Arunkumar rung up Shenay and told him what Mr Jha had said.

Srinivas Shenoy gave a complaint in the local police station also, on the advice of his nephew Leeladhar Pai, who was a Sub Inspector in Special Branch. He told his relatives gathered in his house that she had no mobile phone with her. His nephew Mr Sailesh said that, there was every possibility for a mobile phone with her, and that could be proved, if her luggage was subjected to a search. On his advice, her complete luggage was thoroughly rummaged, and a mobile cover was recovered. Calls were made in that number but it was found to be switched off. On enquiry it was revealed that it was an Airtel number issued from New Delhi. The mobile number was given to the local police and they forwarded the same to cyber cell. During Christmas holidays, only policemen were available in the cyber cell, and the Nodal Officers of of Telecom companies proceeded on leave, and hence Sailesh contacted his friend working in Mumbai Airtel to obtain the details. But, he expressed his helplessness and said 'They will supply the data only to the police or cyber cell on receipt of FIR particulars or other details of the police case'.

Immediately, a copy of the SP's letter to the cyber cell was forwarded to them by e mail, and within a short time all necessary details were collected by Airtel, and forwarded to the cyber cell, Mangalore The cyber cell analysed these data, and relevant details were taken for investigation, such as address of the owner of mobile, details of parties to whom calls were made, from that number, tower locations etc. The tower location was verified and found to be Mumbai. Then the SP sent a message to the City Police Commissioner, Mangalore, for taking up the case with the City Police Commissioner, Mumbai, with all relevant records.

After leave, the Nodal Officer of the Airtel joined duty, and enquired about the Airtel number, and the duty policeman in cyber cell told him, that they have already received the details, through Mumbai Airtel Office. Then he lost his control, and said 'How dare you collect these details over my head. I'll complain to appropriate authorities and supply of further information will be stopped.'.

'I's the missing case of a girl. You had been requested to supply these details urgently, but you ignored it and went on leave. Can we wait for four days in such a case and we sought the help of Mumbai office and got it'. The policeman in the cyber cell retorted. The Nodal Officer was cut a sorry figure and he did not say anything further.

Srinivas Shenoy contacted the GRP station, Goa after a few days, and the Inspector said 'We have received the complaint and will start investigation shortly. Please forward a recent photograph of the missing girl immediately.'

After two days, Shenay contacted Inspector GRP Goa again, and this time he became angry and replied 'If you call daily, that will serve no purpose. Every day, so many complaints are being received here. We are doing our best, and will let you know, as and when they are apprehended.'

Next day Srinivasa Shenoy left for Goa and met the Inspector, GRP, and gave him three copies of the photograph of Saritha, and also the call details of her mobile and other particulars received from cyber cell. The Inspector heard everything and advised him to be patient.

'I's no doubt an elopement case? was she in love with anybody?' The Inspector enquired.

'No, she'd no connection with anybody. She was very silent at home, and spent time in reading and seeing TV.'

'Is she studying there?'

'Yes, for BSc in Ignou. She has no regular classes. Once in a week, she'll visit the coaching centre and collect notes and attend contact classes and she has no friends there'.

'From my experience, I can say that this is an elopement case. Kidnapping cases are frequent, but this case does not fall in that category'. She left the train without even taking the footwears. Her intention was to escape from the train, without being noticed by her grandparents. They would have arranged the elopement from Delhi itself. The boy and his friends would have boarded the train from the same station from which you boarded it. Since the tower location is Mumbai, please go to Mumbai and meet the Police Commissioner, there' The Inspector told Shenoy in an amiable tone.

'OK Sir, I'll go to Mumbai and meet the City Police Commissioner" Shenay said.

'We're helpless and only Mumbai police can help you. I know your grief and mental agony, let God help you'. Shenay shook hands with the Inspector and left.

Then, he dialled his friend Vijay Pande in the Home Ministry and requested him to contact the City Police Commissioner, Mumbai for an appointment and within half an hour he got it.

Srinivas Shenoy told the Police Commissioner the whole story and the Commissioner heard everything patiently and said 'Every day twenty to thirty girls disappear in this city and only ten to twenty percent are detected. There is a special cell to monitor such cases. If it is an elopement case, we can track them and find out later. But if she was sold to brothels, it is rather difficult to trace her out. But, we will do our best in this case. If anybody similar to her is apprehended, we will contact you, and then you will have to come and help us, to identify the girl.'

'Sir, I'm working in the Central Secretariat, New Delhi and my son's working here. I'll give his address and mobile number. He'll come and help you in case any necessity arises. Shenay gave the name and address and mobile number of his son Sunil and left the chamber of the Commissioner.

Srinivas Shenoy went back to Mangalore and extended his leave for a further period of two weeks. In the meanwhile Mohandas made a hue and cry, and blamed Shenay for the disappearance of his beloved daughter. Nimmy took leave for two days and went to a temple at a far away place and prayed for the early return of Saritha. This incident has rattled their family and they even thought of cancelling the visa, and returning to India, but their friends and relatives in Canada dissuaded them from the extreme step.

Srinivas Shenoy waited patiently for any news regarding Saritha but in vain. Sunil used to contact the Asst Commissioner who is in charge of the investigation and he was called twice to identify some suspected cases. Once he was taken to a morgue in a hospital to identify a corpse with some similarities with Saritha and Sunil confirmed that it did not belong to his niece. On the second time he was taken to two brothels one in Colaba and the other at Mahim. Sunil testified that none of them was Saritha.

Srinivas Shenoy returned to New Delhi with his wife. Nothing further was heard about Saritha from Bombay Police later. He used to ring up Saritha's mobile frequently, but it was found switched off permanently. After reporting duty, he was in a desperate mood and had no interest to give more attention to work. Naliny Shenay was in perpetual grief. Nimmy will call her occasionally, and blame them unnecessarily, saying that Saritha was lost due to the carelessness of her parents.

Long two years have passed after the disappearance of Saritha. Srinivas Shenoy remembers her everyday and his mind still weeps in her loss. It remained a mystery, where she went or what happened to her. Sunil met some of her old college friends but they were in the dark about her whereabouts. With the two years Nimmi and Mohandas have made enough money and purchased a luxury flat in the heart of the city. Their second daughter Saranya is now studying for medicine in US. They have made several trips to US.

Srinivas Shenoy has retired from service at the age of 60 and is planning to go and settle in his native place Mangalore. During service, he was very busy and did not get time to visit any of the important places in North India. One day they went to Jaipur by car and stayed there for one week and visited all the palaces. During the return journey they stopped at Gurgaon and decided to meet Mr Rajesh whom they had met during the train journey. Srinivas Shenoy recollected the name of his company -Sreeram Cosmetics. They enquired at many places and finally found out the firm in an alley. They went to the office and enquired about Rajesh from Varanasi, and waited in the office foyer. After ten minutes an emaciated youth with unshaven face and sunken eyes came and stood before them. He was in a shabby dress and his face looked depressed. They could not recognize him and hence asked 'We want to meet Rajesh, son of Nirmal Jha, do you know him?. He is working in this company.'.

'I'm that Rajesh.' He said with a smile on his face.

'Who's Saritha?' Shenoy asked.

'We want to see her. We're coming from Delhi"

Then Rajesh realized who they were and begged pardon 'Excuse me grandpa. We've married and are living here since then. She told me that her grandpa is a wicked man and 'll send goons to kill me and hence our whereabouts were kept secret'.

'We're in great anguish and mental agony for all these two years. We've verified many places in Mumbai including brothels and thought that Saritha is either dead or languishing in brothels somewhere.' Srinivas Shenoy said in a voice choked with emotion. 'Sorry grandpa, very, sorry for the mistake' Rajesh entreated.

They went to his house and it was a single room flat in an old building, and the condition was very pathetic. Saritha was ashamed on seeing her grandparents.

A small girl child was sleeping in a cradle made of sari.

Nalini Shenoy hugged Saritha and sobbed seeing the plight of their granddaughter.

'You could have sent at least a postcard, stating that you are safe and it would have saved us from the mental agony, trauma and grief for the last two years. We have been searching in the brothels of Bombay and morges of hospitals and we did not get any clue as to what happened to you.' Srinivas Shenoy said. 'Sorry grandpa, grandma, we've done a terrible mistake. The elopement was arranged by the friends of Rajesh. They accompanied us in the train. We got down when the train slowed down near Goa for crossing purpose. From there, we went to Bombay by car where we had some relatives, and stayed with them for a couple of days and left for Varanasi. We stayed there for one month and when everything settled down we returned to Gurgaon.'Rajesh said.

'Is your father aware of this elopement and subsequent marriage?.

'He's against such out of caste marriages and hence kept secret from him for several months'.

'When did you start this love?'

'When she was in Mumbai, we became friends through internet and used to chat for hours.

When she came to Delhi we used to meet her near the coaching centre and decided to marry. Our friends offered all support and they boarded the same train from New Delhi'.

'By the by, how did you marry?'. 'We married in a temple at Varanasi and got it registered.'

'Are you friendly with your father now?'

'No, never. He hasn't come to our house and seen Saritha. When the child was born they were informed but they did not come. With their enmity we have learned to live with what we have. After the birth of our daughter Sangeetha, I was laid up with a partial paralysis and nobody came to help us. We've suffered a lot and have overcome all those hardships and privations with the help of god. Life was in great misery for a long time and we have somehow managed to tide over those difficult days. We really thought that our misfortune was due to your anger or curse.'.

'Even though we have suffered a lot we have not cursed anybody. We thought it is our fate and found peace of mind through prayer and meditation. I have retired from service. Today is the happiest day in our life. The very thought that Saritha is alive and leading a family life is a great consolation for us. In fact this is her second birth. We invite you to our house. Shortly we will vacate the house and move to Mangalore'

'OK grandpa we'll come next Saturday. Thank you for your love and affection'.

Srinivas Shenoy informed Nimmy and Mohandas from there itself and they were very much happy and relieved. Sunil was also informed and arranged to withdraw the police complaint.

On next Saturday, Rajesh, Saritha and Sangeetha came to RK Puram residence and stayed with them for one day and went back by Sunday evening. It was a happy reunion. When they were about to go Saritha embraced grandma and wept. and regretted for the mistake on her part.

'OK, those difficult days are over. You are welcome to our ancestral house at Mangalore'.

'OK, grandpa. we can meet there within one month'.

Shenay took them in his car to the New Delhi bus stand and they boarded a bus and left for Gurgaon.

********* END *********

DIFFERENT PATHS BUT DESTINATION SAME

A new private hospital was opened in the silent hamlet of Manalur, in Thrissur district, some thirty years ago. This place is famous for paddy, coconut and the water regulator. There are thousands of acres of paddy fields in this village, and it stretches for kilometres in all direction. The soil is very suitable for coconuts and they grow in abundance in this area. There is a bridge cum regulator to restrict entry of salt water to the main irrigation canal. It also helps to flush out excess water to the sea during rainy season. One side of the bridge is fesh wate irrigation canal and the other side a river with salt water flowing to the sea. In olden times the people of this area used to go out in small canoes to the river and catch plenty of fish. This was the livelihood of a section of the people in the past. Those canoes have disappeared now since most of them have gone to gulf countries and made opulent houses everywhere and the face of the village has undergone a thorough change.

In the initial stages of the hospital, there was only one doctor and a nurse. The building is an old house taken on rent from Sri. Thomas master and the present president of the hospital is one Sri. Vijayanarayanan belonging to the richest family of that village. He has donated a handsome amount to this venture and even provided a free quarters to the nurse and family.

It was Monday, and time 9.30 am. The doctor Venugopal MBBS, was sitting idle in his cabin since he had cleared all patients who came in the morning since 8 am. Suddenly, an auto came to the courtyard of the hospital and stopped and a young girl and her brother got down. They went straight to the doctor without taking OP ticket. The girl was in severe pain and she had closed her eye and the ear with one hand. The face reflected the intensity of pain, and she could not stand in front of the doctor.

The doctor, immediately made her sit on the stool in front of him and enquired 'What is the problem with you?'

'A cockroach went inside the ear a few hours ago. We poured salt water but it is still alive and cause discomfort and pain'. Her brother replied.

'What's her name?'

'Leena'

'Age?'

'Seventeen'

'Address?'

'Peringottil house, Manalur west.'

The doctor himself wrote these details in the register and rose to examine the patient.

The doctor lighted a torch and looked inside the ear carefully and saw the feelers of the insect. It is moving inside the ear causing severe pain to the girl.

'Sister, please bring the tool box'.

Then a talll and slender lady in white sari appeared with a box and Leena lay on the table with the help of her brother Sumesh.

Within no time, the doctor took out the insect with forceps and kept it in a glass tray. But, in the struggle the patient's face which was beautiful like a red rose was distorted and became disfigured. Doctor was alarmed and terrified and sweat rolled down from his forehead. When Leena got up from the table, her brother Sumesh broke into tears and the nurse stood transfixed to the floor.

'Sister, while taking out the insect the facial nerve passing through the ear has been affected, please apply some antiseptic ointment to the affected portion.' Doctor said wiping his sweat from the forehead.

Doctor kept perspiring and the sister applied an ointment inside the ear with a bud.

'Please take rest in the bed inside' doctor asked the girl pointing to a bed inside the room.

She lay in the bed for about half an hour and her brother stood near her with an anxious face.

Then the doctor went to her brother and spoke in a troubled tone.

'Mr. Sumesh, we've to take her immediately to Calicut Medical College. She's a lovely girl and her face has been distorted since the nerve passing through the ear was slightly affected. If immediate treatment is given, it can be rectified. This is only a temporary problem and can be corrected. For this, we require the services of Professor of ENT, Medical College, Calicut. So, get prepared to go to Calicut tomorrow morning. I will come with you'.

Sumesh agreed and and by noon Leena was discharged.

Next day, they boarded the bus from the KSRTC bus stand Trichur by 9 am and the bus fare was paid by the doctor. They reached Calicut by 1.30 pm. After lunch they proceeded straight to the residence of Dr. Jayamohan, Professor and Director of ENT, at Nadakkav.

Dr. Venugopal pressed the doorbell and Namitha Jayamohan opened the door and spoke to him. 'Doctor is relaxing after lunch, please wait'. Then she gave a token and collected fees from Dr. Venugopal.

At 3 pm they were called to the consulting room of the professor. On seeing Venugopal Professor smiled and enquired 'Venu what happened? what is the problem?'

Dr. Jaymohan was his professor and a distant relative and with that freedom he replied. 'Not for me, my patient Miss. Leena's face became distorted by a slight error on my part. While taking out a cockroach with forcep, the nerve controlling the facial muscles was slightly disturbed. Immediately an antiseptic ointment was applied and she was asked to take rest.'

Doctor Jayamohan examined the patient and said 'Don't worry Dr. Venu, this is bells palsy, the 7th cranial nerve has been damaged. This can be corrected within two weeks and admit her in the side room of my chamber today itself.'

Doctor wrote something in a piece of paper and handed it over to Dr. Venugopal.

While going in an auto to chevayoor, Dr. Venugopal told Sumesh 'He is a brilliant doctor but not very popular with his students and patients. He is a good man but his wife is very greedy for money. The naxalites had conducted a public trial against some of the greedy and inhuman doctors and he is one among them.'

'I've heard about this incident in newspaper.' Sumesh said.

Leena was admitted in the side room adjacent to professor's chamber that evening and Dr. Venugopal returned to Trichur, after giving necessary instruction to Sumesh.

Treatment started from next day as per directions of the professor. A lady house surgeon with dreamy and vivacious eyes examined Leena's ear, and applied an ointment and gave an injection.

She's a lean figure with an attractive face.

'Doctor what is your good name?' Asked Sumesh when she was about to leave. 'Nancy Thomas'.

'From which place?'.

'Wynad '.

'Which place in Wynad?'

'Pulpally, Have you seen Wynad?' doctor asked Sumesh.

'I've heard about Wynad, but could not visit there so far. Some of our relatives are there in Ambalavayal, and Cheeral. They have got land from the ex servicemen quota'.

'We 're originally from Ettumanoor, Kottayam. My grandfather came and purchased 50 acres of land there. Cleared the forests and planted coffee, pepper and areconut. My grandfather had struggled a lot, and before he could take the first crop he died. My father made it a big estate and later purchased 30 acres more. I have three brothers and one of them is engaged in assisting father and the elder two are working in Delhi. One brother is working in JNU as lecturer and the other running an advertising agency. I am the only daughter of my parents.'Nancy gave a full account of her family.

Sumesh smiled and Nancy Thomas returned the smile. Sumesh felt something tingling inside while talking to Nancy.

She used to come frequently, to examine and give medicines to Leena. Each time, she used to linger in the room talking to Leena or Sumesh on various subjects.

After two days, the professor came and examined and said 'She is improving and she will be alright within a couple of weeks.'

After professor left the room, Nancy said 'Sumesh you are lucky. Your sister is improving. She is a charming girl and God will help you to get back her beauty.'

'Thank you doctor. How can I repay you for the special care and attention you give to my sister'.

'No question of thanks, it is my duty to give constant attention and care to the patient till she comes round to normalcy.

'But other interns are not like you.

'I believe in God and think that he will take care of everybody. I am sincere in whatever I do. I am praying everyday for the speedy recovery of all my patients here.'

'Thank you doctor, you have a great and sympathetic heart unlike others'.

'By the by, what do you do?'. Asked Nancy.

'I was not good at studies and reached upto 10th standard and gave up studies and started helping father who is running a hotel in Trichur town.'

'Hotel!, hotel is a good and profitable business. One of my uncles is running a hotel in Muvattupuzha town and he has made more money than my father.'

'It may be big hotel,3 star,4 star etc, with bar and other facilities. Ours is a small hotel with vegetarian food, snacks etc and a small bakery of sweets along with it. My younger brother is running a catering unit. He is making more money than us.'

After one week the progress was assessed by professor and informed Sumesh and Leena.

'Very good improvement and she can be discharged after one more week.'professor said with a smile. Dr. Nancy was with him at this time.

'Thank you doctor sir'.

'You're from Manalur, is in't? I'm from Engandiyur and we are neighbours'. Saying this professor laughed and Dr. Nancy and Sumesh joined in that laughter.

Sumesh and Dr. Nancy became close friends.

'Dr. Nancy, we don't want to go after one week'.

'Why?'asked Nancy.

'How can we see Dr. Nancy?, if we go to Trichur after one week?'

'Then, I'll come with you to Trichur.'

'OK, you're welcome. In that case I'll give an offering of 100 wireworks to Triprayar temple.'

Nancy's face brightened and her eye became wet.

'Are you crying?' Sumesh asked.

'Yes, we'll cry if our mind is flooded with more pleasure and joy and that's called anandasru.'

(tears due to ecstasy) Dr. Nancy wiped her eyes and and went to her resting room in a depressed state.

Next mornin, Nancy came and talked to Leena and avoided direct eye contact with Sumesh.

'Are you not feeling well?' Sumesh asked Nancy. But she did not reply and returned to her rest room without waiting more in that room.

In the evening, she did not come and instead sent the nurse to give medicine to Leena.

Next day, she came and talked to Leena only and then Sumesh enquired 'Dr. Nancy sorry for the trouble, excuse me for cracking unnecessary wits.'

'No Sumesh we're too close and talks as intimate friends. It is dangerous and when you leave I cannot bear it. My mind is so simple and soft and it may break with great parting grief.'Dr. Nancy became sentimental again.

'Dr. Nancy I love you with all my heart. I'm only matriculate, but I have a heart to love you and provide everything for you. If you like me I'll marry you and I am not afraid of the consequences.

Dr. Nancy's mind melted like snow and she began to sob.

Leena was fully recovered and date was fixed for her discharge. On the previous day of discharge Sumesh went to the house of professor and paid some money as gift and thanked for his sincere help and care in the treatment of his sister. Professor shook hands with Sumesh and asked him to contact him after reaching home, Sumesh also paid some money to the nursing and cleaning staff in the ward. He put some money in a cover and tried to give it to Nancy when she came to meet Leena. Dr Nancy withdrew her hand and scolded Sumesh severely. 'What is this? I don't want any gift or charity. I am getting allowance and if that is not enough my father will give me whatever I require. If you have so much money give it to the hapless and destitute patients who are rotting here for want of money.'

'Sorry doctor, excuse me for my mistake.' Sumesh apologised.

Next day Sumesh and Leena left the hospital by noon. They wanted to say goodbye to Dr Nancy but she was absent that day.

Sumesh was feeling depressed after reaching home. He had no interest to go to hotel. He recalled the words of Nancy over and over again and did not get proper sleep for some days.

One day, mother asked Sumesh 'Why do you look worried and dejected after returning from Calicut?. Is there any problem?'

'No, nothing mummy'

Sumesh started going to the hotel. He has almost recovered from the mental agony which was tormenting him for so many days. He consoled himself by saying that it is only a day dream and it is not proper to hope for her. She is a doctor from an affluent family and belongs to a different religion.

He despised himself, that he is only a matriculate and no income of his own. The hotel beongs to father and he has to depend on father for each and every thing. If he marries her the society will scoff at him and he will cut a sorry figure in front her and his people. So he came to the conclusion that it is better to forget her.

About two weeks passed, and Sumesh was surprised to see a postal cover on the cash counter table. He turned over the cover to see whether any from address is there. He noted two letters on the backside - NT. He was sure that the letter is from Dr Nancy Thomas. He was really afraid to open it. When nobody was there near the counter he opened the cover and read it with a kind of inexplicable pleasure and ecstasy.

Calicut,
03-08-1985.

Dear Sumesh,

Those two weeks were really wonderful. Your memory still lingers in my mind and gives solace to my disturbed mind. It was like a sweet dream which faded into oblivion in no time,

How are you? how is Leena?. She is really a beauty queen and you look like a bollywood star. Please take this as a compliment.

with love and affection,
Nancy Thomas.

On reading the lette, Sumesh's eye became wet and he was overwhelmed with a surge of passion and he said to himself 'Dr Nancy can never forget me. She is mine and mine only'

For two days he was in a joyful state and he wrote a reply to Nancy's letter.

Trichur,
18-08-85.

Beloved Dr Nancy,

I was in great mental ecstasy on receiving your sweet letter. I do not know how to reply. On the day of discharge of my sister I searched for you in every nook and corner of the medical college hospital, but you were not found out. I thought you had purposefully stayed away from hospital to avoid agony of parting. My mind told me to forget you, because I do not want to spoil your bright career. Since the temporary parting has strengthened the friendship, I would like to inform you that you are mine and mine only.

Yours lovingly,
Sumesh.

Two weeks elapsed, after posting the letter and no reply was received. Sumesh will look at the postman with expectation every day but no reply came. He was anxious and worried and thought of sending another letter to her. Then one day, a lady came to the hotel with a handbag and enquired about Sumesh to father who was in the cash counter at that time. He asked her to wait and sent a messenger to the market where Sumesh had gone to purchase provisions. Within half an hour he reached the hotel and was surprised to see Dr Nancy sitting by the side of cash counter.

'Papa, this is Dr Nancy who was the duty doctor of the ward when Leena was there and she has done a lot for her recovery.' Sumesh's voice faltered when he said this much.

'She has come to visit somebody here. Please take her to sister's house and let her stay there till her mission is completed.' Sumesh's father Gopalakrishnan said.

'OK papa, I will take her now itself.' Sumesh replied.

Dr Nancy was served with tea and snacks and then she was taken by Sumesh to his sister's house at Chembukav in his car.

On the way, she told Sumesh 'My internship is over and I do not want to return to Wynad and now I'm in search of a job.'

Sreelatha received them with great warmth and served them tea and then enquired further regarding Dr Nancy.

'Chechi, this is Dr Nancy Thomas from Wynad and I liked her and wanted to marry her at the earliest' Sumesh said.

Sreelatha was surprised to hear that her brother is going to marry a doctor lady from another community. She considered the pros and cons of the relation and was afraid how he can make it a success. She told Sumesh not to take a decision hurriedly.

Sreelatha liked Nancy very much and told her 'you can stay here any longer. We can try and find out a job in any of the hospitals in the city. My husband is in the gulf and here myself and my two children only. My daughters Varsha and Harsha are studying in a convent high school here'.

Dr Nancy liked Sreelatha for her frankness and friendly nature.

Dr Nancy stayed in that house for about one month. Sreelatha told her father about the love affair, but he had no objections. Thus, they married in the sub registry office, Trichur. and was taken to Manalur for a reception arranged there for their friends and relatives. Dr Nancy had written letters to her parents and brothers well in advance of their marriage stating that she is going to marry a Hindu boy from Trichur who is running a hotel in the town. The entire people in the locality came to see Nancy because such a revolutionary marriage had not taken place in that village earlier.

'She does not look like a doctor' one relative expressed his opinion to his wife.

'I think, she's only a nurse. How can a doctor lady marry a boy who is only matriculate' another relative told Sumesh's father.

'Let her be doctor or nurse, my son has married her and they will live together in this house whether others like it or not'. This was the emphatic reply of Sumesh's father Gopalakrishnan.

Leena was very ecstatic in this marriage because she liked Nancy very much.

News reached Nancy's home and Jeeson Thomas Nancy's father roared like a lion 'A hotel boy has married my daughter, but I will find her out and bring her home. They have applied witchcraft and black magic on my only daughter. Otherwise she would never have agreed to that marriage.'

That house was gloomy and grief stricken. They neither ate or spoke for days. It appeared that somebody has passed away in that house. Mother of Nancy Deepa Mariam George lay prostrate in the bed and father sat in the sofa like a statue. Brother Joyson sat near father and consoled him.

Brothers from Delhi made frequent calls and made enquiries about parents and Nancy.

Mr Jeeson Thomas was very rich and influential in his area. He spoke to some advocates in the High court and tried to file a Habeas corpus petition but they discouraged him and he withdrew from that attempt.

Then, he spoke to some bishops in his community and arranged to send two pastors to the house of Sumesh. They were received with great respect and honour by Dr Nancy and Sumesh. They spent a lot of time in that house discussing various aspects of the marriage. Then they invited them to Wynad for a ceremony in their house.

'We'll think over it father and let you know' Dr Nancy said when they were about to go.

'If they have invited us we should go to Wynad'. Sumesh said.

'No, never' Dr. Nancy.

'Why?'

'If we go you'll never return home alive'.

Finally, they dropped that idea.

After one week, there was news of an accident in the Tamarassery ghat road. A jeep collided with a tanker lorry at midnight and two persons travelling in the jeep died instantly and three others including the driver sustained serious injuries and admitted to the medical college hospital, Calicut.

Dr Nancy recognized the deceased persons and they were workers in her papa's estate with criminal backgrounds.

She thanked God for saving the life of Sumesh from that criminals.

Nancy once told Sumesh 'Sumesh you are lucky.'

'Why lucky?'asked Sumesh.

'The two persons died in the accident 'They had ulterior motives either to kidnap us or kill you' Nancy said.

Sumesh became aghast and asked 'How did you know'?.

'They're people with criminal history and papa has utilised them on many occasions in settling scores with his enemies there.'

Sumesh could not believe her words and in a fit of affection he hugged her and lifted her up.'

Dr Nancy joined a hospital called Karunnya Nursing home as RMO. She worked hard for this hospital for about one year. The work was heavy but remuneration low and mostly night duty.

After one year, she resigned the job and joined a medical college at Coimbatore for DGO. For getting this seat, Sumesh's father paid some amount as donation. At the time of completion of this course, the college got sanction for starting MD in gynaecology and on their request Nancy joined for MD on payment of a heavy donation. Nancy thought this is a worthy course and she can pay back the amount to her father in law by private practice.

At this time, a good proposal came for Leena from Alwaye. The boy is an engineer working in Dubai and both sides liked each other and the marriage was arranged immediately. After marriage, she was taken to Dubai.

During her studies at Coimbatore, her whereabouts were treated as most secret and even close relatives were in the dark about Nancy. Once in a month Sumesh will go there and meet Nancy and come back. Only for very important festivals she will come to Trichur. She came out in distinction in MD and after receipt of the degree she joined a high profile hospital at Ernakulam for two years. By the time, she applied for PSC and got selected as Assistant Professor, gynaecology at Medical College, Trivandrum. Sumesh took a rented house at Goureesapattam and moved to Trivandrum. Dr Nancy became pregnant and the delivery took place there itself.

The child was a baby boy. After delivery, Sumesh's mother went there with a maid for post natal treatment and after three months she went back to Manalur. The son was named as Jeeson on the suggestion of Nancy and others approved it. Nobody knew that, it was the first name of her father.

Nancy was perfect in her duty. She will not demand anything from patients, and whatever they gave she will accept. She will not accept anything from patient, after admission in hospital. She had a ward to look after, even though there was associate professor and professor in that department.

She spent five long years at Trivandrum. She had a lot of patients and her life was very busy. She had to go to the hospital during night on most of the days and she had no time to look after her son Jeeson. Now, there are two maids in the house one to look after Jeeson and the other to prepare food and attend domestic chores.

From the age of three years Jeeson is going to nursery in an english medium school there at Pattam. Sumesh will come occasionally, stay for two days and go back. Nancy gave birth to another child and this time it was a baby girl and she named her as Deepa, the first name of her mother.

Sumesh started a catering unit and it was a big success and he became president of the All Kerala Hotelier 's Association and was a busy person now. Sumesh's father Gopalakrishnan purchased another hotel on Chembukav road and a residential house near it. The new hotel is running with good profit. Now their house at Manalur is in a closed condition, since they have shifted to the new house at Chembukav, Trichur.

Dr Nancy was transferred to Calicut and the residence was shifted to a rented house at Puthiyara near stadium. Jeeson was admitted to 1st standard in an english medium school on Mavoor road. The school bus will come and take Jeeson from home and drop him in front of the house. Dr Nancy was very familiar with Calicut and she met some of her friends there and most of them were pulling on with MBBS only. Two of her friends have taken post graduation and they have managed to become Assistant Professors and others were working as tutors in medical college or RMOs in private hospitals.

Dr Nancy purchased a new car and she will go to hospital at 7.30 am and will be back by 2 pm.

The old maids came with her to Calicut and there was no problem for Nancy in the care of children or domestic affairs. She did everything, for the welfare of the maids and paid them well and treated them as family members.

Dr Nancy has to work in the OP for three days in a week and two days she has to take class for MBBS students. In OP she is very sympathetic towards poor patients and did her best to alleviate their problems. She will not direct them to unnecessary tests in private labs or scanning centres.

Years and seasons rolled by, and her daughter Deepa has become two years old and Jeeson is in II std. now. Dr Nancy is very busy in hospital and her house since she earned a good name as gynaecologist. She used to see patients in her consulting room at home between 3 to 7pm and due to her hard work and devotion to duty she could save a few lakhs and the same was paid to her father in law. Even after so many years, she has not been able to pay even the half of the money spent by him towards her higher studies.

At this time, both of her maids went back to their houses at Trivandrum and did not come back. Dr Nancy sought mother in law's help and Subhadra came to Calicut immediately even though her husband was undergoing treatment for a lot of ailments. Sumesh brought an old lady from Chittoor and she was able to handle everything single handedly. Her name was Sosamma.

She was unmarried and about 50 years old. She was a Christian, belonging to RC wing. She was very pious and wanted to go to church every Sunday. One Sunday, Dr Nancy took her to the RC church and she also took part in the mass along with children. For many years, she has not visited church. Sumesh was very considerate and once he asked her 'If you want to go to church you can go and I have no objection.

'After joining MBBS, I have not visited any churches since I was busy due to various reasons. I used to pray at home and that is enough'

'If you want any portrait of Jesus Christ, I will bring it to you' Sumesh said.

'No Sumesh, thank you for your broadminded attitude' said Nancy.

'I'll tell you a story of my relative at Kodungallur. 'That uncle was in Bombay and married a Goan christian lady, and when he settled in his native village, he made a church for his wife to pray, since she was very pious, and cannot live without praying in church. That is our culture, and no objection in continuing your religion and belief.'

Sosamma compelled Dr Nancy to take her to church every week, and then Nancy said 'I want to come with you every week but I have a lot of other works on Sunday and hence you go and come back in an auto'. From that week onwards Sosamma will go to church alone.

'Mummy are you catholic or protestant?' one day Jeesan asked her.

'What do you want to know? I am neither a catholic nor a protestant, but I am a humanist' Nancy said.

'Can protestants go to catholic church?' He asked again.

'Nobody'll ask whether you are a protestant, pentecost or catholic. Anybody can take part in the mass'. I have seen even Hindus attending mass in certain churches. Is your doubt cleared.'

One day Nancy purchased a framed portrait of Christ and gave it to Sosamma and she placed it on a pedestal in her room and said. 'I will pray in my room and no need of going to church hereafter'.

Nancy was promoted as Associate Professor. She was very happy, and informed Sumesh, father in law and others and then went to the room of Sosamma and prayed for some time standing in front of the portrait of Christ, and seeing this Sosamma was very much pleased. Nancy thought she will be transferred again to Trivandrum, but it did not happen.

Deepa started going to play school and Jeeson is in III std. now. One day, Dr Nancy looked into the mirror and was alarmed to see a bunch of grey hair near the temple. She was now nearing 40. Sumesh looked younger without any trace of grey hair even at 45.

One day an old lady came to her house, for consultation along with a 15 year old boy in a taxi.

She waited outside, along with other patients for about one hour and when her turn came she entered the consulting room and sat on the stool by the side of Dr Nancy, and the boy sat in the chair opposite to her seat.

Dr Nancy asked 'What's your name?'

'Deepa Mariam George'

Immediately, Dr Nancy was startled and looked at the patient and the boy and asked 'Where do you come from?'

'Pulpally'

Dr Nancy immediately jumped up from her seat and embraced the patient and cried aloud 'amma, amma, excuse me amma, I am Nancy your daughter'

Deepa Mariam George realized that the doctor whom she came to see was her daughter Nancy Thomas. She embraced her daughter and wept like a child and kissed Nancy on her cheeks several times.

'Amma what happened to you?' Nancy asked weeping.

'I'm not well for several years, met many doctors at Pulpally and Bathery but no relief. Occasional bleeding and severe back pain. Dr Jayadevan of Bathery asked me to meet you and gave me details of residence, phone number etc. and that is how I came here.'

'I'm happy, that I could meet my amma after so many years'

'I haven't seen you for the last 15 years. You have changed a lot, and I could not recognise you. Do you know what happened following your elopement. Your father sent some criminals to your house to kidnap you. They met with an accident and two people died and three people became seriously injured and the jeep also was completely damaged. Your papa spent about 25 lakhs by way of compensation, medical expense and repair charges of jeep etc. In that worry and tension he had an attack and was in hospital for about one month. Also he arranged a partition of the assets into five sections and nothing was set aside for you'. Fathers' share after his death will go to his sons and such a clause was added in the document in my case also.

'Amma, I don't want anything from you, God has given me a job and a good husband'. Nancy said and then took mother and the boy inside her house. Then Sosamma brought tea and snacks for them.

'Amma, I'll come after 20 minutes. Some patients are waiting outside and let me finish them.'

'OK, I'll be here'

Dr Nancy returned after half an hour. Then amma was relaxing in a bed and the boy sitting by her side and then Dr Nancy asked 'Amma who is this boy?'

'This is Jinosh the son of your brother Joyson.'

Nancy patted Jinosh and asked 'In which class are you studying?'

In X th standard'

'Good'

Nancy then went inside and brought Deepa and Jeeson and showed them to amma.

'Do you know grandma?' She asked Jeeson.

'No, I don't know'. Jeeson said Deepa looked at grandma with a smile on her face.

'Amma do you know their names, this is Jeeson and the other is Deepa'

Amma was surprised to hear that Nancy has given the name of her father and mother to her children.

'This's grandma, say Nameste to her' Nancy asked Jeeson and Deepa.

Then Jeeson and Deepa said 'Nameste grandma' and hugged her.

'How's Chachan (father)?'. Nancy asked. 'He is no more. He had a severe attack six months after the first and he passed away.

'Why didn't you inform me? Nancy broke into tears.

'I told everybody to send a telegram to you, but they refused.

'Sorry amma, my mind was like that of a insane person. You have brought me up and spent a lot of money for my education etc and still I could not show any love towards you. Now, I realize the mistake, but before that papa has left the world. How can I seek apology from him?'

'Leave it Nancy. He does not deserve any love from anybody because he is such a wicked person. He has done a lot of cruelties and God has given him the deserving punishment.' Amma consoled Nancy.

Nancy asked amma to stay with her for few days for conducting necessary investigation etc. and Jinosh was sent to Pulpally in the taxi by evening.

'Had my brothers in Delhi come for the funeral of papa.?'

'For funeral, they could not come, but for the prayer on 41st day of the demise, both of them with families arrived. Actually they wanted to meet you and planned to come to Trichur, but other relatives objected and that plan was shelved.'

'Prior to the marriage, I had sent letters to them, but they did not reply.' Nancy complained.

'Where is your husband?' Amma asked

'He used to come occasionally. He is running two hotels and a catering unit. He is also the State President of the Hoteliers Association. and is very busy. He is a very good personality. His father has spent about one crore for my MD and DGO. Now, I am Associate Professor and after some time I will become Professor and Head of the department. Those, who passed MBBS along with me without postgraduation, will continue as tutor till their retirement. My qualification is really very worthy and even after retirement I can work in any hospital and they will offer me any salary which I demand.' Nancy explained everything to amma in detail.

'I thought you've converted to Hinduism.'

'No, never. They're secular in nature and have no such thoughts about caste and religion. Sumesh is very broadminded and is willing to send me to church every Sunday, but I refused. Then, he tried to bring one framed portrait of Jesus Christ to me for prayer. He is not like we Christians.

'Is it true?'

'Yes, if a Christian marry a Hindu lady he will convert her before marriage and ensure that her share is given to her before marriage. These people are not like that.'.

'I can't believe what you say'.

'Amma, you please stay here with me for a period of four weeks and I will see that you are completely cured.'

She agreed and spoke to her son Joyson and other brothers in Delhi.

Deepa Mariam George was subjected to thorough investigation and it was diagnosed as fibroid uterus on the basis of lab tests and MRI scan. Hystrectomy operation was conducted within one week. On the day of operation Nancy's brother Joyson and family were available at the hospital. Sumesh also had come to the hospital and thus Sumesh met his brother in law Joyson for the first time after marriage. After operation she lay in the hospital for one week and then discharged.

Nancy said to her brother that minimum three weeks time was necessary for recuperation of health and mother had to continue at her residence during that period and he agreed. During the period of rest and recuperation Sumesh brought his mother, father and sister to calicut to see Nancy's mother. They spent a whole day with her and returned to Trichur in the evening.

Nancy's mother once said 'Had I known that Sumesh is such a good boy I would have persuaded my husband to arrange the marriage. Since he belonged to another community we treated him as enemy. To be matriculate and member of another eligion is not a crime. Further the Christians of today are the offsprings of one time Hindus. No body has come from Rome or Damascus.' Amma said.

Nancy's eyes became wet on hearing the discourse of mother,

After convalescence for a period of three weeks, Deepa Mariam George was subjected to a thorough check up and she was found to be OK and in better condition of health and hence taken to Pulpally by Joyson and family.

On hearing the operation of mother the two brothers arrived in Pulpally with their families. They wanted to participate in the death anniversary of their father also. Hence, Joyson arranged a prayer meeting in the orthodox church of Pulpally. Nancy and Sumesh were also invited to the function.

Sumesh and Nancy attended the function with their children and maid Sosamma. They knelt in the church and prayed for the peace and tranquility of the departed soul. After the function Nancy and Sumesh were taken to their house The Delhi brothers and their families befriended with Sumesh and they spoke to their mother 'I's difficult to see such a gentleman like him in our community. In one sense our sister Nancy is lucky.'

Sumesh and Nancy returned to Calicut after lunch and farewell to all their relatives and friends gathered there. Sumesh and family were invited to Delhi by Nancy's brothers.

On the return journey Jeeson asked a lot of questions to his parents 'Mummy are we christians?

Papa and mummy knelt in the church while praying and received blessings from the father.'

'We are neither Christians nor Hindus, but human beings. Religion is only a path and the ultimate aim of all religions are the welfare of the people. This can be achieved if we take any one of the different paths. So, the destination is same but path is different for different religions.' Nancy told Jeeson when the car was speeding past through the highway. After some time, they reached the ghat road. When car started descending through the ghat road Sumesh made a hearty laugh and made a humorous remark 'We are going through a path with full of hairpins and curves and does it reach our ultimate destination of one caste, one religion and one God'.

Hearing this, Dr Nancy made a hearty laugh and all of them broke into peals of laughter.

********* END *********

LIGHTHOUSE

After sunset, the beach road looked dark and deserted. The sea looked calm and a cool breeze kept blowing towards the beach. The lighthouse winked at a distance. Azeez was walking hurriedly to his house. Two Arabs came towards him, from the opposite direction in their traditional attire and walked past him and turned to the bylane leading to the pandikasala (godown). His thoughts were wandering somewhere, and hence, he did not notice them. Suddenly, he heard a loud scream of a woman. He stopped abruptly, and looked towards the beach, from where the cry was heard. In the twilight, he could see two boys dragging a girl along the beach. He ran to the spot and shouted.

'Who' s that?.'

The boys dropped the girl and fled.

Azeez looked at the girl closely and asked 'Who are you, what happened to you?'.

'I'm Zeenath Hamza's sister. They would have spoiled me if you hadn't come.'she sobbed.

'Don't worry, I am Azeez ...deep Azeez, yon neighbour'. Azeez consoled her.

'Allah had sent you here, otherwise they would have torn me to pieces.' She wailed.

'Zeenath get up, I will take you to your house.'

Azeez helped her to stand up. She looked haggard and continued sobbing. They climbed to the road from the beach and began to walk towards their houses.

'Do you know the boys, who molested you?' Azeez asked while walking.

'They are Rahim and Anwar.'

Azeez was shocked. Both of them were from the same same street and belonged to very rich families. Rahim the only son of Rehman Hajee and Anwar the eldest son of Moosa Thangal. They were pampered by their parents and hence they went astray. They are hardly 17 years of age and are roaming here and there after failing in SSLC.

'Zeenath, don't cry, nothing has happened to you. Nobody is going to know this incident.' Azeez consoled her and they walked through the dusky road briskly. The lighthouse winked at them at a distance.

'Why did you come here at this time'?.

'Uncle, uppa is serious and hence I went to umma at Barami's house, but she could not come since some guests have come to their house. Then I ran to meet Hamzakka(brother Hamza) in the porter office. They asked me to go and enquire in the Thangal's pandikasala. Then I went to pandikasala and there I was told that he had gone to load goods in a ship anchored in the outer sea and would not return for two days. While I was coming back, I saw two Arabs on the way, and I was afraid and tried to hide in the beach below, and then I was spotted by the criminals, who were sitting on the beach.' Zeenath said.

'Leave it, by the grace of Allah you are safe. Don't walk alone along this road after nightfall. Criminals are there everywhere and we have to be very careful in future.'

'yes uncle, I'll be very careful' Zeenath said.

'Why are you afraid of Arabs?, they are good and law abiding people'.

'Uncle, in school my friends used to tease me saying that my uppa will give me in marriage to Arabs. Is it true uncle?.

'No Zeenath, you will be given in marriage to a malabari muslim and not Arab. In olden times Arabs used to come to Calicut for trade and commerce and also for building new launches. They used to stay here for longer periods. In that case, they may take temporary wives from poor families by paying a huge amount as meher, to the parents of such ladies. Such marriages are called Arabikalliyanam (marriage of locals with Arabs). The Arabs will leave for their homeland after some time and then these ladies will become more or less like a widow and their life will be doomed. Since, they have not been divorced, they cannot remarry. The Arabs may come after many years or may not come. If they have children, the ladies will have to earn something for maintaining the children and themselves. Hence, most of them will go to work as maids in rich households. Nowaday, people are wary of such marriages and hence very few cases are reported now.

By this time, they had reached the house of Zeenath. Azeez went inside and talked to Sulaimanikka, the father of Zeenath and he was found to be unconscious. Azeez immediately, called a taxi and took the patient to beach hospital. Sulaimanikka was immediately admitted and Azeez helped him as bystander. Next day he was relieved by Zeenath and her mother Saima. Azeez left after paying some amount to Saima for hospital expenses.

Azeez did not say anything to his wife Rehana about the beach incident. He told her about the sudden illness of Sulaimanikka and consequent hospitalisation.

'Why are you looking dull and worried?' Rehana asked.

'I'm worried because I have to go back to the dweep.'

Rehana giggled and said 'It is heartening to hear that your love towards me has doubled after my coming to malabar.'

'Rehana, I am going to dweep only because of you, otherwise I would have resigned the job.'

Then, his son Irfan came running to him from his playmate Shanu and said 'Uppa don't go to dweep. (island). We don't want that job.'

Azeez looked at him and smiled.'What shall I tell your uppapa and ummama there in the dweep?'

'Ask them to come and live with us here.'

Azeez was busy the whole day. He had to take his mother to the hospital for routine checkup, go to sister's house at Feroke, purchase essential items to be taken to dweep and meeting some friends in the city.

That night, Azeez could not sleep. He lay awake reminiscent of the past, his childhood, education, job hunting, selection as assistant in the Lakkadives Administration office, Kavarathi, his love with a dweep girl and the follow up incidents till date.

Rehana was a sweet girl aged 17 studying in 10th standard at that time. She was the third daughter of an schoolmaster named Abdul Wahab. His wife Kousabi is a loving mother clad in burka and is very religious. Wahab master had three daughters out of which the elder two have been given in marriage to locals. They have a beautiful house in Kavarathi town and have two acres of Coconut grove in a distant uninhabited island. Occasionally Wahab master will visit the island in boat with some helpers to pluck the coconuts and bring them to Kavarathi. There are many shops there for taking coconuts without dehusking. Wahab master was getting a good income from his grove and recently he purchased some coconut plantation in a nearby island and these coconut trees were given in lease for jaggery tapping.

In Kavarathi town Azeez was staying in a lodge near the office along with some north indian friends. One day, while going to office he happened to see a girl in headscarf going to school with her friends. He liked her very much and straight away approached her parents. Wahab master was very happy to hear that Azeez was from mainland and that too from Calicut. His other daughters were given to locals doing small scale business such as pearl processing and printing press.

'we are happy to give Rehana to mainland. Please ask your parents to come with the proposal.

'OK, I'll speak to uppa (father) a regarding this and ask him to come to dweep.'

Azeez's father did not like the idea of dweep daughter in law and hence he told Azeez 'If you like the girl you marry her. It is difficult for me to climb the ladder to the ship. If you want to take somebody take your uncle Kunhahmed or brother in law Jaleel. Azeez took his college mate and cousin

Salam to dweep and spoke to Wahab master. From dweep Wahab master, and his two son in laws came to Calicut and the marriage was settled to a date after the annual examinations of Rehana.

For the marriage about fifteen people went to dweep from Calicut. They included Azeez's sister Shamlar and husband, uncle Kunhahmed and wife, cousin Salam, and brother of Zeenath Mr. Hamza etc. It was the first journey in ship for most of them and they vomited and suffered a lot due to seasickness. Some of them found it very difficult to descend to the boat due to heavy rocking of the boat, since sea was rough.

After marriage, Wahab master did not permit him to take a rented house and compelled him to stay with them. Rehana was very shy and did not show her face outside. She always covered her face with head scarf. After a couple of days, Wahab master took them to see their coconut groves in a boat. Kousabi and their eldest daughter Fatima accomanied them. They had taken food and water with them. It was a wonderful experience. They spent a lot of time in the stillness of the uninhabited island. The beauty of the sylvan beach and surging waves is indescribable. On the way back they have seen some coral reefs and a number of atolls.

One day Rehana asked Azeez 'Azeezka do you know the history of these islands?'

'I have heard that you are migrants from Kannur'.

'Yes, it is true. I have heard Bapa saying to a malabari friend doing business here that these islands were owned by Kannur Raja and later it was given to Arakkal Royal family. It was during their rule the migration was encouraged. At the time of migration, the peeople were Hindua but with the contact with Arabian seafarers the entire population embraced Islam. Bapa has also told me about soofi saints who visited these islands during olden days. Azeez heard every thing with rapt attention and then he narrated the history of his own coastal village at Calicut.

'There is a big mosque there and it resembled a temple. People used to say that it is the oldest mosque in malabar. The name of the road in front of the mosque is thrikovil lane. The people of this village is very opulent and you will be surprised to see sprawling houses which are symbols of their aristocracy and wealth. The people still follow marumakkathayam(a system which was prevalent in Hindu society especially among nair community) and joint family system is still prevalent. There are some houses with 150 to 200 members. For marriage of a girl one room will be set apart for the couple permanently and the groom has to live in that house. It is obvious that the people of this area were Hindus in olden days and embraced Islam en masse. With the continuous contact with Arab traders or with the invasion of Tipp, the entire population embraced Islam. They are financially well off. No documentary evidence is available to establish this theory and it is only hearsay. Some old people used to say that the entire people embraced Islam some 200 years ago.

Rehana was eager to see the village of Azeez and she expressed her desire to go to Calicut and Azeez consented. Azeez took two week's leave and proceeded to Calicut with Rehana. Rehana was travelling in a ship for the first time and it was a terrifying experience. They have to go in a boat from Kavarathi port and climb to the ship anchored at outer sea by means of hanging ladder. If the ship is to Bepore they have to climb down at Bepore by means of the same ladder to boat standing below The. Boat will be rocking, when people jump into the boat from the ladder. Unless we are very careful, there is every risk of falling into the sea. If the ship is to Cochin, we can reach the wharf by means of a small bridge connecting the ship and the wharf. The ship was to Cochin and hence Rehana had to struggle only at Kavarathi. While travelling to Cochin Azeez had given her one tablet before boarding the ship to avoid sea sickness and still Rehana was in a dazed mood after vomiting once.

After reaching Cochin, they rested for some time in the Laccadives liaison office and then returned to Calicut by train. Rehana can not forget the first experience in ship. But her fear was dispelled, when she travelled many times in ship from Calicut to Lakshadeep and back.

Rehana was overjoyed on reaching mainland. It took about four hours for the train to reach Calicut. On the way, she was enjoying the landscape, hills, rivers, bridges, paddy fields, coconut groves, arecanut plantation, plantains, various types of cars, buses, huts and multi storeyed houses and people in various types of dress and costumes, temples, mosques and churches. She thought how different is mainland compared to her tiny island with only coconut trees and people of one religion.

The parents of Azeez showed great love and affection towards the daughter in law. Rehana in return loved them very much and did everything for them. She applied coconut oil on the head of her father in law, prepared hot water for him, massaged mother in law and helped her to bathe in hot water. Rahana was like a daughter to Moideen and Razia from the day of her arrival.

'My malayalam is entirely different from yours, but I can fully understand what you say.' Rehana once said to her mother in law. But language was not a barrier between them. The language of love was different and they did not have any difficulty to follow her language.

Rehana befriended the ladies in the neighbourhood and they spoke high of that dweep girl. They called her as dweep Rehana just as they called Azeez as dweep Azeez.

'Will you stay here permanently' the village ladies asked her.

'We'll go back after two weeks' Rehana said.

Then, She did not realise that one day she will be a permanent resident of that village. In olden days, people depended entirely on wireless for sending and receiving messages to dweep and back. There was a wireless station at Vellayil with one Engineer and several wireless operators and also there was a wireless station at Kavarathi with similar staff pattern. Some of the staff deputed to the island have married local girls and settled there after being converted to Islam. It is old story, and after the advent of satellite communication and mobile phones the scenario has undergone a sea change and the wireless towers and the operating staff were made obsolete. With mobile phones and internet the island has come closer to mainland and communication has become very cheap, easy and comfortable.

Azeez took Rehana to many sightseeing places such as Wynad, Mysore, and Ooty. After two week stay at Calicut they returned to the island. Moideen and Razia became very sad when Rehana left for dweep.

Rehana became pregnant, and the delivery was conducted at Kavarathi hospital and it was a baby boy. Azeez's parents did not come to see the new born child. Years rolled by and Irfan has become 5 years old and he was admitted to an english medium school there. When Irfan was studying in 2nd standard Azeez's father Moideen expired, and mother Razia became paralysed. She was completely bedridden and required the help of somebody for her personal needs. Azeez came to Calicut with famiy, on hearing the death of father and Rehana was permanently held up there. Irfen was transferred to an english medium school in Calicut city. Azeez stayed back in the island and he did not want to resign the job without getting another in the mainland.

Azeez had come to Calicut on one week leave and he had to go back on the following day. He had hectic activities before the return journey. Rehana was busy in making sweets for taking to dweep and Irfan was playing with his friend Akbar who was his classmate. After returning from school they were playing together in the courtyard of their house for hours.

'Rehana I'm going to sister's house and will be back very late' Azeez told Rehana.

'Uppa I'll come with you to Ferook"

'No irfan this time I have to go to many other places and can't take you now. Next time I will definitely take you there'.

Azeez returned from the journey by 8.30 pm. Irfan had gone to sleep by that time and Rehana was waiting for him.

'Azeezka one cardboard box is required for packing the sweets' Rehana said.

Azeez again went out, and returned home after some time with a cardboard box. When he came inside his face was found to be very tense and terrified. Seeing the tension on his face Rehana asked.' Azeezka what happened? you look very tense?

'At the grocery shop I had an altercation with some scoundrels.'

'Who was it?'

'I don't know their names, but they are from the same street. They are drug addicts and criminals. They quarrelled with me without any provocation and threatened me with dire consequences'

'If you know them go to their houses and complain to their parents'.

'Whose Parents?, I don't think they have any control over them, otherwise they will not behave like this'.

'Then give a police complaint'

'No Rehana they are debauchers and criminals. We can not fight with them. They'll spoil our family if I do anything like that'.

'We should teach them a lesson'.

'How? leave it. Their parents have enough clout and hence the police will not do anything for us'. Azeez then stopped that conversation abruptly and started to pack the sweets in the cardboard box.

Next day, Azeez left by 6 pm. After Azeez left Rehana had a foreboding, a kind of fear and anxiety gripped her. She had a nightmare in the sleep and suddenly got up from sleep and started trembling. She clearly saw somebody stabbing Azeez with a dagger and his scream fell on her ear. It became feeble and feeble and finally died away when she got up. She looked around and found Irfan sleeping peacefully near her. She then went to the kitchen and drank some cold water and tried to sleep again. She then closed her eyes and prayed to Allah 'Nothing untoward should happen to Azeez. Please protect him from all evils and devils'.

Azeez was stranded at Cochin for two days due to some technical problem to the ship. Finally, when he boarded the ship the sea was found to be very rough, When Azeez called Rehana after reaching dweep she was very much relieved. She did not mention anything about the nightmare.

After one week Azeez called Rehana again. Then she was in a terrified state and was shivering with fear and put down the receiver after saying one or two words. There was no usual gaiety in the speech and was trembling with fear.

Next day, Azeez called again, but she did not take the receiver, After ringing for a long time it stopped. Then Azeez rang up again and Irfan took the phone.

'Irfan where's umma? she doesn't take the receiver'

'Uppa, umma is not well she is not talking to anybody'

Then Azeez called his sister and asked her to go to their house, see Rehana and ring back. She immediately went and met Rehana and called back. 'Ikka (brother) she is gripped by some kind of fear. She is simply lying in the bed covered by blanket and did not answer my questions. There is no usual gaiety or cheerfulness on her face but some kind of dread. She abhors attending telephone calls and does not do any work in the house.'

'You stay there till I come and inform brother in law about it'

Azeez immediately applied for one month leave and left for Calicut. He did not inform Wahab master anything about the plight of Rehana.

Azeez's mind sank within him on seeing the plight of Rehana. She has not bathed for days. Her hair was grizzly. She did not talk to Azeez and always lay in bed. She looked blank and frightened.

He talked to umma and she had a lot of complaints about Rehana.'She does not give me food and water and I am rotting here.'

'Umma she's not well'.

That night she refused to sleep with Azeez and lay on a sheet spread on the floor.

Next day, Azeez took her to a lady psychologist in the city. She spoke to her secretly for about one hour. But the lady did not get any clue. She kept on saying that there are a lot of enemies for Azeez and they are trying to kill him. Also she was getting nightmares daily in which somebody was walking with a dagger to kill Azeez. If Azeez was killed the next moment she would die by hanging. The psychologist said that there would be something behind her fear. Then she asked Azeez 'Have you got enemies here?'

'Yes, I had some altercation with some antisocial elements in our street one day, but after that there has been no further quarrel or threat.

'This may be the reason for her fear, but her problem has to be analysed thoroughly. Then only I can find out a remedy. Please keep a watch on her movements and come after two days'.

After coming back from the psychologist Rehana lay on the floor in the same sheet and slept. Azeez did all the domestic chores including feeding and tidying of mother and Rehana.

After 2 days, they met the psychologist again and this time she counselled for about one hour on various problems of housewives and asked her to face it boldly. 'There may be rubs and frictions in everyday life but it should not be taken seriously. Regarding the enemies, I want to say that we will have to quarrel with several people in daily life but they do not keep the enmity for long and will not come to kill. So be assured that Azeez is safe and no body will kill him'.

While returning home, she was cheerful but after reaching home she became morose and recluse again. Hence next day he met a psychiatrist and discussed the case of Rehana He advised him to take her to a famous counselling centre run by a charitable trust at Trichur. He said the root cause of the fear has to be analysed by hypnotic techniques and then the remedy can be suggested.

Mother and Irfan were taken to sister's house at Feroke and Rehana was taken to the counselling centre at Trichur. They stayed in the counselling centre for five days. In the initial stages she was told that there would be problems in daily life and was taught how to tackle them. She was asked to explain her own experiences and the methods employed by her to tackle the same. for three days they were studying her mind and on the fourth day she was subjected to hypnotic sleep. she was asked questions about the cause of her worry and fear. After about two hours, the questioning was completed and they arrived at a decision as to what is the root cause of the problem. Later, Azeez was briefed by the doctor and psychologist.

'Some two persons came to the house and molested her. They came to make a call to the exchange to register a complaint against their faulty connection and after entering the house they closed the door and molested her. She does not know the names of the persons and she has not seen them before. After that incident, they called her two days consecutively and threatened her with dire consequences if she told the incident to anybody else. She felt guilty conscience and attempted to end her life, but it did not succeed. Her mind made her a patient in an effort to conceal the guilty feeling.'

'Can we file a police complaint in this regard.?' Azeez asked

'Of course, but that will cause more problems. The police will question her continuously and that may aggravate her problem. Please avoid it. Further it will cause a stigma for you and your family.'Please relocate her to somewhere else for the time being and that is the only remedy in this case. If the environment is changed she will slowly become normal.

Azeez thought of many ways to avenge the culprits and waited for an appropriate time. They returned to calicut on the fifth day, stayed one night in their house and the next day Azeez took Rehana r to Feroke and apprised sister and brother in law every thing. He returned to dweep after expiry of leave. He will ring up sister everyday and after one week Shamla said that there was slight improvement in Rehana's condition. By two weeks she became completely normal and the old gaiety and cheerfulness returned to her face. Azeez thanked Allah for his help and told Wahab master and Saima about the illness and recovery of Rehana.

Azeez purchased a small plot from the property of brother in law at Feroke and constructed a small house there and moved to that house. One day, he went to his old house and hung a board there with incription 'HOUSE FOR SALE-contact Mob No. 94476825- -. Many people contacted him and one day, the Barami himself called him and offered a high price. The deal was finally settled and within one month registration was done.

After six months, a news was reported by all leading newspapers that an accident occurred on the beach road, Calicut on the night of a friday. Two boys travelling on bike were knocked down by a speeding lorry and they were admitted with serious head injuries in the medical college hospital, Calicut. The names of the injured are found to be Rahim and Anwar and their condition is reported to be very serious.

********* END *********

STEEL CITY

The first steel city of India lay drowsily, in the Chathisgarh tribal plains of Madhya Pradesh. It is a silent township, without any big vehicles like bus or mini bus and the only conveyance available is, three wheeler open tempo for commutation of people, in the township. It is a microcosm of India, with people from all states and regions. The local tribal people were very backward in education and skills and hence their representation in government service and organizations, both government and private was negligible. They are over innocent and straightforward and hence had to face discrimination in all fields, But now, things have changed and they have achieved great strides in education, and hence, there is great improvement in the poverty and unemployment of these hapless people. The whole area belonged to the steel plant and with their permission many schools, and business establishments have sprung up in all sectors. In addition to this, many temples, churches and mosques have been constructed in goverment land and the people lived in love, amity and co operation.

.

It was a winter evening, in the Bhilai township, in the year 1984. There was freezing cold outside and people were venturing outside wearing sweaters and mufflers. The residential quarter of the Town Administrator of the steel plant, is situated in the first floor of a two storey building in sector I, and from the balcony of this quarter, the power house and the railway station can be seen. There is an open ground in front of the quarters, and always a pleasant wind kept blowing from the north. One day, at about 8 pm, Major Sukumaran, Town Administrator of thei steel plant, went to the balcony and stood there for some time looking outside. The wind kept blowing, and his dress fluttered heavily, and his mind slowly slipped into a reverie.

. He is now one of the most important, and powerful officers of the steel plant. He worked for many years in army as jawan, and then officer, fought with enemy, faced death on many occasions and retired as Major in 1980. He then went to Bhilai, where his brother Ramankutty was working as crane operator in the steel plant He was accompanied by his family and they stayed with brother's family for a short period, since there was no other private accommodations within the premises of the plant.

Major Sukumaran came to know that there is a vacancy of Town Administrator in the plant, and he applied for the same and got selected, since it is a post exclusively for the tough guys, mainly from the army. Then, he was allotted a very nice quarter in sector I. He was bold and efficient and was in the good books of the MD He has to look after about forty thousand staff quarters in Bhilai and other installations within the township. During his tenure, he has evicted with an iron hand many mafias, who had illegally taken possession of Plant's quarters. There was rampant corruption in the allotment and maintenance of quarters, since the opening of the plant. After taking over, he made a thorough study of the problems of his department, and made the allotment of quarters most transparent and reduced corruption in the department to the minimum.

Sukumaran's wife was a Punjabi. During his service in Punjab he had a boss named Col. Surinder Singh. He lost one leg in the war of 1965 with Pakistan, and his family lived in Jalandhar. In the war, Sukumaran also had been wounded seriously and was in army's command hospital at Pune for a long time and finally discharged. He was given leave for two months, for recuperation of health, and during this time he went to the house of his boss at Jallandhar. He was received with great love and affection. He spent the whole day in that family with Col Singh and his family was surprised to know that he had a daughter of marriageable age called. Amritha Kaur. Sukumaran liked her very much, and wanted to marry her. Col. Surinder singh, his wife and his son Amarinder had no objection. At that time, Sukumaran was only Lieutenant and he was inducted into the service through short service commission, when he was a jawan. After joining duty at Ambala, he married Amritha Kaur in a simple function which was attended mainly by service personnel. After 15 years of service, he retired from service in the year 1980 from Jammu. Sukumaran tried to take AMIE for extension of service, but could not complete it, and hence had to retire after fifteen years. At that time, he had three daughters named Sindhu, Sumana and Sujaya. After retirement from army, he moved to Bhilai, the steel city of India.

The steel city of Bhilai has lost the old charm and pride, with the opening of the mega steel plant at Bokaro. In recent times, a lot of other steel plants have sprung up like Rourkala, Salem,. Vizag etc. In the olden times, this was the first steel plant in government sector and there was a large number of malayalees and other south indians like, Tamil, Telugu and Kannada in the work force. The giant Jamshedpur steel plant is in TATA's hands and that is one of the oldest steel plants of India.

During the the period 1950-60, there was a gold rush from Kerala to that place in MP called Bhilai. Construction work of the factory was going on and also the work of quarters for the workers and executives. An uneducated youth named Ramankutty reached Bhilai, from Chalakudy in Kerala, and started work as a labourer in the Rajara mines of Bhilai steel plant. Later, he was transferred from the mines to steel plant. At Rajara, he was living in temporary shed and was happy in getting a job. Years rolled by, and Ramankutty is now crane operator in the steel rolling mill. Now, he has quarters, family and children in sector I. Later, his brother Sukumaran and family came there, and stayed with them for a short period.

Ramankuttty, purchased a hotel named Supriya from a Punjabi, and it was near sector I and entrusted it to his son Preman, who was not good at studies. His second son Pradeep started a workshop, for trucks and tractors. Supriya hotel had big business for about one year, and then declined. One day Ramankutty went to the hotel and studied the problems. Recently, a new hotel named Kerala hotel has been opened in the vicinity, but the real problem was something else. Preman had a love affair with a Telugu girl, and he is not sitting in the counter and goes behind her and spends a lot of money for her. He brought his nephew Aravindan from Irinjalakuda and asked him to supervise the hotel and take care of cash counter in the absence of Preman. But nothing worked. The hotel ended in big failure, and it had to be sold to a Tamilian for a small sum. After takeover by the new management, business boosted again. Preman married the Telugu girl who was studying for degree in Raipur. Even though, he became jobless, she got a job in the plant and became a source of income. Then, Preman turned to a job of bringing silk saris from Banaras and selling them through agents, in the houses of township and found a small source of income. Pradeep was very able and he made a good income from his workshop and the same was paid to his father.

At that time, there was an accident in the factory. There was an explosion and the overhead crane cabin was damaged with molten steel thrown from the bucket (ladle) and Ramankutty and his assistant sustained serious injuries. They were immediately sent to Vellore and was in hospital for about six months. An enquiry was conducted by the plant and found that the bucket contained water due to rains in the previous night and without removing the water molten steel was poured to it and then an explosion occurred and the molten metal in the ladle was thrown upwards and struck the moving cabin. Following this, an order was issued by the MD that the buckets should not be kept outside during night and they should be checked before pouring molten steel in buckets.

When discharged from hospital, Ramankutty was almost like a leper with all fingers chopped off and patches of white all over the body due to burn injuries. He was incapable of doing any work and hence removed from service with some compensation and pension benefits. He had to vacate the quarters also. Hence he purchased about 10 acres of farm lands in far away village and shifted residence to that place. The crop was good for one year but failed consecutively for three years and the same had to be disposed off. Preman's wife was allotted a quarter and hence Preman and family moved to the new quarter and the old one was vacated. Pradeep also moved to the new quarter. When the farmland was disposed off, Ramankutty and his wife also came and stayed with Preman and family.

Major Sukumaran was sincere in his work and hence faced many threats and attacks. One day he went to vacate an illegal occupant of a quarter with only one assistant, It was occupied by a narcotics seller named Karthar singh. When asked to vacate he and his brothers came out with lethal weapons and attacked the Major. But, he escaped since he had taken his revolver with him and still he got a blow on his head. When the mafias attacked with weapons, his assistant ran away and escaped.

One day, a malayali named Joseph illegally occupied a vacant quarter and Sukumaran got information about this. He immediately went to the spot, and evicted the quarter. Mr Joseph did not make any resistance and went away. Later, Mr Joseph was dismissed from service on the report of Mr Sukumaran. The association took up this case and he was reinstated later.

After one month, the MD received an anonymous letter saying that Mr Sukumaran has allowed an unauthorised workshop owned by his own nephew Mr. Pradeep in plant's land. Sukumaran swung into action immediately, demolished the shed and confiscated the machinery. From that day onwards, Ramankutty and his family became an enemy of his own brother Sukumaran.

Then, Pradeep and Preman started a liquor business. The entire liquor business in that district is the monopoly of Sardars. They had so much money, clout and men and nobody can beat them. Pradeep got two shops in auction, but the sardars did not permit them to run it. One day, a group of men came in truck with swords and daggers and completely demolished their shops and taken away furniture etc. A police complaint was registered but nothing happened. Police could not touch any of the criminals.

Sukumaran came to know of this incident and went to the house of Preman and made enquiries. Even though, they were enemies they spoke every thing to Sukumaran. They also informed him of an illegal quarter used by the sardars for stocking liquor.

Next day, that quarter was raided by Sukumaran and party with the help of police. Two sardars were arrested and a lot of liquor bottles were seized. It was a huge blow to the liquor barons and they threatened him with dire onsequences. One day, his quarter was attacked by goons and Sukumaran got bullet injuries on his elbow and they could not do much damage to the house.. because police arrived on the spot within minutes. The assailants escaped, when police arrived.

Immediately Sukumaran was taken to the hospital and the bullet recovered. He had to take rest for about one week. Even though, a case was registered no one was arrested.

Every day, many recommendations will come from the MD, other officers, associations and the politicians, Since, he can not displease them he did everything within the legal ambit. He was not afraid of anybody, and will not take bribe or encourage corruption in his office. He did not do any unauthorised or illegal thing. He resisted all such attempts from superiors with the reply 'I am a soldier and don't compel me in this case'. Quarters were issued strictly on the basis of seniority and eligibility. Unauthorised use of quarters was strictly curbed and immediate action was taken in all detected cases. Maintenance of these quarters were carried out regularly with minimum expenditure since each and every case was supervised by the Town Administrator personally.

For State Officers, like Dy Commisioner, Supdt of Police, Judges and other judicial Officers beautiful quarters have been given, free of rent. For these quarters, frequent maintenance and renovation have to be carried out, as per directions of the MD, since, they are responsible for the discipline and law and order situations of the township.

Maj. Sukumaran's daughters Sindhu and Sumana were studying in Raipur. During this time, Sindhu was in love with a Punjabi boy, But after some time, he discontinued his studies and left to Delhi since his father died in the riot of 1984. Sindhu could not complete her education and returned home in a state of mental aberration. Sumana continued her studies in the same college. Sujaya was in 12th and she came out in first class in higher secondary and was also admitted to the same college in Raipur.

In the meanwhile, many proposals came for Sindhu but she did not agree and said 'I don't want to marry. You can give Sumana in marriage if anybody comes next'.. After some time, a Punjabi Hindu boy came and Sumana liked him and that marriage was fixed. The parents of the boy came and met Sukumaran and Amritha Kaur and both sides liked the alliance, The father of the boy was a doctor named Sethi practising in a room near the market. This marriage was conducted with great pomp and extravaganza in an auditorium in the township. After marriage Sumana was taken to their house at Lucknow.

After a period of one year, Sujaya also was married. The groom in this case was a Bengali settled in Bhilai. The groom's father was a retired Officer and they have a house near Durg. The boy was working in Railways and presently working in Durg station. Sujaya also was happy in the alliance. But Sindu was in disappointment even though she did not express it in public.

One day, a Chethisgadi lady came and complained to Sukumaran 'Sir, I have been cheated by Ram Singh working in your office. I am pregnant and he says he can not marry me. If he does not marry me I will commit suicide by jumping in front of the train'

Sukumaran met Mr Singh and said 'Ram Singh have you any connection with a Chethisgadi girl? She says she'll commit suicide if you do not marry her. Their people will not accept her since she is pregnant'

'It's true that I'm in love with her, but I can't marry her since she's a tribal girl'

'You should have thought about it before you spoiled her. She's pregnant'

This matter was brought to the notice of the MD also and he said 'Don't leave him. You will have all support from me in this regard'

Mr. Sukumaran spoke to the Chethisgadi association people and asked them to file a case against Ram Singh and they did as he advised them. By this time she had given birth to a baby boy. The court examined many witnesses and the lady and the court passed orders that the child belonged to Ram Singh. He had to accept her as wife after birth of the son. Sukumaran immediately allotted a family quarter for Ram Singh and thus that problem was settled.

Pradeep was sitting idle after the flop of liquor business. He had lost a huge amount in that business. He came and requested his uncle to help him find out a livelihood. Then Sukumaran asked him to take a passport and through the brother of Amritha Kaur sent him to Canada where he got a job in Electricity department.

Sukumaran had forgotten Kerala. After becoming a jawan in Indian army, he was outside for many years. When father and mother expired he could not go home. That pain is still there in his mind and wanted a redemption for the mistakes done unknowingly. He wanted to go to his native place. But there is no house there for him to go and stay. He had a sister and it is not known whether she is alive or dead.

He booked three tickets by train to Chalakudy. Amritha and Sindhu accompanied him. They got down at Chalakudy station and went in search of his house. It was on the bank of Chalakudy river near the bridge. They went to the place, but there was no house there. Near that site there is a temple and the house of one Ramakrishna Thampuran belonging to Cochin Royal family. He went to that Kovilakam and enquired. A boy came out and talked to him. He said that 'I am Nandakumar and papa has gone to Trichur and as far as I know that house and property were sold by their sister to a businessman called Peter'. Sukumaran then went to his sister's house at Pudukad. She was still alive and had a very big house there. She is laid up with old age, but recognised her brother and embraced him and wept. Sukumaran also wept with his sister. Sindhu touched her feet and Amritha kissed her cheeks.

'Where were you all these years? We expected that you will come to see father and mother when they were ailing. You did not come even for their funeral, or after that. God's wrath will fall on your head for such sins'

'Chechi I was in hospital due to injuries sustained in the war. I want to do penance for my sins. What shall I do for this?'

'You go to Alwaye temple and do offering and pray for their souls to rest in peace'

'OK chechi, I'll do it" Said Sukumaran.

He stayed there for two days, and visited some of the relatives living in that vicinity. He and family visited Alwaye temple, on the bank of the river Periyar, and did bali and shradh rites, and poojas for the peace and salvation of the departed souls. He also gave offerings to the temple as advised by his sister and then paid a visit to the Ashram, founded by Sree Narayana Guru, on the bank of Periyar, at Alwaye.

He and family returned to Pudukkad and wanted to return to Bhilai after two days. But sister compelled them to stay there for some more days. His niece's son Rajiv was with them. He is an Ayurvedic doctor practising in a clinic there. He is a tall and handsome boy with post graduation in Ayurveda. Sindhu liked him and spoke to him in English for quite a long time. Amritha also liked him. Sukumaran asked 'Do you like him? If so, we can propose.'

Sindhu smiled and said 'Yes'

Sukumaran spoke to his sister and expressed his wish, and she was in favour of that alliance. Thus, in a short time a marriage was arranged and Sindhu was given in marriage to Rajiv and thus her agony was solved. They stayed there for two weeks, and returned to Bhilai by Bilaspur Express leaving Sindhu there with Rajiv.

When they reached Bhilai, the MD had changed. The new MD is very tough to subordinates, and the old conducive atmosphere has completely changed. Sukumaran joined duty and met MD and discussed for a long time regarding various issues. Sukumaran cleared all the pending files.

One day, a call came from MD's office and MD himself came on the line and said 'My son's friend one Rawat is coming to Bhilai to expand his business. Since no other accommodation is available here, you please allot a vacant quarter unofficially. Their company is supplying some raw materials to the plant. He will stay here for six months, and go back. Another thing the SP had called sometime back and wanted a better accommodation and that too in sector I. The CJM also had spoken to me for getting a more spacious accommodation.

'Sorry Sir, don't compel me to allot quarters unofficially. Regarding the demand of SP and CJM

I'll do as desired at the earliest '.

'OK, leave it if you can not do it'

After this, he was compelled to do many unauthorised things but he resisted. Thus the relation between the MD and Town Administrator became very strained and MD began to show open hostility towards him. He was going through difficult days. He is reporting to the MD and if MD's support is lacking, he can not do anything at all.

One day, Sukumaran visited the house of his brother and was surprised to hear that they have moved to a rented house near the drainage canal.

'Why did he shift to a rented accommodation and that too near the drainage canal?' He asked Preman.

'Uncle, they've quarrelled with my wife and left without saying anything' Preman said.

'Bring them back' Sukumaran shouted.

'Deepika is now an Officer. They're ill treating her unnecessarily on all issues. She kept quiet for years and finally she exploded' I'm doing all the household works, looking after the children and then go to work. I've no time to nurse you. Why don't you employ a lady to nurse you'. Then they got angry and left. This is what happened.

Sukumaran left the house without saying anything else. Next day, he visited his brother in the new premises. The condition was very pathetic. The canal is full of filth and dirt of the township and it is flowing by the side of the house. They are drawing water from a well near the canal. The house is a single room tenement.

'Suku, we want to die as early as possible. People treat me as leper and do not come near me and there is a social boycott in this area. Deepika is an officer now, and treats us very badly' His brother lamented. Sukumaran heard everything patiently. 'Suku Pradeep has married a Canadian girl and he had sent some money to us' Ramankutty said when Sukumaran was about to leave.

Sukumaran was very gloom, when he reached home and wife asked 'What happened, you look depressed?'

'A lot of problems. Son could not look after his parents and hence they left the house and moved to a wretched and filthy place. We can not do anything in this regard'

That night Sukumaran could not sleep. He told his wife all about his problems in the office and sought her advice.

'Don't fight with MD. It'll make your life horrible. Tell him the difficulties and if he compels you again request him to give something in writing' Amritha said.

'But he won't give anything in writing. Then what can I do?'

He feared that he'll be caught by the CBI, if he did anything wrong and others will go unscathed and scot free. Finally, he thought for a long time, considered all pros and cons and took a wise decision to seek VRS and go without any blemish in his service and Amritha supported him in this decision.

Next da, Sukumaran submitted the application for VRS and the same was approved. He did not wait for any send off. He met the MD and other officers and friends and said goodby to all.

He bought a small plot, near the house of Sujaya, at Durg, and constructed a 4 bedroom house there. Till then, he lived in a rented house in Durg town. The house was named as Amritha home. For the housewarming ceremony, all his daughters and their husbands had come. They wished a long and peaceful life to Major Sukumaran and Amritha Kaur.

********* END *********

WYNAD BRIDE

In Alappey, there is an old government school on the bank of the backwaters. Most of the students and teachers come to this school in boats from far away places. Vijayanunni master is the seniormost teacher in the high school section and he has been waiting for the HM promotion for many years. His house is located on an isolated island, which has no road access to the mainland. He comes to the school every day in boat.

One day, when he reported for duty the HM gave him a cover and it was his promotion order to a school in far away Wynad district. He exulted on reading the order, and took leave and returned home.

He straight away went to his ancestral house, where his sister Sobha and children are living. His father Padmanabhan Nair is also staying with them. Vijayanunni master is leading a lonely life in a small house constructed in the same compound. He had married a lady from Haripad, but separated some twenty years back on a minor issue.

After that, he never thought of marriage or family and lived for his sister and father.

'Chechi, I've become headmaster' Vijayanunni said in great eccstacy.

Sobha was engaged in some domestic work and she ran out of kitchen to congratulate his beloved brother.

She congratulated her brother with great warmth and love.

Sobha shouted at the top of her voice, and Anil and Babymol rushed to the house from their vegetable garden in the compound.

'Hearty congratulations' they greeted uncle and jumped in joy.

Vijayanunni master went to his father and touched his feet. Padmanabhan Nair is bedridden and he tried to rise on hearing the good news.

'This's really a good news and I congratulate you with all my heart. Where's your posting?' asked father.

'Wynad'

'From Alappey, Wynad is a far away place, but don't hesitate to go. After joining duty, you should marry again. To lead a lonely life is very horrible. I am responsible for your present loneliness and mental agony.' Padmanabhan Nair sobbed silently pressing his face on the pillow.

Vijayanunni went to his house and made hectic arrangements for Wynad journey.

The staff and students of his school gave him a warm send off. Many of the teachers and students spoke about his sincerity, creativity, social and humanitarian activities. One student waxed eloquent on his literary works in the field of short stories and hoped that he will become a great novelist after reaching the beautiful place Wynad. His short stories reflected his loneliness and despair in personal life. He was a lover of nature, and his posting in the enchanting place, will awaken his literary instincts and like Wordsworth he will write on the beauty of nature and will become a great story teller.

Vijayanunni master in his reply mentioned, that he is not a writer but a lover of nature. He admitted that, some of his stories have been published in some journals but that was not enough to become a writer. He also referred to his lonely life. 'I loved my wife very much and still we were separated and this is called fate or destiny'.

Vijayanunni master packed everything in a suitcase and handbag, locked the house and handed over the key to sister sobha. She had made some sweets and gave him a cover, at the time of departure and said 'Many people from this area have migrated to Wynad years ago and they include some of our very close relatives. I will collect their addresses and forward to you later' Sobha said

After saying goodbye to father, Vijayanunni left to Alappey in a boat. His nephew Anil accompanied him up to Alappey bus stand.

After reaching Kalpetta, Vijanunni master took a room in a hotel, made a fresh up and went straight to the school which was in a valley at the foot of a mountain.

The incumbent HM was one Jagadambal and on being relieved she went back to her home district Trivandrum.

After taking over, Vijayanunni master befriended almost all teachers in the high school section and made enquiries about the performance of the school during the previous years. They did not give any direct reply and said 'Performance in SSLC is very poor'

'How many percent tell me clearly'

'33% last year and before that 28 %' replied Viswanathan master with a blush on his face.

'It's very poor. We've to make a concerted effort to improve the result in future.' Vijayanunni master said.

'OK sir, we can try'. all teachers said in unison.

'The house occupied by Jagadambal teacher is vacant and you can stay there if you want' Viswanathan master said'

'OK, thank you master'.

The school is situated on a hillock and if we look from a vantage point we will get a panoramic view of the mountain' Viswanathan master told HM.

Viswanathan master took HM to that point and showed him the mesmerizing sight. HM stood there for a long time looking at the heavenly beauty unfolded in front of him. Chains of mountains stretching for kilometres with their flora and fauna bathing in the golden aura of setting sun.

'I want to go to the top of those mountains and take photos from there. The view from here is really breathtaking, intoxicating, enchanting, glorious and heavenly' HM said

'If you want we can climb those mountains one day. I've gone there many times. Only thing is that a four wheeler jeep is necessary to go there.' Viswanathan master said.

'I 've not seen such scenic beauty anywhere before. It is really wonderful!.' HM said.

'Sir, we can go to the house. I've kept the key with me'

'OK, let us go'

They got into an auto with luggage and went there. The house is on the slope of a hill and it is surrounded by tea estates. From the house they can see ladies plucking leaves with baskets on their back.

The house has two bedrooms, sitting room, dining, kitchen etc. It has a deep well and it will not dry up even during hottest summer. All wells in the vicinity will dry up and people used to say that an underground stream is flowing through the side of this house.

HM liked the house and said 'Viswanathan master how can I repay you for this help'

'It's my duty. You can ask me anything and I'll get it done within no time. I don't want anything in return. It is a pleasure to help people like you.'

'Viswanathan master hereafter I will call you Wiswam and that is easy to pronounce.'

'OK, as you like. I' ll call you only HM'

'OK, that's good. By the by are you a native of this place?'

'I'm also a Travancorean like you. I hail from Pathanamthitta and came here as Malayalam teacher years back, married a lady from here and settled here. After retirement sometimes I'll go back to my native village or remain here till death.' Viswam master became very emotional and began to cry like a child and tears streaked down through his cheek and wet his shirt and dhothi.

'Are you so attached to this place?' HM asked.'

'I'd an infatuation to this place after reading Vishakannyaka and Veerakannyaka of SK Pottekkad. Alos, I'd read so many other books of fiction of terror and ghosts with the backdrop of Wynad.

In addition to this, I'd read many stories of actual migration, hunting for land, wealth and sex and the ultimate human tragedy. Every estate, every plantation, every hill and valley will have to say a story of either cheating, lust, exploitation, conquest, surrender or treachery. Joy'll last only for short duration but sorrow is perpetual. This's life and no use of ego, power and pelf. Everything on this earth will perish today or tomorrow. I've visited every nook and corner of Wynad and I'll tell you a thousand stories of this enchanting place'. Viswam master made a long discourse. HM was very much impressed.

'Is your wife employed?' HM.

'Yes. Sh's a tamil teacher in a Govt. Primary school here. We're living in a line house near the market. I'll take you there one day' Viswam master said.

After some time, Viswam master left for his house and HM became lonely again.

Next day, HM reached the school at 9 am and was surprised to see Viswam master waiting for him.' Thus both of them became too much attached to each other and without Viswam master HM cannot do anything.

HM called a meeting of the staff and prepared an action plan to improve the standard of the school. Each teacher in the high school section was asked to identify students whose performance in the last examination was poor. It was decided to impart special coachings in the weak subjects during lunch break and after school time. Weak students were asked to remain late by one hour every working day and special classes upto noon on saterdays.

Some teachers had objections in remaining late in the evening, but that was settled by the persuasion of the HM.

Lady teachers coming from distant places were exempted from evening classes and they were given class during lunch break.

Some weak students skipped special classes and their parents were called to the office and HM himself spoke to them and convinced them about the urgency of improving the percentage in the next SSLC examination.

Some students were unable to remain late, since they had to cross river, climb mountains and cover long distance to reach home. Such students were asked to remain for lunch break classes and saturday classes.

Another problem was poverty, especially among adivasi sections of society. Such students were traced out and given financial assistance for purchasing books, umbrella, and dress. Special attention was given in the case of midday meal and in each and every case HM was assisted by Viswam master.

Viswam master once asked the HM 'why don't you bring your family here?'

'Viswam I 've no family'

'Didn't you marry so far?'

'Married but got separated on a minor issue. She got married again, but I did not'

'It's inscrutable that divorce is very common nowadays. If she has remarried you also could have remarried'.

'It's true that man proposes and God disposes. In this case i's a case of fate or destiny. The Gods were jealous of our love and affection and creating a trivial reason we were separated' Viswam, I married the sister in law of my elder sister. My sister'd two children and I'd none. My borther in law was a drunkard and he'd a concubine. One day my sister and children came to our house and never returned to his house. My father became very angry, sent some mediators to his house, but failed and then as a tit for tat asked me to send my wife to her house. I know what I did was wrong because she's innocent, but I had to obey my father. It was done to put pressure on him to take his family back, but it misfired. My wife refused to come back, in spite of repeated requests. She applied for divorce and I finally, consented. Within a short period she got remarried and has one child. For long twenty years I led a life of loneliness and mental agony.' HM lost his control and began to sob.

'OK, let us stop here. Gone are gone for ever and no need of repenting. I'll find out a more fitting wife for you shortly'.

Both of them broke into peals of laughter.

HM used to take classes for lunch break and evening. He realized that there is more poverty in Wynad compared to other parts of the state. The students of government school were mostly from the households of plantation labourers, adivasi workers and other backward sections of society. The condition of adivasi homes are pathetic. Most of the adivasi males are addicts to liquor and tobacco. The major portion of their wages are utilised for liquor and a small portion will reach their homes. So, there will be perennial proverty and privation in their homes. It is a herculean task to reform them. Paniyar community is found to be most backward and their children are suffering too much for want of proper food, clothes medicines and other essentials.

One day, a girl student complained to the HM that her house was demolished and bricks sold by father to make money for liquor. Immediately HM and Viswam master visited the so called home of the student named Remani. What they beheld there was very poignant. Remani's father Kelu will not go for work regularly. If he got anything through labour he will remain idle for days together till that money is exhausted. His wife and children are in great penury, and misery. For many days he did not go to work and for liquor he demolished his house and sold the bricks. Remani, mother and others are now sleeping on the varandah of another house. While returning from the house of Remani, HM's mind was grief stricken and he asked Viswam master 'How can these children study when parents are such irresponsible type.'

'Thi's not an isolated case. Most of the homes are like this and children are coming to school without taking breakfast and the midday meal is their only support. They have no anxiety about tomorrow. Out of the welfare funds only 20 % reach them, and the remaining goes to govt. officials and contractors.' Viswam master elaborated.

Next day, HM and Viswam master met the concerned BDO and requested him to arrange reconstruction of the house at the earliest and he assured them that urgent necessary action will be taken in this regard.

Next saturday, HM made a trip to the house of Viswam master. He was given a grand reception by Viswam master and family. There are eight houses in a row and the last one is occupied by Viswam master. The houses resembled the houses in agraharam without any independent rooms.

HM was given tea with sweets and snack, and then heavy lunch with chicken biriyani. After lunch Viswam master enquired 'Let me give a peg of brandy?'

'No Never' HM refused.

'Sorry sir, I used to take one peg on Sunday and my wife is dead against to this and daughter will not talk to me if I take liquor.;

'Viswam master, teachers should not drink and we must show example to the students and public'.

'But this 's secret and my wife'll not tell anybody.

'Master try to stop this habit. It will cause havoc to your liver later. I will tell you the story of so many film luminaries like Padmarajan, Murali, Rajan P Dev, Sarachandra Prasad, Vayalar etc and they had premature death due to drinking'. I strongly believe it is liquor that cut short their life span'. HM said with facts and figures.

'That's cent percent true. I know that drinking is injurious to health, but one peg occasionally will not do much harm. I started this habit about two years ago after we started ginger cultivation with some friends. The place was between Attamala and Mundakkai. During holidays we used to get together in that wilderness. Without some support it is difficult to spend more time there. Thus friends will come with some bottles and we will enjoy holidays' said Viswam master.

'You told me that your wife is a tamil teacher. Is she actually tamilian?'

'No, there are plenty of tamil speaking people here. It is Europeans who cleared forests and planted tea. They brought cheap labour from tamilnadu and were given jobs in their tea estates and quarters called paddy. These labourers didn't go back, and became part of the population of Wynad. In addition to this some Tamil speaking people have migrated to Wynad from the neighbouring districts and they also became part of this district. My wife belongs to the second category. They came to this place about 100 years ago from Palakkad and settled here at Vaduvanchal on Ootty road and have acquired some landed properties there. One of my friends told me that there is a nice girl from Palakkad working as Tamil teacher in a primary school at Meppadi. We proposed and they were willing to give her in marriage to me and my parents who belonged to Unnithan community did not object and thus the marriage took place. My daughter Kalpana is studying in 6th standard.' Viswam master went on talking.

'Viswam master, we have been talking for quite a long time. Let me go back to my house' HM said.

'Santhi please bring tea. HM's in a hurry to go.'After tea HM returned to his house. Viswam master, Santhi and Kalpana waved their hands while he left. Their smiling faces lingered in HM's mind for quite a long time and he said to himself' It is difficult to see such a happy family.

One day, Viswam master came to see HM and spent a lot of time in the office discussing for the next SSLC exam. Surendran master and Joseph master were also with him. They told HM that there is great improvement in the last class tests and most of the students have managed to secure good marks. After this meeting Viswam master took the HM to a place called 900 and from there to the top of the mountain. It is a wonderful place and from there they got a clear view of Nilambur town. It is difficult to go there and since the road is very narrow and full of boulders. On both sides of the road were cardamom plantations. HM got a bite of leech during this trip. That landscape looked like Switzerland wihl hills, valleys and blossoms all over.

'How do you feel?' Viswam master asked HM.

'Very picturesque and scintillating' said HM.

While coming back Viswam master said 'We have to go to a secret place on saturday'.

'What's it?'

'Let it be a surprise, I'll tell you after reaching the destination.

'On saturday morning. Viswam master came to the house of HM in a jeep and took him to the secret destination. After travelling about one hour, they reached an old model tiled house situated in the middle of a coffee plantation. They were welcomed by an old man in the age group of 65-70 years.

'Come and be seated' The old man invited them.

They went inside and sat on an old sofa. Viswam master talked to him eloquently on various subjects related to their school and students and HM thought that he will be a retired teacher.

After the general talk Viswam master introduced HM 'This is Vijayanunni master our HM'.

HM shook hands with the old man, and then he introduced himself 'I am Krishnan Nambeesan, old Hindi teacher'.

'He was Hindi teacher of our high school when I joined duty. He's a good man and a sincere friend. He has an unmarried daughter' Viswam master said.

Then a lovely woman in sari came forward with tea and snacks and Krishnan Nambeesan introduced her. 'My elder daughter'

HM asked only one question 'what's your name?'

'Sunitha'.

He smiled and she returned the smile.

Viswam master later told HM full story of Sunitha. After spending some time they returned to HM's house and Viswam master spent two more hours with him in his house.

'How do you feel?'

'Not bad'

'Say very good, and not bad. She is unmarried and aged 34. Many years back, her marriage had been fixed to a clerk in Canara bank, but that marriage did not take place since the boy withdrew from the marriage. Reason was that her younger sister eloped with a muslim boy. After that, no body came with proposals and Nambeesan master became mentally upset and he came round to normalcy after prolonged treatment. If you like her they are ready for the marriage. Think over and reply.'

'I like her very much and we can proceed'.

Thus, the marriage was fixed for the month of May after the SSLC examination. After the exam HM called all students and asked 'have you done well?'.

'ye s sir, we're hopeful' they replied with confidence.

During vacation HM made a trip to Alappey and returned after two days. He informed father, sister and all others about the Wynad bride. He made all arrangements for the marriage and returned to Wynad.

The marriage was conducted at Guruvayoor temple. Many teachers and friends from Wynad participated in the marriage and Viswam master was everywhere with his wife and daughter. It is he who made arrangements at Guruvayoor such as booking of accommodation, food, transport etc for both sides since they had no experience by conducting marriages there. From Alappey, HM's sister, son, daughter in law, other relatives and teachers from the old school attended the marriage. After marriage, HM and wife were taken to his house at Alappey. Thus, his small house became active again after so many months of closure. The bride Sunitha first made obeisance to the ailing father of Vijayanunni master and then entered the house with the traditional lamp and slept with him in the nuptial bed. The pall of gloom descended on the house twenty years ago, was dispelled by the light of the traditional lamp, with which Sunitha entered the house

'Are you happy to live in a house far away from your parents?' Vijayanunni master asked Sunitha.

'I'm happy to live anywhere with my husband' Sunitha smiled and replied.

After two days, a party came from Wynad with Viswam master and family and after reception the bride and bridegroom were taken to Wynad.

HM's family started to live in his rented house near school. For company Nambeesan master and wife were with them for two weeks. Before they returned to their house Viswam master brought a maid from Vaduvanchal for helping Sunitha. She stayed in the same house and helped Sunitha in all domestic chores.

The SSLC result came. HM was surprised to hear it-87 % pass and 10 first class. On hearing the news all teachers rushed to HM's house. The victory was celebrated with crackers and ladu.

The school was reopened after vacation. HM and other teachers started work with more earnestness and enthusiasm for next year exam.

There was torrential rains, at the time of reopenining and hence attendance was very low for few days. Still they started the special classes without wasting time.

Rains continued till the end of August and then spring came with abundant flowers all over Wynad and the hills, valleys and mountains lay covered under the blanket of flowers. With the change of seasons it's reflection was found in HM's wife Sunitha also. She is going to become a mother and HM's mind was also covered with blossoms of joy and eccstasy and he exulted for many days silently.

Sunitha gave birth to a baby girl in a hospital at Kalpetta. It was a normal delivery and she was discharged within a couple of days. Viswam master and family were in the hospital at the time of delivery and they made daily visit to the hospital till discharge. Sweets were distributed to the entire staff and students of the school. After delivery Nambeesan master and wife came to the house and stayed with them for about one month for postnatal care and treatment. There was much pleasure and joy in their presence and HM once said 'You better stay here and no need of going back. We can visit the house and plantation occasionally. Your age is advancing and to stay there alone is not advisable. We will look after you and your presence gives us much pleasure and peace of mind'.

'Unless somebody's there in the house, the coffee plants'll dry up. There's also some ginger and pepper and constant attention's required for these crops'. Nambeesan master said.

'I 've another suggestion to make. You can either rent out that house or keep it under lock and key. We can go there and arrange necessary works as and when required and pluck the coffee, ginger and pepper when they ripen.'

Nambeesan master had no answer. He was really willing to stay there since Sunitha was most beloved to them and they abhorred to live there alone without her.

Then one day a lady came to the house with a ten year old boy and it was Devika their daughter.

'Excuse me papa, after so many years I've come in search of you, don't turn me out' she entreated'

Nambeesan master did not give any attention to her. Due to her elopement he had became insane and Sunitha had to remain unmarried for many years and had to suffer ignominy from relatives and neighbours and hence she does not deserve any sympathy.

Devika lamented again 'Papa forgive me papa, there is nobody to look after me and my son'

Then Sunitha came forward and embraced Devika and said 'you're welcome to our house. Nobody will turn you out from this house'.

Then HM called her inside and asked 'where's your husband?'

'We were living in Bombay and my son was studying there. One day, my husband came to the house with a Bombay girl and asked me to vacate the house immediately and threatened me with dire consequences if I didn't obey. We were afraid and hence left Bombay immediately.'

They stayed in HM's house one day and the next day Nambeesan master took them to their house.

SSLC result was announced. Their school scored 24 first classes and cent percent pass. It was a landmark victory and congratulations poured to the HM from all corners of the state. DD, DPI and the minister rung up to congratulate and it was a unforgettable and memorable day for the school.

HM was overwhelmed with joy and he told his team of teachers 'We have shown to the world that 100 % victory is not impossible. I thank one all of you in this landmark victory.'

A feast was arranged in the school by HM, in which many of the students and teachers took part. After the feast Viswam master took HM to his house in an auto. After reaching there, he offered one peg to the HM and he accepted it gladly. 'I am taking the drink to celebrate our victory.' After finishing it he demanded more. Viswam master refused, but HM himself took the bottle and poured into a glass and gulped down without adding water or soda. HM was completely in a collapsed state and he said in a faltered voice 'today I am not going home, I will go back to my office.'

Viswam master was in a dilemma and he could not take a decision immediately. The HM was in fully drunken state and it is not proper to take him to his house in this condition. HM slept in the sofa for about three hours and at 8pm he was awaken and taken to his house in an auto. Sunitha became very angry with Viswam master for the first time in their life.'You have made him a drunkard. I don't want to see your face again' she shouted.

Viswam master left the house immediately without saying anything leaving the HM on the floor.

Sunitha's face was red with anger and grief and she beat her chest and lamented.'my life is spoiled and I don't want to live with a drunkard'.

The HM wanted to say something but it was not audible and then he folded his hands and said 'excuse me this time my beloved wife'.

HM was carried to the bed by Sunitha with the help of the maid and he went to sleep in a few minutes. Next day he was shy to face his wife and after a thorough bath he went to the school without taking beakfast. Viswam master came to his chamber and expressed regret for the happenings on previous day and went to his house. Even though it was vacation HM had a lot of work to do. He was in a moody state throughout that day. He returned home by 6pm and Sunitha did not come to received him. The maid brought a cup of tea and drank it and asked 'Where is Sunitha?'

'She's sleeping with child'

'OK, let her sleep don't disturb'.

HM opened the TV and was watching a serial and then Sunitha came rushing to the sitting room and said 'If you don't like me I will go to my house now itself'.

'Sunitha cool down I won't send you there. If you want you can go.'

She began to weep and then HM raised his voice and said 'I am not a drunkard. Our school got cent percent pass and we celebrated that victory. It is not Wiswam that inebriated me. He refused drink to me but in that pleasure and joy I lost my control and drank. You do not know anything about Viswam and without him I am nothing. He is really a true friend. For each and every thing he is helping me without expecting anything in return. It is pure selfless service and that fellow was driven out of my house. What you did yesterday is unpardonable mistake and I don't want you to say sorry to him'.

Sunitha realized her mistake and said 'Sorry, I won't repeat it.'

After that incident Viswam master has not come to HM's house even though there is no change in the friendship btween the HM and himself.

After a couple weeks, the school was reopened. On the day of reopening, Viswan master brought a special news that HM has been transferred to his old school in Alappey. But, Vijaynunni master did not rejoice. He came to the school and did his duty as before.

'I don't want to go. I've so many connections here and my wife house is here and my students for whom I've an agenda in mind and before completion of that I can't go and I'll not go'.

'Sir, what you say is due to your emotion in leaving this place. Don't be carried away by emotion. You have to go and you should go. You 'll not get a chance like this. Said Viswam.

'If I go how can I see my Viswam?' HM broke into tears.

'Sir, you should go to your native place and your aged father is expecting you and so is your sister and family. Don't disappoint them. If you do not go now you can never go and you will have to live here till your death'

'Viswam, I'm unable to take a decision '.

'If you want to see me, please telephone I'll come and meet you. This's a golden chance. I can't escape from this place. I'm part and parcel of this beautiful place and I'll live here till my death. That's different from your case. Your child is in the cradle and you have to bring her up. So please decide to go and don't give a chance to repent.

Finally, HM decided to go back to Alappey with his wife and daughter. A grand send off was arranged in the school in which DEO and local MLA were present. He vacated his house and said goodbye to all his friends and well wishers. Before starting journey he embraced his bosom friend and colleague Viswam master and both of them broke into tears and Sunitha looked at them with wonder and amazement.

********* END *********